Beverley Jones is a former journalist and police press officer, now a novelist and book obsessive. She was born in a small village in the valleys of South Wales, north of Cardiff, and started her journalism career with Trinity Mirror newspapers before becoming a broadcast journalist with *BBC Wales Today*.

She has worked on all aspects of crime reporting (as well as community news and features), producing stories and content for newspapers and live TV. She also worked as a press officer and, later, media manager for South Wales Police, participating in criminal investigations, security operations, counter terrorism and emergency planning for the 2012 Olympics. Perhaps unsurprisingly she channels these experiences of true crime, and her insight into the murkier side of human nature, into her dark, psychological thrillers.

D1578987

Also by Beverley Jones (writing as B. E. Jones)

Where She Went
Halfway
Wilderness

(ebook only)

The Lies You Tell
Make Him Pay
Fear the Dark

The Beach House

Beverley Jones

CONSTABLE

CONSTABLE

First published in ebook in 2021 by Constable
First published in paperback in Great Britain in 2022 by Constable

1 3 5 7 9 10 8 6 4 2

A CIP catalogue record for this book
is available from the British Library.

ISBN: 978-0-34913-474-1

Typeset in Sabon by Initial Typesetting Services, Edinburgh
Printed and bound in Great Britain by Clays Ltd, Elcograf S.p.A.

Papers used by Constable are from well-managed forests
and other responsible sources.

Constable
An imprint of
Little, Brown Book Group
Carmelite House
50 Victoria Embankment
London EC4Y 0DZ

An Hachette UK Company
www.hachette.co.uk

www.littlebrown.co.uk

To Tracey, sharer of the voices

One

Birthday Surprise

The body isn't the first thing I see when I step into the kitchen, it's the length of rope, the knife and the handcuffs. They're lying on the hardwood worktop, making the place look untidy. There's a metallic tang in the air too, in this room that usually smells only of expensive coffee, a flush of open-window salt air or a $60 rosemary candle. Smell is the organ of memory and memory should be clean and reassuring by design, at least, if I have any control over it.

Nose twitching, I call out, 'Eli? Are you home?', stepping forward to put down my grocery bag. Looking at the knife, it's obviously an ordinary Kitchen Devil, cheap in any hardware store, with no place in this streamlined workspace. New, unused, its gleaming incisored edge looks almost eager to be taken in hand, to enjoy its first bite when, by contrast, the handcuffs are well-used, a lattice of scratches around the keyhole.

The coil of rope is clearly new, gathered to a waist by a length of plush, red ribbon, its velvet splash bright on the back of my eyes as I think, *Presents*. From someone with strange taste, granted, but who's still taken the trouble to plan a surprise. Someone who's snuck inside to leave them just for me. Which explains the unlocked back door when I tried my key just now, brown bag hoisted on my hip, trying not to squash the box of cupcakes – Red Velvet, like the red ribbon – Tilly's favourite, for her birthday tomorrow.

Tilly! Where is she? comes the hardwired reflex for her safety, but of course she's not here. My soon to be eight-year-old daughter is at intermediate aikido ass-kicking class in the city with Anoushka, and I'm all alone, in this house, with the gifts. Except I'm not, my head reasons finally, my heart snare-drum jittering to the sudden threat. It's been less than thirty seconds since I sailed down Shore Road in my little hybrid, pulled up in the yard and opened the door, but I'm already the familiar fool I swore I'd never be, the woman returning home to find a possible intruder in the house, frowning at the unlocked door, calling out, *Anyone home?* like a total idiot. I'm the one who freezes in the presence of lurking peril instead of firing her way out of it on her wits, when the suspicion becomes real. Like right now.

Without warning, a ticking fills the afternoon, a count-down reverberating around the winter-light kitchen in segments sharp and clear. As it divides the bursts of my breath, I know I should bolt, but there's a delay between my brain and my anchored feet. It's only when the sun slants in through the picture window, filling it with the glowing weight of the afternoon ocean at my back, that I see the figure on the floor.

It's lying in a classic dead-body pose, invisible crime-scene tape around the one bent leg, one arm out, as if he's sleeping on his stomach. But no one could nod off with that much blood pooling around their head, so much blacker than the red of the ribbon on the rope, a shiny, jet slick the exact shade the edges of my vision are turning. My grocery bag escapes disloyally to the floor, leaving me exposed, as I see by my left foot the blunt, metal baton Eli calls 'the pewter penis', my name etched on the plaque at its base, smeared with blood.

It's not my husband lying there, thank God, felled by the ridiculous award he won't let me stash out of sight in a cupboard. I know this, even though the face is hidden by its uncomfortable angle against the floor. Eli hasn't popped home early with a bottle of chilled Pinot, his bear-like grin a prelude to Tilly's rocket-launch into my arms, yelling *Mommy, surprise!* This man is much slighter and Eli would never be seen dead in stonewashed jeans with frayed hems. He's wearing Converse trainers too, by no means a dignified outfit to take one's final dive out of this world into murder-victim stillness.

So, who the hell is he? And what was he intending to do with all that weird stuff on the worktop? The answer arrives like an Amtrak train, exploding the shock that's held me on the spot, and my feet start pumping towards the door, away from the gifts, from the body, from the knife-edge expectation of a hand on my shoulder.

In all honesty, I'm not that surprised. I've waited seventeen years for this moment, for the vice-like grip dragging me back, branding my flesh with four fingers and a thumb. Not like this though. This is not how I imagined it.

When the inevitable happens, it's not with a hand clamped on the back of my neck, soft and exposed for the first strike. Instead, as I reach for the door handle, a shadow emerges from the family room. I don't scream but the noise that comes from my mouth is a guttural cry, forming wordlessly, its meaning clear.

Not now. Not today. I'm not ready.

Then I'm wide-eyed before the face of a Lookout Beach cop, a blanched and hatless kid in the doorway, gripping me by the wrist, his gun drawn in his other hand as I fight for the freedom I've always known couldn't last for ever.

'It's OK. Are you OK, ma'am? Are you hurt?' he demands.

But I can't answer. I am neither and both, intact, but also not. How can I explain to this uniformed boy that I'm terminally injured, have simply hung on and fought for seventeen years, pushing the sting of sickness back each day, swallowing it down? The fear that I am a bad person and will meet a bad end.

'Is there anyone else in the house, ma'am?' the cop shouts now, as his radio crackles, pushing me outside into the sunshine raining on the iron sea.

When I sink onto the grass, another officer is already there and, out along the shoreline, a siren song of emergency responders joins the fret of seagulls, unused to so much vulgar noise and flurry.

'We're here, now, ma'am. You're safe,' she's saying, as if insistence can make it so, when the only words I hear in my head are from a season long ago and far away, from a face twisted with rage; a voice that spits, 'Just remember, whatever I did to her, one day I'll do to you,' over and over again.

Two

Lucky Lady

An hour and a half later, and I'm sitting in the Lookout Beach Police Station that reeks of Ocean Breeze air freshener and veiled panic. It's not a proper station, just a front desk with pamphlets and a couple of offices behind. The door's locked, the blinds drawn to a squint and I'm adrift in the centre of the spot-lit sofa like a rat on a life raft. It could be worse though. Rats are good swimmers. So am I.

The policewoman has brought me a woollen shawl from the lost-and-found locker, as if cocooning me in scratchy angora will make me forget what I saw on my kitchen worktop earlier, on that curved piece of honeyed grain from a sustainable logging project in Lower Chehalis, a side of tree trunk older than this shoreline-stretched village. I wonder if there are scratches in its hand-polished, mirror shine now, and whether or not the blood will permanently stain the elegant parquetry of the kitchen floor.

Not that that matters, obviously. My mind is simply

flitting about like a bat caught in headlights, bumping up against the familiar. I try to drop a mental blanket over it, hoping it will go to sleep. Bats are not really blind, of course, they just listen better than they see. I do both equally well, as the policewoman closes into a forehead huddle with my erstwhile boy-saviour at the counter.

They must think, because I've been unable to tell them anything useful about the scene at the house and have since fallen into silence, that I'm in shock, shooting sidelong glances at me, trying and failing not to stare, to assess, to judge. How do I appear to them right now? I wonder. Like a cat probably, one of those creamy Siamese ones with pale blue eyes, expensive, aloof, poised. Playing along, I sit a little more upright, resisting the urge to smooth my hair back from my eyes, as the woman stage-whispers, loudly, 'Jesus, what in God's name is going on? Must be a sex pervert, right? I mean, did you see the *size* of that knife?'

'No shit! Course, there have been reports of prowlers in that area lately.'

'That turned out to be the UPS delivery guy, Danny. You know the GPS problems we get here.'

'Yeah, OK, Dolores, that one time, but it's not the only one, right? You just never really think . . . I mean, in a place like this. That's the sort of shit they get up to in the city, am I right?'

'You *are* right. I mean, who knows what he had planned for her, if he hadn't been disturbed? She's one lucky lady.'

Their heads swivel in unison now, to detect the aura of all the good fortune I must possess, presumably not to have been trussed up, raped and gutted like a fish on my own bit of original feature flooring. Their faces are full of fuzzy, cottonwool sympathy, this pair who sound like a 1940s stage comedy act, in name if not in action – Dolores and Danny, partners in crime. Their expressions are exactly like those of the greyer, crumpled detectives I met years ago, in that 1960s-built, cement monstrosity of a police station, that banal nightmare of concrete walls, water-stained polystyrene ceiling tiles and long, lightless corridors.

They brought me a can of Coke that night, when they first questioned me, *under caution*, DI call-me-Maureen and DC no-first-name Davies. Then came the pints of tea and biscuits, the usual British lifesavers. In later days, the tea stopped and the questions grew dry and repetitive, their sharp edges sticking on my tongue, their sour taste filling the air, hours into the interviews, the never-ending spool of questions and recriminations.

At first Detective Inspector Maureen reminded me of a hamster, plump and cuddly, but those little buggers have sharp teeth. She always put sugar in my tea, even after I'd asked her not to; her eyes missed nothing and she was the one who first said, 'You're lying, aren't you, young lady? You've done nothing but lie all along.'

When Lieutenant Andy, a familiar face from the friendly community events at Tilly's school emerges from the back office, I raise my eyebrows expectantly. Andy always reminds me of a racoon, a ranger racoon in a flat hat, one who says 'Go safe now, folks,' as he chucks a salute. I bite back a smile, the three coffees I've been mainlining clearly making me twitchy, over imaginative, something no one will ever say about Andy, Dolores or Danny I suspect. If I could read his lips, I'd guess Andy Mackenzie, who I've never heard get even close to uttering a curse word when he hands out plastic police badges to the kids during 'good citizen' classes, is saying something like, 'Holy shit. What a hot fucking mess!'

I check my text messages and voicemail for the tenth time, and, seeing no notifications, wonder if I should ring Bright Brothers again. Where the hell is Elias? I know he's out on site in Portland today, checking the final touches to the housing project in Slabtown. I've instructed Bridgette to tell him to call me, *urgently*, the minute he resurfaces from approving the tweaks to the armadillo shields of solar panels that came with the zoning permissions. Why hasn't he answered any of my messages? I need him here, *now*, while I sit like a fish caught on a hook, waiting to be stunned by a blow to the head or thrown back to the currents by Andy's next words.

I'm not worried yet. I'm safe here, in more ways than one, my disguise intact – the one I refine every morning when I apply my nude lipstick and mascara, choose some subtle silver earrings and skinny jeans, throw on a pale blouse and pastel scarf. It's carefully cultivated, this character, a work of performance art, years in the making. It says *nothing to see here, nothing you're not used to, nothing unexpected, move along.*

Because I look exactly like everyone else in this blustery beach-front town and the ones like it, scattered like pebbles along the coast. I'm thirty-two and 'in great shape', a 'well-groomed' career woman with an impressive husband and two homes – a mom certainly, a MILF maybe, though no one here in this Oregon village would be vulgar enough to use a phrase like that.

To the easy eye, I belong here as naturally as marion-berry pie and Tillamook ice-cream, like Sasquatch and filberts (which I still think of as hazelnuts), as familiar as fried oysters and artisan beer. Nothing I do today will betray the intrinsic difference between the inside and outside of me, here on the Pacific Northwest shore, the far-flung edge of the New World, where America gives up, folds down on itself and falls into the sea.

This is the boot-edge of civilisation for thousands of miles, the ocean swelling onwards towards Japan with nothing in between, keeping its secrets. Here in the top left-hand corner of the U S of A, I concluded my own journey of discovery, not unlike the early nineteenth-century pioneers Lewis and Clark, who dragged their skinny arses from Missouri, through forest, flood, dys-entery and starvation along the Oregon Trail, to find a passage west. Here they founded communities, hewing the heart out of the virgin forest, seeking freedom by shoving aside and squeezing past the peoples minding their own business for millennia.

Centuries later, it's still a place people come to run away from the slavering things hot on their heels, to reinvent themselves. That's why I'm here, in this linen, cashmere costume, in this method-actress performance, honed to hypodermic precision. If anything, only my vowels betray my original, alien Britishness, still there on the tip of my tongue, as I think of the best way to ask Lieutenant Andy when I can just get the bloody hell out of here.

Because I don't want to sit on this sofa one minute longer, cornered, hemmed in. After all this time, any room can still feel like a cell if I'm told I can't leave. I swallow the surge of anxiety that hurls my breath against my chest, worried it'll overwhelm me if can't get out of here soon. Not because I think *he*'s coming for me, of course. I know that now. That the things I saw in the bizarre tableau at the house earlier, and the things I did all those years ago, are not connected. How could they be?

I had a bit of a scare that's all, a post-traumatic flash-back, muscle memory flexing – a calf cramp to grit my teeth at, shake out and breathe through. I mustn't over-react and drag everything from that murky past kicking and screaming into this polished present. I'm OK, right here, right now and I know what I want.

'Andy, I need to get out of here. I need to go to Portland and get Elias, right away,' I state, trying not to clench my hands into fists when he shakes his head and says, 'Not a good idea, Mrs Jensen. You're in shock. And you shouldn't be alone right now.'

I'm not *in* shock, I want to correct, though I *am* shocked. But I know he means I shouldn't be alone *right now*, when someone clearly came to my house to do bad things to me today and we don't know who or why. He doesn't say this, just explains, 'We need to go over your statement again and some detectives are on their way out from the city. They want to talk to you.'

'Can I call Mary-Kate, then?' I counter. 'I could go to the Project and they could talk to me there.'

'I don't think that's a good idea either.'

It seems I'm full of bad ideas tonight, like the one to skip out my husband and daughter to get home from the city a day early. But I can't think of a better thing to do right now than collapse on the bony shoulder of Mary-Kate, my friend and neighbour along the loose string of beach houses on Shore Street. MK does not conform to Lookout Beach's low-key aesthetic and neutral palette, dressing like a dizzying Dior convention mated with a pina colada at Coachella. She smokes real cigarettes too, loves dairy and red meat and does not wear SPF year-round. These are the last legitimate forms of rebellion in a community that thinks single-use water bottles are akin to satanism and meat is not just murder but the weapon of our own human genocide.

MK will make it all better. She'll pour me a pint of Pinot to 'help take the edge off', make me laugh. She'll make me *feel* lucky, tossing her balayage blonde mane alongside the words, *that kinky bastard*, about the man on the slick kitchen floor, *got what was coming to him. That's karma. Good job the cop was there to shoot his ass!*

But that's not what happened, not as I'd first assumed when the police surrounded the house earlier, that Officer Danny had somehow dealt with my intruder before I arrived. From listening to them talk, it seems he was merely responding to a routine call. He arrived moments before I did, found the back door open, and the man was already on the kitchen floor. So, who did the deed? Who killed him? And who brought the fun-time torture toys to the party?

'I can't stay here, Andy,' I plead, squeezing a single tear from each eye by staring for as long as I can at the sweat beads on his temple, then blinking ferociously. It's never been easy for me, turning on the waterworks. I'm not a weeper, a sobber, a snotter. I think DI Maureen thought it was a sure sign of my guilt. *Look how cold she is. She hasn't*

11

even cried! But I've developed useful techniques since then, adding, 'I'm going crazy here,' with a hitch in my breath.

Because Grace Jensen is a woman who's never encountered this sort of vulgar crime before, never been a victim or otherwise. She'd be upset now that she has, wet-eyed and even a little hysterical. I add a tremble as I clutch Andy's hot hand, pleading, 'Please, Andy? I don't feel so good. I need to lie down.' To seal the deal, I soften my knees and incline to one side like a listing ship, until he gives in with, 'OK, OK darlin',' anything other than having to watch me pass out on his couch and explain that, on top of everything else, to Elias when he arrives.

'Maybe I can get someone to take you up there, to the new beach house,' he offers. 'The detectives can catch up with you there, if they want to. Danny . . . ?'

He summons my saviour, looking even younger in this fluorescent light, with the suggestion, 'Why don't you take Mrs Jensen to her new beach house, let her get some rest until we can locate Mr Jensen and the detectives get here. Stay by her side and stay in touch, yes?'

'Thank you. Thank you,' I say, aiming for somewhere between grateful and brave, 'I just need some space to . . . *process this*,' a useful phrase my American friends employ when they are, you know, *'trying to deal'*, aka trying to get a fucking grip.

'Andy? Do you have any idea who the man is?' I ask, sniffling. 'Do you know who . . . I mean . . . what happened? Was he waiting for me? Do you think he was . . . ?'

'We're working on it, darlin'. We don't know much yet. Best not to speculate,' guiding me to the door, both of us glad I'm leaving.

Three

Secondary Players

Fifteen minutes later and Officer Danny and I are grinding up the loose gravel track to the wooden fence that surrounds the Project. It's almost full dark now and it's a relief to see its camouflaged angles emerge from the woven curtain of hemlock and Sitka spruce beyond the windows of the patrol car. Everyone else just calls what is soon to be our new home 'the new beach house', though that's hardly fitting, as it sits on a granite ledge above the booming surf and a scratchy crescent of pebbles, so much more to me than the 'toes in the sand', soft summer days that name conjures up. This is my new life, my refuge, nothing between me and the forgetful September sea outside its windows except 800 square feet of almost invisible hardwood, tinted glass and subtle dark steel under construction.

It's my Project, my work of art, a difficult labour of love that began even before I was as old as Tilly is now. I can't believe it's almost fifteen years since Mum showed me the pictures of Fallingwater, Frank Lloyd Wright's beautiful house in Pennsylvania, a masterclass in glass and canti-levered girders elevated over a waterfall. It took up twelve slides in one of her many reference books, as sleek and alien to the old, cluttered world I'd been used to as if a spaceship had landed in the woods.

In that intake of breath, a fascination was born, along with the desire to become an architect. Then, ten years later, after Elias and I met admiring the futuristic lines of the Seattle Space Needle, he took me to Fallingwater and promised he'd build me the home of my dreams. The Project is the result, with the help of Bright Brothers' con-struction expertise, Wright refracted through the prism of a sleek, Bauhaus aesthetic, that Eli has let me sketch, draft and design, every last elegant line of it.

It's not the first of its kind in Oregon, but it is unlike any-thing here, close to Lookout Beach and its kitsch, arts and crafts, English-village-through-the-lens-of-folk-America aesthetic. It's still a work in progress, though. The bones are up, the glass and slate skin watertight, but the interior floors and walls are incomplete. Except in here, where I've made a den for myself with cheap second-hand furniture, because I like to work with the impressionist view of the ocean, blurred through branches and swathes of sea fog. I have my draughtingboard, my sofa, my little fridge in the back room, a hotplate where the kitchen will soon be.

The bedroom, up in the mezzanine, is almost fin-ished and has a 'holding' king size with clean sheets. Eli and I slept there once or twice, after the first phase was completed in the spring. Sometimes I nap there in the afternoons when I come to sketch, when Eli's in the city and Tilly is at school.

It couldn't be further from the house I spent my childhood in, the sticky, chocolate-box charming village of flower-choked stone and giddy, tilted roofs pitching towards the sea. Hugging the bent backs of the dunes, our cluster of cottages clung to the skirts of the South Wales coast clothed in centuries of stories; weathered tales of farmers and Roman soldiers, fishermen and finer folk, wool merchants and privateers. Once, a medieval settlement was swallowed whole by ravenous sandstorms, legends and tragedies layered so thickly in the ground itself, that sometimes it was suffocating.

I was in love with it all then, my father's lamplit bedtime tales of maidens and heroes, of ancient curses and eternal love promises, picking my way to and from school through the canting streets, scouring the dunes for Roman coins and fairy rings, and visiting silent stone circles keeping their secrets. What child wouldn't have wanted to live somewhere so magical, in our happy cocoon of privilege, meaning we never really had to acknowledge one of the poorest housing estates in the poorest part of Wales, existing a few miles down the road.

I thought I'd add my own stories to its history until we wrote a different one, over that single, tarnished summer: the primary players – two girls, two boys, as they often are. But there were so many to blame, in such a picture-postcard place. *How could it happen here?* they asked afterwards. *They're such nice kids, from such good homes. The Cracknell boy's father is a doctor. They go to church all the time, for God's sake.*

But why not there? Why not us? Any architect will tell you that the surface of something cannot guarantee the state of its heart. Rot, black mould, leaks can live beneath the facade of buildings, fractures swell in the ribs of walls that smile with climbing wisteria. Just as jealousy, longing, shame and confusion lurk under the skin. As Mum said afterwards, packing my suitcase, trying not to cry, there's a lot to be said for starting from scratch, creating your own clean space with no stories jostling inside.

And this is it. My blank sheet. My space to fill. My story to invent.

'Wow, that's quite a view,' whistles Officer Danny, as we climb the steps into the impressive open plan area spanning the front of the Project. 'Very roomy,' though I can tell it's *too fancy* for his tastes, sitting gingerly on the old sofa as if inside an art installation, scared he might sully it with his khaki pants and boots. You'd think, from the cow eyes he's making, that he's an old farm boy, fresh from milking Tillamook's famous dairy herds down the coast, when I know his mum and dad are realtors, aka estate agents, and their house worth almost as much as ours.

As he witters on about his brother who's just moved to Bend, his newborn 'super cute' nephew Jake, it's clear I make him nervous, or my money does, or my narrow escape. Little does he know I've had narrower. While he prattles about the Seattle Seahawks' upcoming football season, his words become waves of static on a far shore and I tune out, staring at the black heave of the Pacific that's merged with the pooling of the sky.

There's a bald eagles' nest up there, in the jagged trees on the ridge. They don't bother us in their homemade bowl of sticks and twigs, their perfect symbiosis of sustainable form and function, and we don't bother them. We avoided building in nesting season and used low-impact techniques to protect the colony. Along this coast laced with State Parks, we are an anomaly with permission to build. We've sourced everything from producers and local artisans within a fifty-mile radius. We support the ecosystem in all its forms. This is our green and sustainable brand. Look what good and thoughtful people we are, how seamlessly we blend in and belong to this quilted heartland with barely a dropped stitch.

I can almost believe it, until my reflection, refracted by the lamp on the floor into a layered image of an almost familiar face, stares back at me and mouths, *You are full of shit, Laura Llewellyn.*

I jump when Officer Danny's radio pulses and an electronic voice inside informs him that the city detectives are at the front gate. That was fast.

'Wait here, ma'am,' he says, with restored formality, quickly reappearing with a man and woman who look like an advert for a dial-a-detective company. Each is clad in a black suit, white shirt and his-and-hers lace-up brogues, like agents from the nineties TV show repeats we'd watch in the dark, close, tea-and-biscuit dens of our tweenage bedrooms. This pair are not the attractive main leads though, they're the supporting players, nosing around underlit warehouses, flashlights flaring, the ones who get killed off before the first ad break.

Not everyone is a character in one of your stories, Laura, I hear my mother caution, clear as day, in my head.

'But, of course they are, Mum,' I'd always grin back, usually scribbling in one of my many notebooks for later reference. 'Existentially, everyone is a supporting player in someone else's story, aren't they, Dad?'

So here come tonight's secondary players in the latest instalment of *The Laura Llewellyn Show*, as Mum always joked, doing a fake drumroll on the kitchen table. First the senior detective, who introduces herself as Rose Olsen, a pin-neat Native American officer of about my age in a well-cut, white blouse that could be last season Yves Saint Laurent. I don't usually 'do designer' as it's considered quite crass here, to flaunt your money, unless it's with your subtle address or your 'bit of boat' down at Netarts Bay, but in my line of work it pays to know quality. Her pink and pasty underling calls himself Chad White, a nonentity of a name which suits him, a plump hairless baby with a soft, blond down on his head so it looks like he's still fledging.

He smiles. She doesn't. Well, OK then. Let's get to it.

I suspect, right away, that something about me irritates the hell out of Det. Olsen. I can tell from the narrow gauge of her professional gaze, sliding over me, toe to crown. Maybe it's because she was just about to clock off her shift for a Friday night beer in Portland's gentrified Pearl District, but has instead had to drive down to the god-damn coast. Or maybe it's the slightly 'earth mother' look I'm sporting today that grinds her gears – hair in a lazy plait, loose linen blouse, buttery leather loafers – on some basic and guttural level it offends her.

After Oregon was the New World, and before it became the hipster heaven of today, this state was full-trip hippie land, with communes flourishing alongside famous photos in *Time* magazine showing shoeless kids and their kaftan-clad, Summer-of-Love parents seeking to flee *The Man*. There's still a ghost of that in the handmade earring, hemp shirt trade and it's no accident that Oregon was one of the first states to legalise weed. Olsen probably hates all that crap, the modern incarnation, commodified, normalised by the cannabis dispensaries that are opening up in former joss-stick-scented gift shops.

If it smells of patchouli, she probably loathes it. Her 'don't fuck with me' haircut would send a flower-child running for the hills. She's the embodiment of a city downtown block, no fuss, no muss, no window boxes or wind chimes. She looks like she does her homework on time and the dog has never eaten it.

Earth to Laura, intervenes Mum's voice, as everyone looks at me, waiting to be offered a seat, and Grace rises to the occasion, thanking them for coming, offering a hot drink. I think of the detectives who threatened to send me to prison back in Wales, wondering which of these two will start to prickle with sharp questions first. Whose voice will start to edge with sandpaper like DI Maureen's did? Who'll fill the role of bad cop today? Pound to a penny, or buck to a dime, it'll be Ms designer blouse. But we won't get that far, because I haven't done anything wrong.

Not this time.

Once the preliminaries of my statement are out of the way, Detective Olsen raises her eyebrows into her spirit level-straight fringe, or bangs, as I've never got used to calling them, and waits for me to speak. I've seen this technique before, pausing for the suspect to volunteer information, to lead the interrogation. But I'm not a suspect now so I can ask, 'So, the man in my kitchen? Do you know what happened? Do you know who you're looking for yet?'

'First things first,' says Olsen. 'I'm sorry to have to tell you this, but the casualty in your kitchen was Mr Walter Lennon.'

For the first time on this day of the unexpected, I am genuinely surprised as I ask, 'You mean Mary-Kate's husband, Walter? My neighbour?'

'I'm afraid so, yes.'

'Walter Lennon? Jesus!' interjects Officer Danny, closing his mouth following Olsen's lip-stapling stare.

'Yes, we had to secure the scene before we could move him. When we could, and he was cleaned up, the local doctor recognised him at once.'

'But, I mean, that's awful,' I say. 'Then, I need to call her right away. MK, his wife, I mean. She must be . . . I mean, she'll need me there.'

'I wouldn't try to call her just yet. Mrs Lennon's at the hospital.'

'Of course. But she'll need me. Has she seen him? Has she been told he's dead? Oh God, has she had to identify him? His body?'

'Oh no, Mrs Jensen,' she corrects, 'I'm glad to say he's not dead. Not yet, anyway. Mr Lennon is still unconscious. He has a serious head injury but he's stable. We haven't been able to speak to him but we're hoping he'll wake up soon and, in due course, tell us who assaulted him.'

'I see,' I stutter. 'I mean, let's hope he'll be all right.'

One eyebrow disappears entirely under her bangs as she asks, 'Until then, why do you suppose Walter Lennon was in your home this afternoon? Were you expecting him to drop by?'

'No. No, I wasn't expecting anyone.' I shake my head, letting the news sink in.

'Was he the type to just come over to shoot the breeze? With you or your husband? Did he call by for a beer, talk about the game, that sort of thing?'

At 4 p.m. on a Thursday, when he knew Elias would be in the city? I think, but say, 'No, he doesn't really pop by. He's away quite a lot with his construction company. MK calls in from time to time, if she isn't working up in Portland.'

'So, they live here but are often away? I thought Mrs Lennon doesn't have full-time employment?'

That's true, Walter is so rich MK doesn't need to work but she dabbles in what she calls 'this and that', to keep herself occupied. Recently that's meant freelance selling of very on-trend cannabis oil beauty products to her contacts in the spa industry. I have a whole box of freebie CBD toiletries in my utility room she sneaks back from her conference trips to Portland. Though this new-wave stuff is strictly the non-active end of the cannabis market, she's not averse to some more recreational stuff too, but I don't want to tell Olsen that.

'She sells beauty products on commission,' I say. 'She's here at the beach a few days a week and we hang out, though Walter mostly keeps to himself.'

'So, Walter and your husband are not friends?'

The truth is that Eli thinks Walter is 'kind of a dick'. He's never really been one for 'chillin' with the guys' or the keggers and football scene at college. He thinks Walter's an aging frat boy, coasting on Southern charm and conspicuous cash, and has been known to have me pretend he's out for a run on the rare occasions Walter's called round to ask if he wants to watch the ballgame on his 77-inch plasma and partake of a few 'brewskis'.

There doesn't seem any point in explaining this to Olsen though, not when the man might still die at any moment, and I feel a spike of guilt about disparaging his frayed jeans. Even with his wads of money, he self-confessedly 'dresses like a hobo' at home because it was good enough for his old dad in the auto shop, and he often volunteers to take on Tilly in sweaty bouts of beach soccer, usually 'getting his ass handed to him'.

'No, I mean . . .' I shake my head again. 'Walter was in the city a lot.'

'Did he have a key?'

'To our house? No, why would he?'

'Well, neighbours do sometimes, you know, for emergencies? Or if you're out of town and someone needs to check on the place. Mrs Lennon doesn't have a key?'

I shake my head once more.

'So, why do you think Walter Lennon might have called by today?'

'I don't know. I can't think of any reason, but maybe MK sent him round for something?'

'But,' she consults her notes, 'you've said that the yard door was unlocked when you came home. You told Andy Mackenzie you didn't use your key to gain entry. Which means Mr Lennon could have let himself in.'

'I doubt it.'

'But someone must have let him in, as there's no sign of breaking and entering.'

'Except for the knife and the handcuffs,' I correct. 'The stuff the other man left.'

'Other man?' She looks intrigued, waiting for me to continue.

22

'Whoever did this to Walter. The pervert.' When the silence stretches between us, I almost laugh. 'But you mean, you surely don't think *Walter* brought the rope and the knife? You can't think . . .'

'We don't know anything yet. We are, of course, keeping an open mind.'

Well, I would hope so, because it's absurd to think that good old Walter, La-Z-Boy-lounger fan and Long-Island-iced-teas-on-lawn-chairs guy, would creep into his neighbour's house like a *Dirty Harry*-era stalker with a sex-toy kit. Walter's the victim, as am I. Unless they are trying to suggest . . .

Then I feel it in my ribs, the metronomic knock, knock, knock of bad news, even before Olsen says, 'Well, as unlikely as it seems, we have no sign that anyone else was in your home today, Mrs Jensen. Nothing else is disturbed. We're waiting for forensics and fingerprints so it's very early days, but, so far, we have no evidence of anyone in the house today, other than you both.'

'But then, who hurt Walter?'

'That's the real question, isn't it?'

And in the white glare of the lamp bouncing off her black pupils, I see the interview room light that flared when DI Maureen asked, 'So where were you that night, Laura, when the others went to the woods? Did you go to the riverbank? Did you watch?' That was the moment I knew what she was thinking, that she was looking at me as the one with dirty hands, a doer of grimy deeds. That she knew I was hiding something.

This woman has the same look, though exactly what she's implying is unclear.

Focus, Laura, Mum warns, and I hear myself saying, 'Well, it's obvious whoever attacked Walter brought the items with him. He must have disturbed him while he was . . .' *waiting for me to get home . . .*

Olsen sniffs, pauses for a moment as she scribbles in her notepad, then says, 'So, let's just clarify, you were expecting to be alone at the Shore Street house tonight? Your husband's in the city? He works there frequently while you and your daughter live here all week?'

'Yes, he works from the city office two or three days a week, when he stays at our town house, and from his home studio for the rest. He's been up there since Tuesday. I was there too, and had Tilly with me. She had a bit of a cold, so I kept her home from school. She was feeling much better today, so our assistant took her to her aikido club and I came home early, to tidy the house for the party tomorrow.'

'Ah yes,' she looks at her notepad. 'You came home to prepare for Matilda's birthday?' Her tone makes this decision sound at best bizarre, if not downright reckless.

'Yes, it was a last-minute decision.'

'So, no one knew?'

I shake my head again, the repetition starting to make me woozy. If I plead a concussion will she fuck off now? Actually, will everyone just fuck right off? *Language, Laura*, says Mum, and Grace bites her tongue.

'So, Mr and Mrs Lennon didn't know you were cutting your stay in the city short?' asks Olsen.

'No, I . . .' Now she's insinuating something else. Or is she? I'm not sure at this precise second, because my pulse has acquired the whoosh and rush of the ocean at my back, the glass wall behind pressing up, the waves beyond pushing in. I don't like the crush of being cornered. Of wondering if I should tell the truth, or if I even know it. But I tell myself, this is not then, this is now.

'No, I mean. I didn't tell anyone else. I was going to tidy up the house and then relax on my own until tomorrow.'

'Relax, on your own . . .?' she repeats, as if this is something someone like me could hardly need to do. Someone so privileged, with two houses, building a third. How stressful could my life be, that I would leave my daughter and husband to drive alone, two hours, to an empty house? How can I explain that, once I leave the choked outskirts of Portland, I love the roll of the car along the lanes shrouded with dense woods and dells, savour its rise and fall over the edges of the Tillamook State Forest, the meanders through the hills, past homesteads and meadows in the farming wetlands?

During that drive I can breathe, stretch out inside this stiff shell of mine, snatch time to pause the performance, stop worrying if anyone can see a crack, spot something trying to sneak out. In my metal cocoon I can eat M&M's from the glove box by the handful and lick my fingers clean if I want to. I can put Radiohead or Nine Inch Nails on the phone 'stupid loud', as Tilly would say, and sing along like a screeching banshee.

Grace Jensen does not curse, but in there I can yell *Seriously, motherfucker?* when a pickup tailgates me or an absurd, gas-guzzling tourist SUV cuts me up. Sometimes I sit in silence, rolling through the shadows and sunspots, the sweep of the windscreen wipers becoming the beat of solitude. Occasionally I yell, scrape my throat raw. Only in the deep swerves of the tracks, you understand, in the low, logging hollows when no car is in front or behind. If a tree falls in the forest and there's no one there to hear it, does it make a sound? Is it the same for a woman's scream?

If so, it's only the pines lending an ear here. Not Det. Olsen, that's for sure. Not goddamn Rose Olsen with her sharp, black eyes, who's looked at my house, my clothes, my 'Project' for twenty-seven minutes and already written her own narrative; spoiled expat, bored Oregon coast rich-bitch, and I can't even blame her. I've done my job too well, enforced the impression my life has been charmed and cosseted, until 4 p.m. today, that is.

'It's been a busy week,' I reply, eventually, hating the sound of excuse in my explanation. 'I work at my husband's firm – Bright Brothers – too, as an associate architect, well, mostly interior design now, and I've been finishing a project up in Portland this week. Though I mostly work here during the school term.'

'Yes, I see.'

'Yes, we mainly use the city house as a work base, or to escape the tourists here if we're not taking a vacation,' I run on, aware I'm babbling.

'Ah, yes, *tourist season*. That can be . . . challenging,' nods Olsen, for the people who can't escape to the spa lodges of Washington State or the beach front of Santa Barbara, her little smile seems to say.

'Then, we come back for the new semester and have a little birthday party here.'

'Not now, obviously,' she frowns.

'Of course not. Actually, I suppose I need to make some phone calls, tell people it's cancelled.'

'I doubt that will be necessary,' she says.

She's right. No one will expect there to be a party tomorrow afternoon. Everyone will know about this by morning, if they don't already.

'So, to confirm, no one had a key?' asks Olsen, redundantly.

'No.'

'But do you have a Hide-a-key? You know, one of those things disguised as a rock you can keep in your yard, in case you ever lose your set.'

'Uh, no. Though I do keep a spare key hidden in the birdfeeder. I've only used it once, when I locked myself out. I think it's still there.'

'Does anyone else know it's there?'

'I don't think so. Only Eli.'

'Could someone have seen you using it?'

'I doubt it. The back is screened pretty well.'

'Yes, it's pretty private. Then I have to ask you this, Mrs Jensen,' she says carefully, a show of professional sympathy, 'can you think of anyone who might want to hurt you? Anyone who might be responsible for today's events?'

Then I mime the function of thinking long and hard, even though, as I cast my eyes up to the ceiling, furrow my brow, I can only think of one answer to that first question and one answer to the last. And I can't say his name out loud. I struggle to even think it. I don't want to recall his long, ink-stained fingers, his cool grey eyes or the light in his smile. I really don't want to think of the sneer in his voice or the rage cracking there.

'I can't think of anyone,' I answer, the sound of the keypad activating on the door to the ground floor preventing any further reply, as Elias's voice calls my name, heavy steps repeat on the stairs and he bursts towards me, crushes me to his chest. It takes a moment to escape the scratch of his beard and weathered Norse god embrace, before I can ask where Tilly is. Thankfully, it seems she's still with Anoushka in the city, already stuffing herself with Voodoo Doughnuts probably, because, if I know our treasured but sweet-toothed, East Coast assistant (don't call her a nanny, not because she would mind, but because I am not the sort of person who wants to say she has a nanny), she never can resist the urge to play tourist.

'I was going to swing back to the city to get her after work but when I got your messages I came straight here,' he explains. 'Jesus, baby, are you OK?' Elias asks, cupping my face. It's only when he registers the three officers in the room that he pulls back and holds out his hand in a formal shake.

'Mr Jensen,' says Olsen, rising, though not far, as she barely reaches his shoulder. 'We've been trying to call you for some time.'

'I thought you'd never come,' I chide, as he explains how he'd had to unexpectedly drive out to Astoria this afternoon, to check on some timber cuts.

'When I finally got the call from Bridgette, I came straight here,' he adds, knowing there's little phone signal on the winding coastal route north of here, so he doesn't need to explain why I haven't had a call. 'I'm so sorry. I'm here now.'

And I'm sickeningly glad of that. Seeing him always feels like stepping off a swaying boat on to stable ground. That's how it felt the day he came and sat next to me on the observatory level of the Seattle Space Needle, its saucer soaring above the low-rise city and silver expanse of Puget Sound. He had his own sketchbook in his lap, but his huge hand reached out and rested on the page of mine for a moment as he said, 'I don't mean to bother you but these are really good.'

Something shifted inside me that day, as we 'went native', drinking Stumptown coffee as he introduced me to Dutch baby pancakes at Tilikum Place Café, the weight and solidity of him steadying me, binding me to this country long after my student exchange visa expired. Now he's my mooring in fair weather and the only port I'll ever want in a storm, which is just as well, as surely one is on its way.

To underline the point, the wind starts its slow rise up the water-cut creek below us, winding from the sea slough that slopes into its mouth, its rough singing echoing around the bones of the house. Back in Gwyn Mawr on the Welsh coast, my grandfather, often over for snoozy evening tea and ramblings, had a word for that unsettling song, straight from the depths of the wind's throat, the chorus that rose into a shrieking around the houses – *Cyhireath* – a warning of what's on the way in the old tongue.

He was a former Army sergeant who worked at the prisoner-of-war camp in Island Farm, near Bridgend. It was the site of one of the biggest German POW escapes in wartime history when seventy men tunnelled to temporary freedom and he'd laugh when he'd say, 'North wind tonight, little one. That sound always put the wind up them Jerries, all right. Not so big and bad then, at the sound of trouble brewing.'

How right you were, Grampy, I used to think, it's always

brewing somewhere. But, for now, Elias is here and I'm so grateful to him for being him, and for being mine, I don't care what Olsen thinks. As I lean into this muscular slice of rich man in a soft designer suit, she cannot know he's not as smooth-seamed as he's learned to appear either; that he's polished himself to this sheen since he was raised by a single father, a 'blue collar' engineer, who made sure his two sons appreciated the roughness of JCPenney cotton on their necks and getting their fingernails blackened in builders' yards long before college.

When we first met, it was this hands-on honesty that attracted me to him, every grain of who he is etched in his smile, like a great Northwest pine sliced down the middle, the rings and weather of his world marked on him. In this way my Elias is not like Silas – *my Silas*. There, I've thought his name, recalled his smile spinning out behind him in the sand dunes and sea spray of my memory.

No, Eli Jensen, son of Norwegian immigrants, twice removed, is anything but the boy who once lived across the road, in the damp half-timbered end cottage. Unlike that boy, with his prickly confidence, and enthusiasms that ebbed and flowed with his allegiances, Elias does not say one thing and mean another. He does not make promises he cannot keep.

'Perhaps we could continue this in the morning?' he asks now. 'I think my wife's been through enough for one day,' and I'm touched he thinks I can stand so little.

'Probably a good idea,' says Olsen's baby-fat colleague who, until now, has not spoken. With a nod from her, he hands Elias a card, saying, 'We'll be in touch in the morning, but if you think of anything significant before then, do let us know. Can you stay somewhere close by tonight in Lookout Beach? Can you let Officer Landon know your whereabouts?'

We nod at Officer Danny, acknowledging that we are politely being told 'not to leave town'.

'We'll let ourselves out,' says White.

'I'll be in the patrol car outside,' adds Officer Danny. 'Sheriff's orders, so holler if you need me.'

There's something reassuring about that, though why would I need anyone else now Elias is here? When he holds me, waiting patiently for me to speak, muttering, 'Jesus, if anything had happened to you, I don't know what I'd do,' I know he is telling the truth. He is as open as a halved heart and his is melded with mine.

This is what matters.

Silas is not here tonight. He was not in my kitchen earlier today either. He can't have been. There is no connection between this and him, and a fall night when I only ever called it autumn. It's a coincidence, the fiction of my conscience. Just because a red ribbon and a rope were found at the crime scene all those years ago, that has nothing to do with the gifts on my countertop today.

But if Silas, and all that came with him, is buried with the past, whoever brought the gifts to my kitchen is still out there in the howling night. And right now, no one knows who he is, why he came, or what he will do next.

Four

Cap Goch

You could say it all began the day I shared the story about the Cap Goch, the tale that keeps running through my head as I rest it on Elias's shoulder. We know we can't stay here all night, with no hot water, no food, but, somehow, we're still glued to the Project's tatty sofa by an unspoken urge to hold the moment. I'm glad Tilly is tucked up warm on Anoushka's sofa bed tonight, until we can decide what to tell her and explain why we can't go home. Slugs of bourbon in coffee mugs help us deny the reality of what's happened today. Though, for me at least, it can't hold back what came long before.

It's the wind song, the salt smell and the night black that have raised the dead. That and the feeling of everything starting to simmer and smoke in the gaps between the day's events, beginning with the tale of a long-dead man in a red hat, with a sharp knife.

Eli has never heard the folk legend, about the innkeeper on the River Ogmore, and, as far I'm concerned, he never will. I won't tell it again and neither will my parents. We know our roles too well, hands, feet and tongues dug in and braced against what is behind us in our own ways. I suppose it's a miracle we've remained so close really, at heart, if not in the miles of ocean that separate us fifty weeks a year, that my parents are still together, when Liam's mum and dad separated soon after the scandal and Silas's father killed himself.

Back then, I was always grateful that scatty, smiling Dad was nothing like straight-up-serious Dr Huw Cracknell. When things turned bad, Dad's background in English and Creative Writing helped him 'process' it all, or 'reframe his narrative' as he would have put it, into something he could live with. Silas's father on the other hand, scalpel precise and Bible severe, couldn't even begin to handle it, choosing a rope and a barn beam, despite the likelihood of eternal damnation because of it.

You could say it was partly my dad's fault, what happened that summer, because years before he told me he would always love me but I had to tell the truth, no matter how bad it was, he told me many stories, including the one about the Cap Goch. It was the third of twelve tales in the book of local legends he'd gathered and published some years before for his PhD.

The tome, with its array of colourful and creepy characters stalking the lands and netherworlds from Sker to St Donat's, Crack Hill to Candlestone, never left my bedside table and was largely responsible for my mother's complaints I was 'away with the story fairies' for half my childhood. Often literally, as I roamed the dunes in nighties over shorts and T-shirt outfits, muttering rhymes and incantations, beachcombing with Dad until the house was full of shells and sea glass, driftwood and salty charms my mum would periodically clear out and disperse.

By the summer of my fifteenth year, I was long past dressing up in princess pinafores and pirate hats, galumphing through the dunes in search of wronged maidens and bold buccaneers. But somehow, I still viewed the world through a lens of those heroes, villains and happy endings, even as we fledgling teenagers splashed on our bodyboards among the estuary's white crests, slipping like seals through the murky green swells in £200 wetsuits. Even as we rolled our eyes at how boring everything suddenly was, twisting with newfound awkwardness inside our scuffed-up designer trainers and artfully ripped hoodies.

Secretly, I would've been more than happy to keep drifting like that for years, keep coming top of my class, winning every Eisteddfod competition with my detailed historical stories and, once a year, raising the swim trophy aloft with Silas holding the other side. I thought the kids who'd followed us through those years of surf competitions and swim parties, stealing warmth and light from us at the beach bonfires, would keep clapping, clustering towards our flames, that is, until everything changed the August we spent at the rickety cottage in the dunes.

It was nothing more than run-of-the-mill teenage rebellion that prompted Silas to bring booze along one afternoon, well, to tell Liam to get some; gentle Liam, tall by then, shooting up like an ear of tousle-haired seagrass, one of life's sidekicks, quick to smile or agree to whatever Silas wanted. We were only playing at experimenting, hiding away in our crumbling club house, the three musketeers, as Dad joked, because we were always found together, usually deep in some form of enterprise.

That is, until Priss joined us. Priss with her plastic baggies of weed, who'd moved to Gwyn Mawr that July toting a harsh Norf London accent and a sniffily pierced nose. Priss, with her hundredweight of black eyeliner, who turned heads in our Best Kept Village, 1996, 1998. She made no secret of the fact she thought we were so very provincial, so soft, *so Welsh, for fuck's sake – sheep-shagging, harp-playing, leek-munching twats*, but she was still drawn to us because we were the sagging social centre of our scene, even if it was 200 miles west of the one she was used to.

Late starters I suppose, sheltered, soft with money and learning, how we snickered when she showed Liam how to roll the weed into the newly bought papers, when she suggested we take shots of whisky and play truth or dare. Then how we groaned when she got high and told us she could read the tarot cards if we wanted, that she could 'sense things', even see the future.

'Goth bullshit,' I remember Silas scoffing, sprawled across the broken earth floor of the abandoned cottage that had previously only had room for three.

'Lame,' I American-drawled, like the TV teenagers we admired, taking just a little puff of the beery spliff, as she held the pack towards me, saying, 'Pick a card, any card, Princess Lolly Pop. Or is it Pirate Pissy Pants now?'

It was gloomy inside the old walls but I know my face was electric hot then, when Liam snorted and Silas yawned, 'Fucking hell, give us a break, Madam Zorah.'

Because I knew they were thinking of the mortifying photograph that had circulated through our youth club two weeks before, feeding my blush even as Silas shot me a sleepy, sympathy wink. Though both his eyes were anything but slow as he watched Priss's skinny fingers moving through the pack, her purple lipsticked mouth puckering.

It was seven o'clock then, but autumn was already knocking on the ends of the August evenings, sliding in through the window cracks, blowing on our bare legs. Silas lit the stumps of candles we kept hidden in the wall recess and rolled out a blanket for me.

'Pick a card, if it's all bullshit,' challenged Priss, when we were settled again, 'or are you afraid of what you'll see in your future?'

And there it was, that pinprick more subtle than the direct smirk I'd detected at the end of the previous term, when Mr Jones had introduced her as the new girl whose dad would teach us history in September. Not wanting to show her I was deflating, I remember pulling a card out, tossing it on the floor, only for it to reveal a hoary skeleton.

'Death, wooo!' wailed Liam. 'It's all up for you, Lolly Pop!' the name Silas's little sister Abi had given me years before when I'd first joined the Surf Club and had somehow stuck.

'Fuck off, twat,' I grinned, because the more we swore at each other that year, the more grown up we felt.

'Death does not have to mean death the way you think it does,' smiled Priss, with the indulgence of a deity not sitting on a rolled-up anorak. 'It can mean rebirth, renewal, a metaphor for things about to change. An awakening.'

And, as she grinned at me, sly and wolfish, her eyes flicked towards Silas. She thought I was stupid, that I didn't suspect. But I did.

'Wake up to this, then, and roll me a refill, yeah,' drawled Silas, using his knife to idly scratch a pentagram on the stone edge of the old hearth, 'or it'll be Ouija boards and voodoo dolls next.'

Priss just smiled. 'When we lived in London, we used to creep into Highgate Cemetery and set up a Ouija board on Christina Rossetti's tomb. They were really into all that, you know, the Victorians – spiritualism, the afterlife. One night we held a séance and heard unearthly voices.'

'Told you,' Silas rolled his eyes. 'Was it Karl Marx's ghost, dying of capitalist-inspired horror, or George Eliot turning in her grave?' because, we were, after all, reaping the benefits of a modestly private education, aimed at easing us into Oxbridge.

'It's true. We all heard them,' insisted Priss, her eyes glowing. 'It was horrible. The strangest thing I've ever heard.'

'I'll tell you something horrible,' I said, keen to make Silas look at me instead of her again, as it should be. 'It's a true story. A tale of horror and murder, right here in Gwyn Mawr.'

'Oh yes, go on. It's cool,' said Liam, knowing the tale I was about to recount from whispers and skipping games in the playgrounds, from Halloween chants and jump-scares in the hide-and-seek streets. 'It's got slit throats and beheadings in it. There's even a rhyme to warn you that, if you misbehave, the Cap Goch might come and get you.'

On cue, he chanted: '*Don't say his name. Don't stay to eat. Don't close your eyes or fall asleep. Stay on the road, stay on your feet. Or he will come and bury you deep.*'

'That sounds like fucking kids' stuff,' said Priss, feigning boredom. 'Nothing cool ever came out of this dump.'

'Wait until you hear the story,' said Liam, unfolding both arms towards me, as if introducing a stage magician. 'Tell it, Laura.'

So I did, and it had everything to do with what came next. And nothing at all. Though DI Maureen didn't believe the last part. 'But Laura,' she repeated, peering through her pink-rimmed eyes, as if trying to understand, 'what sort of game includes a knife? A rope? What sort of sick mind would think up such a thing?'

That was a complicated question with more than one answer. I'm still not sure I know the whole truth – if there is such a thing, listening to the wind shriek around the Project, glad when Eli says, 'Come on, let's get going and get some food inside you,' so, at least for a few hours, I don't have to think about what came next.

Five

Tsunami Alert

By 8 a.m. it's already a beautiful sunburst of a day. It's a myth that the Pacific Northwest is constantly shrouded in cobweb drizzle and this morning is shaping up to be a reminder of how magical the coastline is when you can see it. Except it's hard to appreciate the raw wonder of a shiny, salt-washed sunrise when I'm fidgeting in yesterday's clothes, mainlining espresso, and Elias is using the Tideline Inn's wi-fi to read news stories about the violent prowler on the loose.

It's less than twenty-four hours since I found Walter Lennon on our kitchen floor but, as we feared, Lookout Beach is in what passes for uproar. The local rag/community newssheet has it plastered across their website in caps, MAN CRITICAL – ATTACKER SOUGHT, and it's being bandied around the Lookout Beach Facebook feed in anxious exchanges between mums and traders, with *Shocked!* and *Concerned!* headers. Exclamation marks a go-go!

Maria Weathers, the local nightmare busybody, has put

the news report on her *Go Moms!* webpage and some of the details have leaked out – an intruder with a knife is mentioned, which can only have come from someone close to the scene; a blabby paramedic perhaps, a slack-tongued cop chatting with colleagues or whispering with loved ones, warning them to lock their doors and windows.

There's no mention of a rope or a red ribbon, thankfully. There's no mention of me by name. But the screaming giveaway will be the police camped out on our front steps.

Bob Turner, the Tideline Inn's manager, clearly knows what almost happened to me yesterday and has no idea how to react. Last night when we arrived from the Project, he'd simply given us the 'some adult time' smile and issued us a room key, but he's become better informed since then, as have his staff, constantly finding excuses to come in and gawp, topping up the brimming juices on the breakfast bar, checking on the groaning hill of fresh sourdough rolls.

Thankfully, we're the only guests here, except for two wind-burned out-of-towners, staring mutely at their avocado toast and his 'n' hers pastry baskets. The summer is officially over. We're well past the final push for September's Labor Day, the late American equivalent of a bank holiday, and the Tideline Inn, and the dozens like it, are switching to wooing romantic escapers, fireplaces lit and beach bonfires stacked high in readiness for shortening evenings, Octoberfest and Halloween.

They call it the secret season here, the 'shoulder' months when this stretch of coast empties out and the mists roll in. Then the weekenders from the city materialise, wraiths wrapped in cashmere sweaters and quilted jackets, to appreciate the waves and wind before the residents hunker down for the slow season. But there are so few real locals here now, the original locals living further north on the white-capped expanse of Willapa Bay or inland on the farms. They gather and shuck oysters there, pump gas, haul and fell trees in mildewing villages and fallen industry towns, rusting into the landscape, sanded down by the sea, strung along a coast road.

The citizens of Lookout Beach are mostly incomers – artists setting up colonies, second homers and exhausted city slickers who've decided this is a better place to raise their tech-addicted kids, in this purpose-built piece of the American dream. Except now there's a stain on it, of violence and perversion. The fact that their perfect village is no better than anywhere else is a tsunami of realisation, far more immediate than the one expected to one day emerge from the Pacific void, engulfing anyone too slow to flee inland along the meticulously marked evacuation routes. A constant reminder that, at any moment, a wave could rush in and swallow us whole.

This is going to be a long day, I realise, dipping a knob of sourdough into my organic poached egg. I'd really like to get out of here, get my winter wetsuit on and thrash myself out into the wide, rolling bay in my kayak. I could even slip into the water and activate my arms and legs in the booming surf that serves as a silencer for the high velocity thoughts in my head.

Not too far out, of course, just hugging the barnacled rocks that slide this bay into the next, keeping away from the currents at the distinctive, rocky Oregon sea stacks squalling with gulls. Then I'd go limp, watching the town from the water, the retreating doll's house-sized strings of clapboard and pine, black windows unseeing because I'm invisible on the ocean.

It's out of the question, though. It would be, even if the police weren't still at the Shore Street house where my wet-suit is. Elias would never have it. He hates my penchant for 'wild swimming' and 'boating' as he calls it, at the best of times, and has good reason to remind me that even the surfers are cautious of the riptides and surges along this beach, that the cold can cut like iced teeth, chewing you in half in minutes, and at least one careless person drowns every year.

No, today Grace Jensen must play the victim and hope to make it through until darkness when she can hide from the looks and glances. This is just the beginning. It will get worse. I should know. It's new to Elias though, and he's not sure how to deal with it, except to remove himself from it and keep pushing onwards.

'Let's blow this joint,' he mutters, an in-joke phrase beloved by his old dad, as he rises to his feet, blocking out the morning sun.

My thoughts exactly.

'You're sure about this?' he checks again as he drives me, at exactly two digits below the snail's-pace speed limit, towards the hospital in Cannon Beach. To be fair, he has asked if I want him to come with me to see MK at the hospital, though I know he doesn't want to. Watching his mother die in one when he was only fourteen has under-standably put him off, so he's relieved when I tell him to go find a coffee shop with decent wi-fi to do some work.

He still flanks me all the way from the car to the front steps though, his gaze flickering around asking, *Who is close by? Who looks like they should not be here? Is it safe?* I've done the same thing myself, many times over the years.

'Call me when you're done,' he insists, as I nod and tiptoe upwards to kiss his cheek.

'It's all right, Officer Landon will give me a ride back to the Project,' waving at Officer Danny parking up the patrol car behind us, though he must be dying for a sleep, a shower, a shave.

I should be scared. Perhaps I am. Elias obviously thinks I'm not scared enough, but he doesn't know I'm not taking any chances. That I have a gun in the slouchy leather handbag Grace calls her 'everyday purse', her vocabulary, like her behaviour, acclimatised now, so she calls a lift a 'ride', the rubbish the 'trash', and tells Tilly to keep her bike on the sidewalk.

Good old Laura, on the other hand, is not taking any polite chances, hence the Glock nestling in the inside zip pocket against her leg. I've kept it close to me since college, hidden away out of sight in a shoe box. Elias doesn't know and wouldn't disapprove, exactly. Being from North Oregon he grew up with shotguns and rifles, or at least with people who didn't think twice about keeping one in the gun cupboard or hall closet. But he doesn't want one in the house. Why would he need one in the safest little bolthole south of Seattle?

Besides, Grace is a mom, worried about school shootings and the political pull of the evil NRA. She wouldn't inherit a college friend's Glock, in her final university semester in

43

Seattle, because that friend's dad got his daughter a better one for graduation, or go to a clearing in the wood to practise popping holes in rubbish bin targets. The idea alone would scare her, the noise prompting her to raise a hand to her mouth, muttering, 'Oh my!'

I raise my hand now, but only to wave to Elias, who won't walk away until I'm through the double doors. Lookout Beach is too small for a real hospital and, as never fails to amaze me, all healthcare is private in the US. We're lucky to have excellent insurance, included in the Bright Brothers' package, but whatever poor old Walter is having done to save his life will cost MK tens of thousands of dollars. Before he's even recovered, or, God forbid, been buried, the bills will start to arrive.

Giving birth to Tilly here cost us 17,000 bucks. While I'm not saying she wasn't worth every penny, I'm just wondering how much saving a whole life costs.

Sipping the fresh espresso in my hand, sitting in the lavender-scented private lounge, I scan the doors of the high dependency unit for Mary-Kate. This is the woman who welcomed me as a neighbour six years ago by turning up on my back step in a neon yellow kaftan carrying a bottle of tequila. Since then she's been my safety valve, my anti-mommy-routine conspirator when shots, cynicism and oversharing need to be liberally applied.

It's unsettling knowing that, behind those doors, she's waiting to be told if her husband will live or die, or if his brain will bleed until it robs him of who he is. I can't imagine what she's going through, or bring myself to wonder if she hates me now, because it's more than likely that Walter saved my life yesterday.

Whatever the police uncover, whoever the suspect is, Walter's in there, tethered to tubes because of me. If he hadn't disturbed the intruder would I have been found today, by Elias returning home, trussed and violated, the rope taut around my swollen wrists?

I ignore the flash of memory that splinters my vision, a pair of black cotton knickers, a black padded bra, gagging on the sour smell of vodka and vomit it conjures, the blood on the leaves, red, black. I close my eyes but that only accelerates the heave in my stomach so I snap them open again.

Don't close your eyes, don't fall asleep, chants Liam.

Fuck off, twat, I mutter.

I haven't really slept in years. I didn't last night, imagining Tilly and her blonde curls bouncing into the kitchen, finding me there, offered up as a twisted sacrifice. My skin crawls to think of my little girl in that room, when, since she was born, I've tried to keep her away from the discolouring effect of this world, always looking into her pale blue eyes for signs of the stains of my DNA.

So far, it all seems to be her father, in her looks at least, everything about her guileless and clean, a tomboyish bundle of laughter with a love of pirates and beachcombing and paddling until her feet are blue. If she can read it, swim in it, kick it or get dirty in it, her delight is boundless, which I suppose she gets from me.

Today she is eight years old, has woken up at Anoushka's, and no one will properly explain why she cannot come home and have her pirate birthday party today. It's hard to explain to an excited eight-year-old that it's because of the forensics team taking apart our home.

She's borne it well, though, under the promise of Blue Star Donuts. I'm not sure exactly when our not-a-nanny finds time to study for her PhD in Native American Folk Art, but I'm glad she's so flexible in emergencies and will keep Tils entertained until we're allowed to drive to Portland tonight and I can bearhug her skinny bones until they almost break.

The thought is cut off as Mary-Kate suddenly emerges through the swing doors, and I see at once that her usual air of neon floral confidence has collapsed.

'How is he, honey?' I ask, getting to my feet, as she falls into my arms like a felled tree. After a moment my blouse is soaking and I realise my whirlwind of colour and don't-give-a-damn friend is crying, silently, into my shoulder.

My stomach clenches, as I ask, 'What happened?' eventually pulling her down into a seat, handing her the wad of Kleenex Grace keeps handy in her purse, alongside Band-Aids, wet wipes and painkillers for headachy school-run moms. 'Has he been able to tell anyone what happened yet?'

'No, honey. He's not conscious. He hasn't come out of the coma because of the pressure in his skull. They don't know if he'll ever wake up,' her voice fighting the slow squeeze of medication, probably Valium, which they seem to give out like M&M's here. Me, I don't even take paracetamol. I don't want to be dulled and blunt. I want to be sharp. That way, whatever happens I'll feel it all. I deserve to.

When the door to the corridor flies open, I jump, until I realise it's just our friend Belle, bowling to the rescue. She's the polar opposite of MK, the stay-at-home mom who made all the pirate hats for the cancelled birthday party today; Captain Terrible for Tilly, Bosun Brilliant for her son Seb, Tilly's bestie, etc., and all the other kids who would've been rolling up at our house in six hours' time were it not for the police cordon.

If we hadn't all ended up living next door to each other I'm not sure the three of us would ever have become friends, but somehow it works. MK always determined to make sure Belle gets drunk and eats non-vegan at least once a week, Belle never tiring of looking after MK's 'holistic wellbeing' and me bridging that gap with a foot in both camps.

I'm glad to see Belle now as she exclaims, 'Oh my God,' from across the room, billowing boho beads and hand-dyed linen. 'How's Wally?'

'He's not good, hon,' manages MK through Belle's sudden and strangling patchouli hug. 'He hasn't woken up yet.'

'Jesus, this is just so awful. I mean, poor Wally. And you, Grace, honey. Jesus, are you OK?' throwing her arm around my neck so her deck of bangles grazes my cheek. 'Oh my God! Do they know who he is yet, this guy in your house? And did Wally just wander in on him? I mean, he must've interrupted this creep in the middle of ... and hitting Wally like that. I mean, a knife, a rope ...'

Her thoughts drift into sex-slasher movie territory and I wonder how she knows all this, before remembering that Seb's piano teacher Polly Jackson, fond of Belle's bran muffins, is head of the town council and will have been updated by Lieutenant Andy, officially or otherwise.

'I mean, holy cow!' Belle explodes. 'Maybe he saved your life?'

And I'm grateful to her for airing the obvious elephant stinking out the room, though I counter, 'We don't know anything yet. What matters now is how Walter is, right?'

'Sure, sure,' Belle agrees, transferring the bruising hug back to MK. 'It's just such a *thing*, isn't it? Like fate or something. I mean, like, wasn't Wally supposed to be in Bend this weekend, MK? You said he was coming back on Monday?'

'He was,' mutters MK. 'I guess his work retreat was cancelled.'

'So where were you when this was going on?' demands Belle. 'I mean, did you see him go over to Grace's place? Did you see anyone suspicious?'

'I was walking Oprah,' MK mutters, meaning their dopey labradoodle, which seems weird because I could've sworn I saw her hairy silhouette against MK's first-floor blinds as I walked up my path. That's her lookout spot, her nose-art, snot doodles a permanent glass fixture, no matter how often MK breaks out the Windex.

'Walter wasn't supposed to be coming home,' MK wails, her sobbing reaching hurricane proportions.

'Maybe he was looking for you, at Grace's,' says Belle, with her usual sledgehammer tact. I mean, I love her but sometimes she has the verbal grace of Donald Trump, 'and that's how he stumbled on the guy. Thank God, in one way, you know, but Jesus, poor Wally.'

There's not much to say to that, beyond pointing out that no one ever calls Walter 'Wally', which would serve no purpose.

Easing MK back down onto the sofa, Belle whispers, 'I wish I had a gun at home, you know, just for protection.

I know guns are bad news and all, but this creep is still out there, right? Who knows where he'll show up next? This sort of thing just doesn't happen here, not to people like us. And, like, why you, Grace? Why your house? Did he just pick one of our places at random? Could it have been any of us? It makes me sick. I had to take two Xanax last night just to try and sleep.'

I feel the weight of the gun in my purse but ignore it, asking MK, 'What can we do, honey?'

'What can anyone do, except wait?' she sniffs.

'Maybe you need to go home, get a change of clothes, a shower?' I suggest, but she vetoes that immediately, insisting, 'I can't leave here. I can't leave him.'

'Of course not. Then maybe Belle could go get you something to eat and drink, something other than coffee and vending-machine candy?'

'Yeah, sure, good idea. You have to keep your strength up,' says Belle, gangling to her feet, eager to have a task. She reminds me of Liam in that way, always wanting a job, then to be told he'd done that job well. And he always did, until he just couldn't bear to do it any more. Not even for Silas.

By the time Belle returns with a decaf soy latte, orange juice cup, an egg-filled breakfast wrap and a bag of goji berries, MK has fallen asleep on the sofa, her face cradled on her snotty arm.

'Probably best if we just let her rest a while,' I whisper.

'Sure, sure,' she whispers back. 'I'll stay for a bit. Seb is at Jungle Jim's for a couple of hours. I know, I know,' she grins, 'kind of like expecting Harry Potter to enjoy an afternoon at NASCAR but I figured I'd be needed here.'

Then she shoves a patchwork hobo bag at me, saying, 'I brought you some clothes too, a sweater, a shirt, some bathroom stuff, you know, till you can go home.'

'Bless you, honey,' I smile, patting her on the arm, pretty sure I can smell my own sweat on this two-day-old shirt.

'When *can* you, you know, go home?'

'That's up to the police.'

'Yes, this must be a nightmare. You're bearing up so well. But I saw Officer Landon. Guess he's your body-guard now.'

'Yes. Until they figure out who they're looking for.'

'And why he picked you. I mean, your house, out of the three of ours, all of them back to back.'

'Why do these psychos do anything they do?'

'True. Is Elias freaking out? It must be so hard for him, being so close by when it was happening but not here to, you know . . . protect you.'

'What do you mean?' I ask.

'You know, yesterday. In Seaside. Elias being only min-utes away but, well, that's a lifetime, right? Were it not for Walter, in the right place at the right time . . .'

I'm not sure what she means. I'm also a little bit narked that everyone seems to think I'm so bloody helpless. Is it out of the question I might have fought back against my intruder? But I don't say this to Belle. It's the first part of her sentence I respond to when I state, 'Elias wasn't in Seaside yesterday afternoon. He was in Astoria.'

'Oh, right, sure.'

'What?' I ask. She has an uneasy look that I don't like. In my experience women who willingly contribute to the bake sale every fourth of July, and stand on a windy stall

50

outside the firehouse selling community-grown zucchinis (aka courgettes) for charity every Friday evening, lack a talent for subterfuge.

'I just thought I saw him at Seaside yesterday, that's all,' she replies. 'I had to run up there to get those awful sugar balls Seb likes for the bake-sale cupcakes, and some cotton candy. But I might have been mistaken. I'd been in a tear all day, up to my elbows in icing sugar. Anyway, what are you going to do now?'

Good question.

We sit and wait with MK while she sleeps. When she wakes and wants to go back in to see Walter again, we hug and stare at the doors as they close behind her.

'Let's blow this joint,' I say.

'Thank God,' says Belle. 'I hate hospitals.'

Six

Bad Thoughts

There's some time to kill before Belle has to collect Seb, so we drive along the coast road in her green mom wagon with the nonsensical sticker, 'I brake to bake', on the bumper. We park at the beachhead outside the village, where you can walk through a cutting in the cliff onto the rock escarpment tidepools or across the tussocky grass to the sand. I need air and wind, and a yawning Officer Danny, who dutifully follows us in his patrol car, gives the thumbs up and a 'Just for ten minutes, then, ladies,' when we ask if it's OK.

Belle seems nervous, though, walking through the shedding leaves and evergreen heads, glancing around as if the Boston Strangler might leap out from behind a Sitka spruce at any moment. But surely no one is going to bother us with Officer Danny at our rear and the constant stream of elderly, wiry trail walkers passing in ones and twos, nodding with mild curiosity?

'Don't worry,' says Officer Danny, reading our minds,

'I'm sure whoever did this is long gone. I wouldn't be hanging around here if I was him.'

As we pass the little bridge over the brook, high and fizzing with the first autumn rains upstate, I fill my lungs, watching a bald eagle loop lazy rings from the bluff, like water draining down a plughole.

'Isn't that where Ashley Weathers had her accident, back during spring break?' says Belle, gesturing to the trail that surfaces from the scrub on the headland. Nodding, I think of the daughter of *Go Moms!* Maria, who slipped and smashed her head playing some sort of tag up there. She spent two months recovering and the sight in her right eye is not what it was. She's a grade above Tilly and wears glasses with one extra thick lens now, a cautionary tale about respecting an environment that can turn on you in moments.

'Maria's all over this home-invasion thing, of course,' sighs Belle, as we stroll on. 'The *Go Moms!* chat stream is going postal. She's talking about setting up a neighbour-hood watch, like she'd actually peel herself away from nightly hot yoga, or Brad from his home gym, to walk the streets with a flashlight. Dear little Ashley is devastated there's no pirate party, of course. She posted a pic of herself in her costume on the stream, with a sad face for Tilly, then messaged me to ask if she could have her badge and hat anyway.' She grins. 'Irritating little brat.'

Tilly hadn't liked Ashley much either, before her accident. Probably because Ashley is almost a better swimmer than Tilly at Otters Club, and because she used to make fun of the twisty big toe on Tilly's left foot she broke when she was four. Tilly went through a phase of saying she hated her, yet when she heard about the accident she was inconsolable.

'It's nice that you feel bad for her,' I said, pulling her into my arms, proud of my empathetic girl.

'It's not that, Mom,' she sniffled back. 'I think I made it happen. I wished she'd fall off a cliff, like a thousand times, and then she did and I made it happen with my bad thoughts.'

'You didn't really mean for it to happen,' I soothed. 'Besides, it's what a person does about the bad thoughts that count. And you've never done anything bad, right? So that makes you good inside.'

Because, though I'm fairly sure this rationale doesn't apply to me, I'd never believe anything dreadful about my girl. Even if she turned eighteen and was accused of becoming a serial killer I'd side with her every time, because that's what Mum and Dad did for me, the gift of faith they gave me. That's why they upped and left everything they'd built in Gwyn Mawr after the trial.

They couldn't name us in the newspaper stories, of course, nor in the sombre talking heads the TV reporters delivered from the imposing court steps. We were under eighteen, in theory still children, our identities protected, at least until after the verdict when the judge lifted one of the reporting restrictions because of the 'severe nature of the crime'. But it didn't matter. Everyone knew who we were; our classmates, their parents, the people we'd lived alongside since birth, the dads who'd superintended beach barbecues while the mums slathered us in sun cream and cheered the beach races and swim contests.

There could be no forgiveness, and forgetting would take

more than one lifetime, so, that spring, Dad announced we were leaving, taking a little holiday, spending the summer in a rented house on Lake Windermere. I remember the sound of Mum crying during those months, behind closed doors as she worked from home, laptop keys clattering, while Dad took on A-level tutoring at the summer school.

I was just another anonymous, solitary kid, puttering about on the lake. No more long sun-stroked evenings on the warm sand for me, on the lookout for pirates from the towering grassy head of the 'Big Dipper' dune; no more damp Welsh afternoons, warming up in tracksuits in front of the gas heaters of the old concrete-clad Surf Club house, eating cheese and onion rolls, with Liam peeling apart a Battenberg cake and throwing away the pink parts.

That summer I was alone on the cold, saltless shores of an inland sea, unable to pick up a book and transport myself to the world of stories any more, the words swimming away, meaningless. All that had shattered with the hammer edge of the judge's words, no room for the old me in the suitcase and boxes we loaded into the Fiesta.

When autumn began kicking leaves in our faces, rattling letterboxes, we finally moved to Northumbria so I could restart my GCSEs. There we rose to the challenge of being an ordinary threesome from 'Cardiganshire', relocated for Mum's job, lecturing at the school of architecture. While Newcastle was a long way from the shores of South Wales, it was only a hop over to the Northumberland coast, where I eventually joined a kayaking club to drown my memories, fill the gaps in my head where my stories had once been, on the waters of Whitley Bay.

Mum also stepped in when she saw my old books

untouched on the dresser, when Dad's suggestions we look at the folk stories of Northumberland or visit Hadrian's Wall were met with a disinterested shrug. Never a great lover of fiction, she was a great believer in the immutability of angles and equations, of things we could corner and calculate, and she encouraged me on a new path, away from the stories and English studies I'd loved. Instead, she offered me a new perspective, in the solid behaviours of stone and metal, the alternate poetry of Frank Lloyd Wright's Fallingwater, of Walter Gropius's Bauhaus school in Dessau.

Together, we built a new way to live. I even asked them to use my middle name, Grace, after my nanna, so I could rebuild myself, and never once did they think I didn't deserve the chance to be different or better, or believe I had done anything other than tell the truth.

That's what kept me level and sane back then and I'm determined this incident shouldn't upset that. I have to keep an even keel for Tilly. The police are bound to catch this crazy guy soon. He might have done it before. He might even have a police record they can check, fingerprints on file, or they'll find a witness, a traffic camera that will lead them to him. I just have to wait for an arrest and it will all blow over. If Belle will just stop asking questions for five minutes.

'So, have you noticed anyone weird hanging around, lately?' she whispers, with a backward glance at Officer Danny. 'Anyone suspicious, like maybe watching you at the market or something?'

'No, Belle, honey.'

'Those enviro protestors haven't been back, have they?'

'No, the phantom windshield stampers have not been back,' I confirm, referring to the Take Flight organisation, keen on hampering the planning permission for the Project. We love the eagles round here but they *really* love the eagles. One of them came all the way up from whatever commune in Salem to paper my windshield with polite objections printed off on what looked like a twenty-year-old inkjet. That was four months ago, though, and they're much happier since we've explained all the protections in place.

'I don't think breaking and entering is in the purview of people who use emoji sad faces to express their feelings,' I smile.

'No, I guess not,' concedes Belle. 'I heard there was a prowler, though, just last week.'

'There wasn't a prowler. It was the UPS guy.'

'Yeah, they said that, but how do they know?'

'Because his name's Marvin and he delivered my fabric swatches, on the third try.'

'Oh yeah, the new guy. He called at mine first.'

'Course he did. I still have that box of craft stuff you sent for. I'll drop it over when I can.'

'Sure, whenever. I'm glad you're OK, honey. I'm sure this will all blow over. I mean, the officer's right, he's long gone.'

Then, as a dipper skims down across the flat sand, and Officer Danny hangs back a little to speak into his radio, Belle leans in and asks, '*Do* you have a gun, Grace? You know, just in case?'

And I laugh as I punch her on the arm, saying, 'Of course not. What would I do with a gun?' making a fond, *you Americans, all trigger-happy* face.

'No, of course not, I just mean, well, look out for yourself is all.'

Never done anything else. I nod.

'I'm afraid we're gonna have to wrap this up, ladies,' says Officer Danny, as he re-holsters his radio at his belt. 'The city detectives want you where they can find you while they complete the scene review.'

I bet they do, I think, as Grace smiles obediently, and we head back up the beach.

Seven

The Ticking

It's 4.13 a.m. I know this because the LED on the radio alarm clock blinks like a beacon in the blackout-dark bedroom. Elias is beside me, hand heavy on my hip, breathing from a deep underwater space I hope is dreamless.

There's a patrol car sitting across the leafy street. Not Officer Danny tonight but an unknown Portland cop, drinking coffee from a takeaway cup, no doubt muttering about what a waste of his Saturday night this is. He's probably right. The townhouse here in Willamette Heights, where Eli's dad lived until he died five years ago, is bolted up tight and true, the alarm system set. I hope Tilly will remember that and not decide to wander downstairs in search of the remains of her cupcakes at the crack of dawn or we'll have a rude awakening.

She was so good and grateful tonight when we collected her from Anoushka's and she launched into my arms, then when she unwrapped her new half-shell wetsuit and booties downstairs, ripped the paper off her birthday books, my heart almost exploded every time she smiled. Yet, throughout our trip to Gino's Pizzeria tonight, in lieu of her abandoned party – balloons at the table, a sundae topped with cherries – I kept thinking about the knife and the rope bound with red ribbon back in Lookout Beach. It must be a coincidence. I mean, those handcuffs – we never had a set of those. And I mustn't make assumptions. Allow myself to be paranoid. America is full of pervert weirdos, right? What are the chances of this being about that after so long?

So I close my eyes, trying to mirror my breathing to Elias's, to banish the sound of a clock counting off the seconds with a tick-tock judgement I can't ignore. It's skin-crawlingly loud in the wet, windless night, but I don't climb out of bed to consign forgotten clocks to wardrobes or watches to sock drawers. I know the sound isn't out there, in the room. It's in my head.

I first heard it when I'd jolt myself awake in the middle of the night, convinced water was pouring into my nose and throat. I was in my first year in Seattle by then, and literally sleepless there, though not in a quirky and romantic way like that idiotic movie. Luckily, I didn't have to share a dorm, my halls offering single rooms for exchange students. I could never have slept in the same vulnerable space as a stranger, inflicting my tendency to splutter awake, confused, suffocating, on another girl.

The Pacific Northwest had seemed the perfect place to escape to, emblematic of so much still wild, untamed. Because, in almost five years in Newcastle, through A levels and then those first college terms studying architecture and design, I'd never really lost the feeling that my misdeeds were tight on my heels. Surely it was only a matter of time before someone recognised me, some reporter turned up on the doorstep or some angry vengeance seeker confronted me on the screeching Metro or fog-lapped Tyne quayside?

I thought maybe that spectre would flounder in the ocean as I headed for the American horizon, freeing me from that police interview room where they'd kept me as long as the law would allow. A period of limbo, of days of waiting and hoping, of sticking to my statement as the dark crept up to the windows, wide-eyed at the spectacle inside – an impassive girl on one side of the desk, a middle-aged police officer with a bad perm on the other.

'Tell us what really happened,' DI Maureen would ask, again and again. 'Tell us, Laura, the truth now. Who brought the knife? Why that place? Why did you lie about being there?' her calm voice the only noise in the room to break the silence, the stretching, flexing, clenching silence that tied my tongue. Except for the hum of the wall heater and the tick, tick, tick from the poker face of the electric clock on the wall . . .

During that first term, even though I had made some decent friends, and I'd already met and arranged a first, then a second and third date with the strapping yet sensitive postgrad who would later become my husband, I found myself waking to the sound of that clock, searching every inch of my dorm room for the source. I'd hear it in the lecture halls, in the exam room, everywhere the hubbub of the city, the chatter of voices, fell away.

The campus doctor told me it was tinnitus. She checked me for ear infections and fevers. A psychological counsellor said it sounded like auditory hallucinations, brought on by anxiety, common for those so far from home. But it wasn't any of those things – it was a countdown; part of me was waiting for the day someone would find out who I was. Part of me still is.

It's not likely. It's not probable. It can't be Silas. But there are others who might want a chance to add their own epilogue to the story of the Gwyn Mawr Cult, as we became known. People who crawled out of the woodwork to blame and hate and warn us we would burn in hell, even before social media took hold and the authorial God of Facebook and the like of *Go Moms!* were all powerful.

There were phone calls in the night when it all came out, threats, letters stuffed through our door along with envelopes of shit. Everyone had something to say, except us, forbidden to speak to any of the other families, to get in touch. Whoever it is, whoever is left to chew it all over once more, it seems like they might want to say it in person, soon.

Maybe it's something to do with the messages I picked up on the answering machine tonight. Not the 'you evil bitch', 'you sick twisted liar' variety Dad deleted for weeks before we moved from the village; a man called Neil Morrow, from an architectural magazine that carried a feature on me a few years ago. They did a 'women on the way up' article when I helped design the Flat Rock house near Bend, then presented me with the same pewter penis for 'newcomer of the year' that left a sizable dent in Walter's head.

I think I spoke to a woman called Bree something then, not this Neil Morrow who has a weird accent, a hint of Britishness about it, perhaps? In which case, is he merely pretending to be from Portland? Could he be a reporter from back home? Does he know something about my life across the waters and is sniffing out a story?

But it can't be that, I tell myself. *Stop fretting, Laura*, Mum's voice orders behind my clenched-shut eyes. Word must have got around about the incident in Lookout Beach, that's all, though that's bad enough with the awards ceremony in a few weeks. Elias is being honoured this year because, when he's not letting me build my dream house, his heart is devoted to sustainable social housing and the belief of the German-born Bauhaus school that environment can mould community and character. It was the topic that kept us chatting through our first beer-lubricated seafood platter at Seattle's Pike Place Market and ever since.

The shiny school and social hub Bright Brothers has just erected in Slabtown is exactly that, sustainable housing for low-income families around a central wheel of stores and green space – biophilic, as they call it now, breathing architecture. Where the visionary British newbuild disasters of the 1960s, the post-war edifices that descended into slum housing estates, failed, Elias knows he can succeed, on the spot where Portland once housed its own slums.

Though he hates the idea of getting a special mention at the awards, climbing on stage, making a speech, he's agreed to go so I can put on a dress and clap like crazy. So this Neil Morrow guy might just want a soundbite from the proud wife. But either way I won't reply. If you speak even once, or even if you don't, the press keep calling.

The thought amplifies the ticking in my head now, so loud it threatens to rip through my skull, as I climb out of the king size and into the bathroom down the hall, pulling the door behind me. I get into the shower and turn it on, sitting cross-legged on the floor as the cold jets stream over my head, breaking the familiar rhythm of panic.

This is what I did on that October night in Gwyn Mawr, took off my clothes, got in the shower, soaped up, tried to scrub myself clean. As if I could rub off my outer skin, uncover the person I had been hours before it happened, that I thought I had been all my life until that night – a good person.

That's what Mr Kamal, the barrister, did so well at the trial later, painted a picture of a wholesome young woman led astray, tempted off the narrow path of virtue onto the wide slope towards hell.

'Look at her,' he invited the jury. 'She could never have willingly been party to anything that happened by the river that night,' his every move and statement reinforcing that I was young and naive for my age, romantic, foolish.

'Look at these stories she's written,' he insisted, showing my school notebooks to the court, each one wearing my heart on its sleeve and on the pages. It was clear I'd been 'bewitched', he said, in a predictable female way, easily led, in the thrall of a cold sociopathic personality.

He meant Silas. My Silas. As he still was then.

He showed that photo of us to the jury too, the snap Priss had found so damned funny at the cottage and when it was circulated around youth club then the school. The one where I was a happy, smiling child, dressed as a pirate, with tricorn hat, stripy jumper and drawn-on moustache. The one where someone had spilled half a shandy on me in the Anchor pub, where we were rattling our charity tumblers for the Surf Club fundraiser.

They didn't mention it when I gave evidence, the wet patch on my crotch, I mean, or the jibes it had triggered – Pirate Pissy Pants. The image was only used as evidence of the long friendship Silas and I had shared, him standing next to me scowling, refusing to put his pirate costume back on, while Liam, on my right, and a foam octopus, which was really Coach Turner, vied for the widest grin.

Mr Kamal used it as proof of my good, charity-full heart, the reason he could believe what I said, and evidence of Silas's selfish and cold one, even though we were twelve years old and it was merely a moment caught in the camera flash.

But I can't get stuck there, where it happened. Where the police and the lawyers painted their own pictures of that night, then rolled us all up in a verdict tied with a bow as neat as the one on the worktop yesterday afternoon. I have to gather myself together and be ready for what comes next. Tomorrow, I go to the Central Police Precinct to try to tell the truth.

Eight

Stranger Danger

It's much easier these days, getting fingerprinted. We don't roll our pads on inky cushions any more, simply apply them to a blue screen at the points indicated, like you do for Homeland Security at airports since 9/11. It's so clean and convenient that, if you ever need to get it done, you could be forgiven for thinking you weren't in a proper old mess.

Tilly is disappointed, though. She was looking forward to the mucky bit, only perking up when a lady officer says she thinks she can find some taffy in her desk, if it's OK with Mom? I nod and smile for Tilly's sake, maintaining the air of a game, a day out in the city that began with a fun ride to the Police Department in a black and white patrol car.

'It's just easier this way, as you're here in town,' Det. Olsen had said in her 8 p.m. telephone call yesterday. 'We'll bring you in at ten tomorrow.' Not an order but not a request either. Now she repeats her reassurance that this is 'for elimination purposes only', to compare our prints against any found in the Shore Street house, but to me it feels like a reboot of the time I stood in the clanging Bridgend custody suite, Mum and Dad rigid next to me, hands dirty in more ways than one.

Now Det. Olsen watches, as Det. White directs our fingers and clicks keys and buttons. He's taking his time. I think he's still learning.

'So, you don't have any leads yet?' asks Elias, as he steps up to replace me at the scanner.

'The situation at the house is still under scrutiny,' says Olsen, no Yves Saint Laurent blouse today, just a classic black turtleneck. In true Pacific Northwest style, the weather has changed in an eyelid slip and the temperature dropped ten degrees overnight.

'But you *are* looking for the intruder?' Eli persists, impatience starting to bubble on his stoic face. He knows how much his size can intimidate people, that even the slightest show of annoyance can be amplified as aggression when you have hands like a lumberjack, so he's practised in making sure he remains physically still and calm. He likes hands-on solutions to problems, though. He'd be out there himself if he could, searching the backyards and highways, questioning neighbours, looking for suspects. He needs to know everything is being done to protect his wife and daughter from this weirdo, housebreaker, sex attacker and I adore him for that.

But Det. Olsen isn't in the mood for reassurances, making a noncommittal face as she says, 'We're still hoping Mr Lennon will be able to clear that issue up soon. The doctors say he's improving a little.'

'Clear it up? You mean give you a description of the man who attacked him?'

'Tells us what he remembers, yes.'

'Sure, but you don't need that to keep looking for this crazy SOB, right? I mean, you can check traffic cams and look for witnesses? See if there was anyone suspicious in the area?'

'I assure you, we're following all protocols, Mr Jensen,' says Olsen with an everyone's-an-armchair-cop sigh, Elias's reply reduced to a huff as White asks him to place his other hand on the screen.

'So, you're both sure no one else had a key to your house?' she asks, as White nods that we're all done.

'Yes, of course,' says Elias, as I nod again. Two nodding dogs are we, but Elias's hackles are rising.

'And,' she consults her screen, 'you were in Astoria until five p.m. on Friday, until you spoke to your assistant Bridgette, then you drove straight back to Lookout Beach?' which she knows is the case, as we have just signed our official statements while Tilly asked White a million questions about beating up bad guys and if he knows any martial arts.

'I already told you I was,' says Elias levelly.

'You did. Except no one can completely verify that time period, Mr Jensen. Why is that, do you think?'

'I was out and about, between meetings, I guess, and doing a lot of driving. Like I said.'

'Yes, you did. And Walter Lennon told his wife he was going to be in Bend until Monday but then he wasn't. People seem to change their plans all the time, don't they? Lucky for Mrs Jensen, clearly.' She smiles but I'm not taken in by it. Then she adds, 'Not for him, though. Poor old Walter who just called by.'

She doesn't think there was an intruder, I realise, just like she hinted two nights ago. In the back of her mind she thinks the players in this story are already accounted for, as they so often are, she just doesn't know the roles they've assumed yet. Because, let's face it, from her point of view what's more likely – that some random psycho targeted me in my home with a rape kit, or that this story could be explained away if everyone just confessed and clarified their part?

That's more or less what the Crown Prosecution Service said in their opening remarks all those years ago, that the jury had to acknowledge this was no murder out of the blue by an unknown assailant. Stranger Danger did not come into it, not as Lieutenant Andy teaches Tilly and her classmates, as they taught us back then, reminding us *don't talk to people you don't know, don't accept gifts from them, don't get in their cars, go to a safe place if you think someone is following you*, because the victim died at the hands of someone far nearer to home.

They knew it was one of us. They just had to prove which.

'Yes, lucky for Grace,' nods Elias, in response to Olsen's comment, 'if you can call it that. But someone must have seen something? Lookout Beach is a small town, good people. We have good neighbours.'

He means rich neighbours, certain neighbours who tend to notice anyone new or different from the usual Lookout Beach mould, anyone they consider to be 'not from here' and 'not our sort'. Last week MK shook her head in disbelief as she told me she'd heard that it was the seventy-five-year-old grand dame of the local theatre club, Daphne Wallis, who had called the police to report the prowler who turned out to be Marvin, the UPS guy. He's pretty new on the route and happens to be, *whisper it*, as Daphne certainly would, *black*. He's not used to the satnav routinely sending deliveries to the wrong addresses at our end of Shore Road and was a bit lost.

It's transpired that it was also dear old Daphne who called the police on Friday afternoon, just to let Lieutenant Andy know that a man was sitting in an unfamiliar car close to my house. The man looked scruffy, *not our sort of caller*, she said, because it's all about tribes in the end, isn't it? The *people like us*? Even here, in Portland, Oregon, the Beaver State's City of Roses, so determined to support the last gasp of social rebellion, hipster hair, body piercing, complicated coffee and that belligerent *Keep Portland Weird* sign embroidered in paint and lightbulbs across the walls of downtown.

Except, the more everyone tries to stand out the more everyone looks the same. When everyone is edgy and tattooed, eco-friendly and switching to a carbon-free footprint, perhaps the most glaringly obvious and suspicious thing you could be is rich, white and boring. Like us. Enter Olsen.

'We've carried out door-to-door enquiries,' she sighs eventually, 'but, well, Mrs Wallis, who was walking her dog, only recalls seeing the white man in black clothes in a grubby black car. Otherwise, there's only ocean at the back of your lots and, because of the layout of that part of Shore Road, with the Lennons' and Ms Belle Cooper's houses on the southern end, no one has a direct line of sight.'

It's true, we bought the house for its privacy. Mine and MK's are both two-storey stacks of Pacific Modernism, built as a pair in the 1930s for the wealthy daughters of a local alumnus developing the brand-new beach front. MK had an article on her place in *House Beautiful* a few months back, a feature boldly asking if the craze for 'mid-century modern' was 'passé-d its prime'. The third house was originally a bungalow for summering guests, the kitsch arts and crafts 'cottage' which Belle rents.

'But what about Mary-Kate?' I counter.

'She was also walking her dog but says she didn't see anyone, which isn't helpful.'

'Has she gone home yet?'

'Yes, this morning, actually.'

'And us?' asks Elias, checking his phone buzzing in his pocket. 'Can we head home to Shore Road now? I need to check in with the office. We also need some clothes.'

'You can go home later this evening,' Olsen confirms. 'Sorry to inconvenience you for so long. We're just finishing the . . . *tidying up* a while longer.'

Is it my imagination or is that remark aimed at me?

'But is it safe?' Eli demands. 'I must say, you don't seem very worried about this, Detective. I mean, is there any chance this guy, whoever he is, is going to come back, to finish what he started?' giving my arm a little 'sorry honey' squeeze.

'It seems very unlikely. I'm sure you don't need to worry about that.'

'But you're going to leave a patrol car outside? To keep

an eye on things until this is resolved? I'm not taking any chances with my wife and daughter in the house.'

My phone rings before Det. Olsen can answer, and I clock that it's my mum before hitting reject.

'There's no reason for you to stay here any longer. Thank you,' says Olsen without answering the question. 'You're obviously both very busy. Your big build must be nearly complete?'

'Yes, the first residents arrive at the Slabtown hub in fourteen days.'

'Of course. Duty calls,' she nods. 'We'll be in touch,' as she beckons Tilly and her chaperone back and escorts us through the security barriers onto the street gusting with fitful rain.

When I walk into my kitchen again, only forty-eight hours have passed, but it feels as if everything has shifted sideways, somehow. Stepping up to the counter, I put down my sack of items from the market, Elias close behind me, carrying Tilly who's floppy-drunk-tired following a post fingerprinting day of cooing at the floaty, cuddling antics of the sea otters at the Oregon Zoo.

'I'll take her straight up,' he whispers, as I open the cupboard, pull out the coffee and feign normalcy.

It would be possible to think nothing had happened in here, were it not for the tell-tale, chemical ghost of the police forensics team. Otherwise, they've erased their tracks well, the counter cleared, the coffee maker and cups exactly where they should be. There's a slightly lighter shade of wood grain on the floor where Walter bled onto the parquetry, but that's all. And the pewter penis is absent from its niche on the shelf.

I'm not fooled, though. It's impossible not to see them picking their way through the spot-lit scene of our kitchen, dusting, bagging, tagging. They must have been all over the living room too, glancing into Eli's study, re-checking doors and windows, casting an eye over our bedroom where I haven't made the bed since we tumbled into the car almost a week ago, heading for Portland.

It's impossible not to think about the last time the police searched my bedroom, how I'd been teenagerly mortified by the box of tampons they'd see in my top drawer, the dirty knickers I'd meant to throw in the washing basket but left straddling the chair. I'd been hot and itchy at the thought of the Edwardian dolls and scuffed teddies keeping vigil on my dresser, worried that the uniformed men would snigger, thinking me childish.

Worse was the knowledge that my sketches, based on the tale of the imprisoned Maid of Sker, the legend attached to the seventeenth-century manor house just down the coast, were Blu-Tacked to the walls for all to see; worst of all, was the likelihood they'd read my notebooks, filled with the stories I'd concocted about wronged maidens roaming the dunes for their lost loves. In each of those tales a single hero – Captain Carruthers – repeated his swashbuckling adventures, his brooding good looks replicated in the sketches. I wondered if DI Maureen would realise he looked a lot like Silas Cracknell, in period britches and a slyly cocked hat.

I wasn't immediately worried what else the forensics team would find in my room, as we waited at the police station that night, but I was overconfident because that's not where they found the bloodstained sweater. They found that stuffed in the washing machine, in the pantry.

As I try to focus, spooning coffee into the espresso maker, I realise I still need to call Mum back. I haven't told my parents about any of this yet and I'm not sure I should. I could just say we've had a break-in, a burglary, like we've told Tilly so far. It'll only make Mum anxious, and there's nothing she can do about it. Though, as the room fills with percolating Guatemalan roast, I wish she were here to distract me right now, to make hot chocolate like she used to when I was stressed from studying. I wish Dad were here too, so he could tell Tilly stories about heroes and villains, embracing twenty-first-century feminism by applauding her demonstrations of wrist locks while Eli laughs and joins in.

I've always been grateful that Eli and my parents get along so well. I think he genuinely enjoys it when they come out every April so Dad can get tipsy on organic Willamette Valley Pilsner and Mum eat her weight in sustainable seafood. Tilly loves that her Gramma Lew (the closest she can get to Llewellyn) is clearly very old, but still sparky enough to jump up and down on the dockside, shouting tips and encouragement, as we practise paddling on the Tillamook river.

It tightens a vice in my throat when I watch Mum directing Tils's sculling technique, one eye always on the currents, because she was a keen swimmer and boarder in her day. In fact, it was her love of the water that led to me becoming friends with Silas, because, when I turned nine, she enrolled me in the Surf Club she'd been part of as a child.

Until then Silas had only been known to me as the moody boy from the year above, who lived three houses down. But he was the swimming star of the 'Sharks' age group and he let me join his circle because of the thing that happened with his sister. Abigail was just two years younger than him, and that day he'd left her in 'Dolphins' while he splashed around with the boys near the estuary. One minute, she and a skinny girl were sitting on a wedge of rocks waiting for the others to get their kit on, the next there was a yell and trilling screams.

The skinny girl, her face a red screech of hysteria, was already being pulled from the far side of the rocks by one of the more alert parents, but little Abigail was drifting away on the green turning of the vast spring tide. We all knew the dangers of the rips on that part of the coast, drummed into us from the time we could paddle, but something had happened and Abi's head was sliding with the cold undercurrent from the enclosed bay channel into the mouth of the open water.

Kicking out for the line of froth that marked the point of no return I wasn't afraid. I was strong and sea-fit, a plucky heroine in my head and heart, who'd already saved dozens from imaginary shipwrecks along that coast. By the time I closed the distance between me and Abigail I was winded and stiffening, flashing through what I'd learned: *Go limp, stay upright, float with the current.* I knew they'd already seen us, that help was jostling into position, I just had to keep us both afloat long enough for someone bigger to arrive.

'Don't let me go, please don't let me go,' begged Abigail, sopping red curls stuck to her face, solid icy hands on my neck.

'Don't grab,' I insisted, 'go limp,' tucking my arms

under hers, holding on to my body board. 'Relax. I've got you. I've got you.'

'Good job, Laura!' Coach yelled when the inshore rescue boat arrived and strong hands hauled us into its low belly, banging on my back like a midwife clearing a baby's airways. Then everyone was gathering around on the beach, clapping and cheering and I was so happy I could have burst.

At the end of the season I received a 'special award' for bravery, which was brilliant because I'd always known I had it in me to be a real heroine. But the best thing was that Silas slouched over to me the next Monday, after class, with the words, 'Thanks for saving the little shit yesterday. Wanna do rescue drills next week, with me and Liam? You're a really good swimmer, for a girl.'

And that was it, we were a trio from then on, a captain, his first mate and willing bosun Liam, up for adventures and searching for buried treasure. I'd gained a shadow for a bit too, Abi at my side at every swim practice, a willing slave we took full advantage of as the years passed, bringing us all Cokes or Tangos from the ice-cream van in the car park, smiling shyly saying, 'These are for you, sweet Lolly,' then 'Lolly Pop' after my favourite order of an Orange Maid.

Silas would always roll his eyes when she begged me to tell the tale of how I'd saved her to the new recruits again and again. God, I felt like dying, when I caught her eye after the trial, saw her trying not to sob while her dad helped her mum into their car. She was just a teenager. How had she dealt with it all? What must she have thought when it all came out? Her own brother? His best friend?

How I'd let down everyone who ever believed I was good and true.

To defeat the thought, I abandon the spluttering coffee machine and creep upstairs to Tilly's bedroom, pausing at the door to watch Elias stroking her hair. Here alone, in this toy-stuffed half light, the sleek interior design of our statement home gives way to the clutter of childhood. Bunny ear slippers. Mermaid pictures. Doofus the plush dolphin folded under one arm while the revolving glow of the nightlight sends smiling crabs swimming around underwater walls.

She's still so young in many ways but one day, far too soon, she'll wake up and declare she wants to go to Banana Republic to buy that cute top the other girls are wearing, or, more likely, join an environmental activism group to lobby senators about climate change like Greta Thunberg. I try to halt time, sitting on the bed next to Eli in the warm spot he's made, the hot heart where our family lives. Then I lean in and kiss her.

'Tuckered out,' whispers Eli, as I draw the door behind me after a moment and we slip downstairs together.

After he finishes making the coffee we sit in the glass picture window, staring out at the black nothing where sky and sea have secretly met, until he says, 'The police think you were sleeping with Walter.'

'I know.' I nod, after a moment, catching sight of Grace Jensen's usual clean and guileless reflection in the glass. Typically to the point, no subterfuge, Elias has put his finger on exactly what I feared Olsen was insinuating with all those, *How did Walter get in? Your husband was supposed to be in the city*, questions. Because it's all about sex, isn't it? Or everyone thinks it is. Once you're old enough to understand anything.

Elias hasn't wanted to raise this, but he needs to now, I understand that. Even though it's the stupidest suggestion in the world.

'I know. Crazy, right? That's insane,' I smile.

'It is?'

'Yes, it is. So, don't let Olsen get under your skin.'

He visibly relaxes, as I push him the last of the box of Blue Star doughnuts we brought back from the city as a treat.

'But then, why *was* Walter here? Why did he come around? It's all so weird,' taking an iced ring while I take a bite of buttermilk old-fashioned, letting the sugar comfort us.

'They think you attacked him. You know that, don't you?' I add between chews. Because I've just realised this myself. That's why they were so hung up on where Eli was at five o'clock that day. 'They think you probably caught me and old Walter going at it, or just before the dirty deed. They think it's a classic jealous husband thing.'

'I know. Crazy, right?'

'Is it?' because, right now, that explanation makes more sense than any other has in this forty-eight-hour window of strangeness. On one hand, it's simply ridiculous that Eli would hurt anyone. At the same time, it's perfectly logical that he'd come home early that day, found Walter in our home and jumped to conclusions. This great bear of a man, enraged, blinded by red mist, triggered by the red of the velvet ribbon, the foxy face of Walter in the henhouse, then a push, a shove . . .

He doesn't know his own strength . . . Olsen thinks so.

But it *is* crazy. Things are often not what they appear to be. You can knit them together any old way you like to create the picture you want, but the simplest explanation is not always the correct one.

'It's insane,' Elias confirms. Then I relax too.

'Jesus, Grace,' he says. 'I mean, who brought those sick things into our home? I can't bear to think about what he was going to do to you. This is serial psycho stuff, right? I bet he's done this before. You don't suddenly do something like this out of the blue.'

'I guess not.'

'And, I mean, why you? How the heck did he pick you?'

'It was probably just random,' I reassure him, though I should be the one who needs reassurance. 'I mean, he couldn't have known I was coming home, right?'

'Unless he followed you or something. Listen, you should keep an eye out, in case you see someone acting weird. Though if he's got any sense, he's long gone from here. If I ever get my hands on the sick . . . Thank God for Walter, I guess. I hope those cops are not going to waste time trying to make this about me instead of getting out there catching him.'

'I wouldn't worry. They always rule out the husband or boyfriend first. And you have a solid alibi.'

'You make it sound like I need one?'

Everyone needs one, I think. That's what we got wrong back in Gwyn Mawr. We didn't have good ones. We hadn't realised just how much we'd need something other than each other's loyalty.

'You'll be ruled out anyway,' I smooth. 'No one really

suspects you,' as I try not to think of Olsen's crow-black eyes, peck, peck, pecking at me.

'Of course. But you must make sure you lock up properly from now on, honey, that at least. And we should get better locks.'

But no one broke in, I think, recalling the spare key that was still in the birdfeeder outside. Olsen returned it to me in a little plastic baggy, after it had been dusted for prints, with the instruction, 'Maybe put this somewhere safe from now on.'

'How do you think Tils is taking all this?' asks Eli, finishing off the other half of my old-fashioned.

'She thinks Walter is a hero for taking on a burglar and is ready to aikido the crap out of anyone who breaks in here again.'

'That's my girl,' he grins. 'My girls,' squeezing my hand.

Outside in the night, Officer Danny dozes in his car and the Cyhireath starts up its old familiar song.

Nine

Rule of Three

At last I'm alone, dipping along at a gentle speed, my borrowed paddle and kayak carrying me through the bends of the Tillamook river in the warm, autumn sunlight. It might seem strange that I'm out here, so soon after what happened in my kitchen, but it's a bright, white Wednesday, filled with sea mist, singing with the lure of the cool, damp shallows, and I could wait no longer.

There are no leads yet, no more sighting of the intruder over the last week, but Officer Danny, who dutifully followed me all the way down the coast today, is leaning on his patrol car at the jetty behind me. Since we are, after all, what passes for the Portland great and good, Lieutenant Andy has authorised a continued babysitting shift and I've built up a bit of a rapport with Danny by supplying him with Thermos cups of darn good coffee.

I convinced him to let me kayak today, promising to stay on this meandering stretch, peppered with pods of learners and leathery old hands, just for some 'me time', asking him not to tell anyone about our secret outing. Because Elias doesn't know I'm here while he's reluctantly in Portland, wrapping up a few things, leaving me with instructions to stay close to Officer Landon.

As I shift my left paddle out of the water, taking the smooth curve away from the slow-water sailors, I finally inhale some of the space I need to clear my head, hoping no one will say anything too stupid to Tilly about knives and stalkers and creeps. The principal called some of us moms in for a huddle-talk a few days ago about not sharing gossip and scaring the kids and it's worked so far.

If Tilly knew I was going AWOL, she'd much rather be here than caged in a classroom today. She's very good on the water, unafraid of failure, screwing up her face to perform a perfect Eskimo roll every time we practise in the protective curve of this river. She'll recite the relevant parts of the survival 'rule of three' too, without really appreciating what they mean – three weeks without food, three days without water, three minutes without oxygen – all it takes to die, dehydrate, drown.

Normally, I love to share this world of sunlight and slow currents with her, and, in the right season, take her out to sea, hugging the coves and sloughs, lifejacketed and helmeted, tethered at my bow like a lone duckling. She likes it best when we can snatch glimpses of the Tillamook Lighthouse, or Terrible Tilly as it's known, because of the tribulations of its lighthouse keepers and the ships it failed to guide home.

'That's me,' she'd grinned, at six years old, 'Terrible Tilly,' and her pirate name was born.

But I'm glad of the solitude today. It's hard to explain

the electric irritation that marches under my skin when I have to spend endless days in the company of other people, when I can't switch off and reboot so I don't overheat and short out. On those days, when the routine and certainty every hour brings crushes in, I think I might implode in a massacre of bone and blood if I have to smile, 'practise gratitude' and 'be thankful to the universe' even one more time. Even looking into the eager faces of my own daughter and husband can feel like an endurance event, which I sometimes think is further evidence I'm a bad person, but there it is. *Like it or lump it*, as Mum used to say.

The best course of action is to take preventative measures before the blow-up occurs. So today, I paddle, though knowing Officer Danny is watching from the deck downstream is making it difficult to forget that this isn't over, the investigation, for all intents and purposes still at square one. Though not a square exactly, more a shifting triangle and that's the most unpredictable thing of all when someone else is doing the geometry. Someone like Det. Olsen, who believes it's a question of Eli, me and Walter in the other universal rule of three – two's company and three is overcrowding.

But how do you know who's the third wheel, the unwelcome addition? Especially if you started out by inviting them in? That's how it began in Gwyn Mawr, because Dad said, 'Do me a favour, Lo. Be nice to Priss Hartford. She's had a tough time. Her mum died of cancer a few years ago and it's not been easy for them. I told her dad you'd help her make friends this summer, before school starts again. It's difficult being in a new place.'

So, to please him, I invited her round, even though I

didn't think I'd have much in common with a girl who, even at first glance, seemed more grown up, more spiky, more cynical that I imagined I could ever be.

'You've got some real kids' stuff in here,' I remember her saying, the first time she eyed my bedroom. 'Why've you kept all this baby stuff?' poking at my crackle-covered fairy stories and folk tales, raising a pencilled eyebrow at my costume-drama DVDs. 'If you like the supernatural you should read Clive Barker, Stephen King or Poppy Z. Brite instead of this old crap,' tossing my Edgar Allan Poe and Sheridan Le Fanu paperbacks aside. 'I could lend you some. Get you up to speed with, you know, popular *adult* horror.'

I swallowed her slights as part of the cool-girl act I hoped would fade as we became friends, but the sneer never really left her, not even after I introduced her to our classmates, showed her all the walks and hangouts, even took her on the bus to Bridgend to go shopping.

'You're not much good at being a girl, are you?' she remarked once, fingering the racks of tarty nylon tops in River Island, evaluating my jeans and hoody combo. 'You don't really dress up much either. And you don't seem to have many girl-*friends*.'

No one had said this to me before, pointed it out so brazenly, but I knew she was right. I'd never really needed girls because I always had Silas and Liam. The girls I'd got on best with were the ones at Surf Club, and they went to the comprehensive school on the other side of town. Over that past year, my few sporty classmates had stopped coming to swim club, self-conscious of their imaginarily plump thighs or chubby tummy rolls. Though Willa and

Dawn, who I'd known since first year, were still good for chatting with, eating lunch besides, their conversation was increasingly alien to me, about clothes and youth-club snogging crushes on sixth-form boys.

A gulf was yawning between us, one Priss was levering open, exposing the soft, pink flesh of my worst fears. I wasn't cool any more. People didn't really like me now. I was last season. Out of fashion.

'You know, you could stand to, like, put some make-up on, once in a while,' she grinned, holding a shade of dark plum gloss up to my lips, deciding against it and choosing a lurid pink. 'I could give you a makeover?' Fingering a scratchy black tube top with bust padding, 'We could even make you some tits?' causing me to bolt out of the shop, cheeks afire.

'So, what will we do all summer, Laura?' she'd asked later, as we ate slippery ice-cream sundaes at the tired Italian café she'd proclaimed 'retro, but definitely shit retro'.

'Swim, surf, you know,' I offered.

'Christ! This really is Sleepy Hollow, isn't it?'

'Washington Irving, 1820,' I said automatically.

'What?' she laughed. 'You're such a geek. You know who Johnny Depp is, right? You like hot guys, I assume?'

And that was it. I wasn't even smart any more, I was just a geek.

So she kept on, her words like sandpaper scouring layers of skin off a raw sunburn. If I hadn't promised Dad I'd be nice to her I'd probably have told her to sod off.

'So, who goes to this Surf Club then?' she asked at last. 'Who do you hang out with?'

So three weeks into that summer holiday, Priss met Liam and Silas. She spent the session sipping orange cups on the sand, sniggering at chubby Abi as she scuttled off to fetch us pop refills, ignoring everyone else through her aviator shades as she watched Liam and Silas race between the buoys in the bay. She never got into the water herself, never risked that eyeliner running, or wetting the long black T-shirt over denim shorts that barely contained her smooth white thighs. Instead, she lounged around while I was paddling, pounding, pumping my legs in the cool, thick summer swells, feeling more and more ghost-like the harder I tried to tread water.

'Your boyfriends are actually only fifty per cent lame, you know,' she observed, peering over the top of her shades at Silas, towelling off. 'Summer's looking better already.'

'That's your new friend, then?' said Silas later, eyeing her up and down in his own bored, unimpressed way. 'Takes herself a bit seriously, doesn't she?' as we helped Coach tidy away the floats, mimicking her sliding her sunglasses down her nose and squinting at me.

She ended up following us to the cottage that night and, somehow, became the fourth of our gang, seeming amused by Liam's puppyish babbling and tales of swim triumphs, name-dropping books and films she claimed to like with Silas. Even when I didn't actually invite her, somehow she'd turn up at the doorway with something to smoke that she'd rather impressively scrounged from a guy called Kev she'd met hanging out by the rusting kids' park behind the housing estate where she lived.

Then, when term started again, things changed. She stopped coming to call for me in the evenings and sometimes, when Liam and I would turn up at the cottage as we'd arranged at school break, ready to drink and pretend to be grownups, neither she nor Silas would show up.

'I was at home. I had a project to hand in today,' Silas would mutter, when I'd ask him at lunch why he'd 'bailed' on us.

'My dad was on my back,' Priss would say, if I saw her next day. 'He grounded me until my homework was done.'

By then she'd started lounging around the art room at lunchtime, a chair pulled up to our table, mine and Silas's table, watching him blackening the pages of his sketchbooks with mournful abstracts full of shadows and peering eyes, proclaiming, 'Cool' and 'nice composition'.

And Silas? He still hung out at my house now and then, we still watched his favourite horror movies on DVD when his dad was at church and couldn't disapprove. He still helped me with my photography club collages and with the developing chemicals, but . . .

Once, when I called around to show him some new seascape photographs I'd taken, I thought I could smell something in his bedroom, that strange, strong perfume Priss used to wear, like liquorice or burnt caramel, the smell of autumn here. Woodsmoke, taffy, pumpkin spice.

I saw the spot on his wall, a postcard of Hieronymus Bosch's *Garden of Earthly Delights*, where that photograph of me in my pissy pants had been tacked for years before it found its way outside into the world to humiliate me. He said he'd taken it down and lost it, that it must have been someone else's copy, but I knew then that she'd done it, that little bitch Priss – she'd taken it, copied it and passed it around my year like the weak joke in a Christmas cracker. That meant *she'd* been in his bedroom and what else would they have done in there, all alone?

Everything suddenly seemed to be ending with the falling of the leaves, that time in the cottage, when I'd told Priss the story of the Cap Goch, the last time things felt halfway normal. It already seemed forever ago that I'd leaned into the glow of the candles by the cold fireplace, to conjure up the age of carriages and carts for her, of travellers laden with cash and bolts of cloth hurrying to and from Bridgend's thriving woollen trade, only to fall foul of the most notorious innkeeper that ever drew breath.

'No one recalls his real name but he was known as the Cap Goch because he always wore a red hat or stocking cap,' I'd begun, just as Dad always did when he told the tale. 'More than two hundred years ago, he was the landlord of the New Inn by the river near Ewenny, close to the "dipping bridge" where sheep would be shoved from the parapets for a dunk-wash in the slow water. But he was far from a generous host. With his band of cutthroats, he'd murder hapless travellers in the night while they slept, or snatch them from the roadside, strip them of their valuables and dump their bodies in the river.'

Priss gave one of her usual disinterested sighs, though I could see she was intrigued. 'OK, so how did he kill them?'

'Slit their throats,' I said matter-of-factly. 'Sometimes the bodies were found mutilated, others dismembered. One without a head too.'

'Where?'

'Where we took you last week, to go paddling, down by the sacrifice stone on the riverbank.'

'You mean the river, right where all the kids were swimming?' She looked delighted.

'Oh yes,' I played up, getting into my stride. 'Or on the beach near the river mouth at low tide. Though the exact location of the inn is lost to history – it was demolished in the late 1800s – it was believed to be right near the bank.'

Her eyes were as wide as saucers by then, though that was probably something to do with the spliffs we'd shared. I began reeling her in, each word a hook tugging on her curiosity.

'So, they caught him in the end?' she asked, gesturing for me to continue.

'Well, no. You see, there were rumours of missing packmen and drovers for years, and bodies that turned up in River Ogmore, but there were no police back then. If people were suspicious how could they prove it?'

'But the slit throats, the dismemberments?'

'Well, they were lawless times. Loads of footpads and highwaymen and robbers about. Some say the Cap Goch got away with it, lived to a ripe old age, others that he was hanged for stealing a sheep after he left the inn and it fell into disuse. But, years later, they excavated the ground and found dead bodies and decomposed corpses, even far into the fields around, sometimes buried three deep or upright, feet first, packed and stacked like lamb cutlets.'

I paused for effect in the dancing candle glow, Priss's face instinctively inching towards mine, before continuing, 'For years, people swore the land was haunted, that they heard cries in the night pleading for their lives. In the late nineteenth century, they say satanic rituals were carried out at the sacrifice stone near the shell of the inn, because the Red Cap was a devil worshipper who'd sold his soul to Satan and become a powerful evil spirit. They believed he would grant their wishes, at a price, that they could harness his luck and prosperity by sacrificing sheep and goats on the stone in exchange for a good harvest. Others say young girls were strapped to the stone, their throats bound in red ribbons, to acknowledge the Cap Goch's legacy and seek his evil favour.

'On Halloween night, it's said you can hear him laughing and his victims pleading, if you're brave enough to stand at the stone at midnight, that is. But take care not to close your eyes, because if you fall asleep he might come for you!'

Then with perfect Gothic timing, the tarot cards flew from Priss's hands as the Cyhireath gusted in through the half-rotted door and blew out the candles.

'Your faces. Your faces!' I remember Silas crowing then, rocking with glee. 'Well done, Lolly Pop! That was one hell of a tale, as usual.'

'*Don't say his name. Don't stay to eat. Don't close your eyes. Don't fall asleep,*' chanted Liam, eager to show he hadn't almost shat his pants. '*Stay on the road, stay on your feet,*' Silas joined in, beating his hands on his thighs for the big finish, '*Or he will come and bury you deep,*' before they descended into unmanly giggles.

I didn't mind the laughter, though, because Silas was grinning at me like I was the only thing in the room again.

'You're a star, and no mistake,' he laughed. 'Laura Llewellyn, you're full of shit. I guess that's why we love you.'

And there were the words I'd clung to for so long – *he*

loves me – reminding me of the moment he'd kissed me, back in the budding spring, hip-deep in art photos and graphic novels on his bed, an awkward nose-bump of exchanged saliva, no more than twenty seconds long. First, he'd kissed me, now me loved me. In that fleeting moment I was the noise and heat of a fifteen-year-old flare exploding into the night sky.

He was *my* Silas, mine alone, the one I'd carried out expeditions to foreign lands with in the sand dunes, paddled across oceans of afternoons beside. The boy who'd make me cheese on toast at his house after swim practice, just the way I liked it, with a quick splash of vinegar, who'd talk for hours about TV and movies, his crush on brainbox Agent Scully, indulging my dreams of being a writer or artist because they were his own.

I was on a high as Silas said, 'Cheers! To Lolly Pop and the Cap Goch!'

'Smile, Priss,' I demanded, raising Silas's old Nikon he let me use, on its strap seldom far from my neck, like a pistol, right in her face. Ready, aim, fire! Catching her scowl, recording her defeat, or so I'd thought.

'Now, this tale of the Cap Goch,' the prosecution asked later, 'do you expect us to believe that this is a coincidence? That you had nothing to do with these photographs,' calling them up, one at a time on the slideshow screen, the faces of the jurors darkening, giving a little gasp or two. 'I'm sorry, they're not easy to view, are they? Imagine what kind of person would take them . . . ?' letting the question hang there. 'The victim may even have been still alive in these shots . . .'

I push the slideshow of blood and accusations into my

wake with my paddle blades, trying to fight the tick-tock panic that clicks in in my head, suddenly wishing I could keep paddling upriver for ever, stroking my way inland faster than Officer Danny could follow. Then I could vanish into the heart of this state where bears and beavers and maybe even Bigfoot lurk, alongside the ghosts of the tribes who fished these waters before the settlers arrived for pelts and timber. If they're still there, those old, quiet ones, they won't ask me any questions, impose any rules. They won't understand my foreign tongue, anyway. I'll never have to bite it or use it to explain anything again. Not even to myself. Wouldn't that be a relief?

But Officer Danny will get anxious if I'm out of his eye-line for too long. So, like a good, nervous, near-victim, I perform a neat turnaround and let the current float me back towards the safety of dock.

Ten

Something and Nothing

When I approach the landing stage, I realise my body-guard is not alone. Det. Olsen is waiting for me, hand on hip, mobile phone in hand, as out of place in this leafy, watered world in her dark suit as a statue of check-shirted lumberjack Paul Bunyan and his axe would be in New York's Times Square.

Motherfucker, Laura mutters under her breath, before Grace can reassert herself, my briefly claimed calm evaporating.

'Mrs Jensen,' nods Olsen, as I scull alongside the dock. 'Out and about, I see?'

'Yes, I just needed a change of scene. Danny, Officer Landon, is still chaperoning me. I only went to the first bend.'

I'm apologising again, as Olsen's eyebrows vanish into her bangs once more. I'm pretty sure she doesn't think I'm in any actual danger here, she's just pissed off she's had to schlep all the way from Portland for whatever reason she's about to reveal. I don't have to wait long.

'I just wanted to update you, to tell you that we've found no viable fingerprints in your home except those of you and your family,' she says, making no attempt to help as I haul myself out of the kayak and Danny and I pull it up behind me, trailing water and river weed. 'Except some of Walter Lennon's prints and one of your nanny's, Anoushka Sullivan.'

'I see,' I nod, pulling off my lifesaver and tugging on my sweatshirt. 'Not even anything on the knife, the rope or handcuffs?'

'No, there were some smudges on the handle of the knife and the cuffs, but only a couple of partials we can't run through the system. Rope is not a good fabric to draw clean prints from, I'm afraid.'

'So, nothing, then? You came all the way down here to tell me that?'

'You weren't answering your cell and I thought you'd want to know. If there *was* an intruder, he left no prints.'

'*If* there was an intruder?' I echo, sitting down to pull off my water booties and get back into my board shoes.

'Yes, Mrs Jensen. We still can't account for a third party.'

'But Daphne Wallis saw someone in a strange car.'

'Yes, but it's not illegal to have a beat-up car and sit in it by the ocean. Anywhere except Lookout Beach, maybe,' she gives a wry smile. 'Mrs Wallis didn't see anyone actually enter your yard,' she adds, sitting down on the wooden plank bench next to me.

Here it comes. Fire away.

'Look, Mrs Jensen. Is there something you want to tell me? Anything at all?' she asks, with a sudden air of confidentiality. 'About you and Walter Lennon, perhaps? Now is the time to let me know if there is. We all do things we're not proud of. No one is perfect, right?' adding a sympathetic smile. 'Hell, I'm not. I know it can be difficult sometimes, when things get out of hand, if someone gets hurt, especially. Sometimes it feels impossible, in the heat of the moment, to admit it, but afterwards, well that's when you realise the best thing you can do is explain what really happened.'

I start for a minute, even though she's not talking about me and Silas and Liam and Priss, trying to ignore the twang of the raw nerve she's just plucked; this cop, this lazy pile of suppositions in her last-season blouse, trying to dismantle the image I've worked so hard to sustain – good wife, good mother, good person. What right does she have, trying to tell my story?

'If you've got something to say, why don't you just say it, Detective?' I sigh.

'OK then,' all business now. 'Were you and Walter Lennon involved? Were you having an affair? Did you come home early to be with him?'

Now Danny Landon looks awkward enough to leap off the dock, though he jumps to my defence instead with a, 'Now hold on a minute, Detective . . .'

But I cut him short with a raised hand, laughing, 'Well, that's certainly the stupidest thing I've heard this side of Christmas. You know, Detective, maybe you should spend more time trying to catch the pervert who broke into my house than concocting fantasy stories about me and my neighbour.'

'You haven't answered the question, Mrs Jensen,' she

insists, her eyes flinty again. She was hoping for an out-raged denial that would have told her she was right.

'No, I was not involved with Walter Lennon,' shaking my head. 'There, does that satisfy you?'

'Oh no, Mrs Jensen, I'm afraid I'm far from satisfied with this whole business.'

'That makes two of us.'

'Really, because, for a woman who was almost attacked in her own home you seem very calm and collected. Calm enough to be out here on the river today. It seems to me that perhaps you're not that worried about your attacker returning. Why might that be?'

She's got a point. Would a genuinely scared woman do this? Go off on her own? Perhaps I'm really not frightened enough, not because I still have the gun in my purse, but because whoever it was that chose my kitchen, perhaps part of me thinks I deserve it – that maybe time has caught up with me, my comeuppance is due.

'Just because I'm not a trembling mess, doesn't mean I'm not concerned, Detective,' I say, as calmly as I can. 'Maybe I just don't want one sicko to rule the way I live my life?'

'Or could it be because you already know who attacked Mr Lennon and you're not in any danger?'

But I don't, I really don't, I want to yell. I want to slam my fists on the bench, to stamp my feet screaming, *I don't know who did it. It can't be Silas. It can't be him!*

'That is ridiculous,' I insist, trying to tune out the tick-ing crescendo in my head, the feeling of water rushing up all around me.

'OK, let me read you a description of a person seen at

your property on the afternoon in question – six foot four inches tall, broad, dark jacket, possibly a beard.'

'That's it?' I ask. 'Just that? Because that's a thousand men in the Pacific Northwest.'

'It could also be your husband Elias, couldn't it?'

Now she's getting to the point.

'Yes, I suppose so,' I concede, 'but it's so vague it could be anyone. It could be Charlie, there,' gesturing to the guy who runs the kayak rental stand I've hired from today, to save the fuss of dragging mine out of the garage and strapping it to my car. We wait while big, bearded Charlie retrieves the kayak, carrying it back to the racks with less effort than it takes to tote his masterfully groomed lumberjack chin bush.

When he's out of earshot, Olsen continues, 'It's just that Mr Lennon woke up this afternoon. He's groggy but was able to recall certain details about the man in the house and these are them.'

'He's awake? Well that's great news.' I'm genuinely pleased. 'But if he meant Elias, why wouldn't he just say so? We've lived next door to the man for years.'

'Yes, it's a basic description at the moment. He's still quite confused. He remembers being in your kitchen. Seeing a vague shape, and then recalls a struggle.'

'Does he remember why he was there?'

'He can't quite recall the period of time before his assault. He says he thinks he saw a dark car pull up, down the street, and someone sitting in it for a while, then maybe walking towards the house. He thought the person might have gone into your garden so he went to check.'

'Well that's a start, at least. No licence plate, I presume?'

'No, but as I say, we're hoping more details will come back to him as he recovers. The doctors are very hopeful the memory damage will not be permanent.'

'That's a relief.'

'Yes, it is, but it does mean that if you have something to tell us now, *voluntarily*, that he remembers later, well, you'd be obstructing justice, not to mention making a false statement regarding a crime.'

'Well, I hope he does remember soon, because then he can tell you what BS your theories are, Detective. Thank you for your effort but I need to get back to collect my daughter now.'

'Of course, lucky she wasn't with you that afternoon,' she muses. 'That she was in Portland with your husband. Except he wasn't in Portland, was he? He was all over the county, it seems.'

That's when I remember what Belle said, at the hospital last week, about Elias being in Seaside when she was buying Seb junk candy, half an hour before I walked into that kitchen. To Olsen I say, 'You know where he was, Detective. It's in his statement.'

'If your memory improves at all, do call me right away, Mrs Jensen,' she responds, tossing the words at the back of my head as I walk to my car.

As I drive away, and Officer Danny pulls out behind me, I watch her staring at the water, shaking her head at the gliding terns.

I'm jangling with unspent annoyance by the time I collect Tilly half an hour later. Belle was on school pickup today and Danny dutifully follows me the fifty yards through the scrubby trees at the back of my house to her 'cottage', before sitting down on a lawn chair. It suits Belle, this homey, clapboard folly, a pastiche of a Cape Cod cottage with a picket porch. How the rich liked their whimsy back then, when they didn't have to live in it.

Tilly loves it over here, in this American quilted and cushioned haven, the exact opposite of our mid-century-modern minimalism, with its throw rugs galore for impromptu tent making, craft supplies in boxes and wall-to-wall carpeting. Sure enough, when I open the screen door and knock the glass, I see Tils and Seb stomach surfing in front of the old-fashioned fireplace in a makeshift den. I lift the latch, as I usually do, to let myself in, but the bolt is shot home on the other side. I guess Belle is still unsettled by the incident at my house and isn't taking any chances. When I give a wave, Tilly, eating what looks like one of Belle's weird carob ball 'treats' gets up to let me in.

'Hey, Mom!' she grins, offering a waist-crushing hug, returning to the TV as I go towards the cramped kitchen.

'Seen MK today?' I ask Belle, ably julienning courgettes at the counter, her fingers a blur with the blade.

'No, she still won't leave the hospital for long. I took her some snacks last night and we had a coffee. Walter woke up today, though, so that's good news.'

'Definitely,' I nod, picking up a sliced carrot and crunching it, 'though I think it might be a slow recovery.'

'Yes, baby steps, right?' she smiles. Baby steps is one of her things alongside 'practising gratitude', some self-help wisdom about small efforts. As her New Age fluffery goes, it's the most practical.

I'm dying to ask her about Seaside and Eli again, but

don't want to just throw it into the conversation. Once elegant, the first Victorian promenade town in this part of the world is now a 'family-friendly' sprawl of slot-game parlours and souvenir shops, not unlike Margate or Blackpool, just with more dramatic scenery. We always bypass it when we drive up the coast so quite why Eli would ever stop there is a mystery.

'Belle,' I ask airily, as she chops mushrooms, 'remember at the hospital last week, you said you saw Eli in Seaside on the afternoon of the incident?'

'Oh yes,' the knife flashes.

'Where was that, exactly?'

'Well, it was Seb who saw him. Or said he did. We were rushing along and he pointed and said, there's Uncle Eli. I didn't actually see more than the back of a head.'

'So, you didn't see what he was doing? Who he was with?'

She stops chopping, leaning back to wipe her hands on a dish cloth before asking, 'Why? Is something wrong, G?'

'No, it's just, well, it's not Eli's kind of place and he didn't mention he'd been there. He told me he was in Astoria all afternoon.'

'Right. Well, I shouldn't worry. You know Seb. His glasses were probably steamed up. Probably someone else entirely.'

'Yes, probably. It's just the police, they seem to have this idea that Eli might have been here around that time, from the description Walter gave of his attacker. It does sound a bit like Eli.'

'Yeah, but Eli wasn't here. I mean, his car wasn't here when I left with Seb or when we got back. I told the detectives.'

'They asked you?"

'They've asked everyone questions, hon. That's what they do, for all the good it's done. That woman cop is kind of a bitch and, if you ask me, she's doing exactly nothing while this guy's still out there.'

Then she almost drops the knife as the trees in the yard crack and sway in the wind suddenly racing off the sand, before grinning and saying, 'I guess I'm still jumpy about the whole thing. Stupid huh? Silly old Belle.'

'You're not silly, B,' I smile, though, give or take a few years, in her boho blouse, barefoot, turquoise and silver-heavy fingers, she looks exactly like the hippie girl who gets strangled by the sex attacker in every seventies serial killer movie to the sound of a jazz flute.

But that's melodrama, not life, and I don't want to make a song and dance about it, or where Eli was, as Tilly and I walk through the trees to our backyard. It's strange to see MK's house in darkness across the fence, no Oprah-woof to greet or warn. Belle took her to the dog sitter for an extended playdate with Ralph the Labradoodle, so Tilly can't rub her ears through the picket gate. With affection to spare, she runs ahead at the sight of her daddy, backlit in the door, and I smile, biting my tongue. After all, speccy Seb, delightful as he is, once claimed to have seen a mermaid off Oswald West rocks.

My intention, when Eli releases me from his beard-prickle crush, is just to get inside and get the dinner on without any more complications. But as the spaghetti hits the water, I hear the words, 'Eli, were you in Seaside on the day of the incident?' coming out of my mouth, sounding like an accusation.

Reaching into the Smeg icebox, Eli stops with a carton of organic tomatoes in one great paw before answering, 'No, honey. I told Olsen I was in Astoria, remember?'

'Right, sure. Just, what were you in Astoria for, again?'

'Photo-voltaic plates – the solar panels for the Grant property.'

'Right, right. You said timber cuts though, that night at the Project.'

He closes the fridge door and reaches for the salad bowl.

'Yes, those too.'

Tomayto – Tomato, I think. OK. 'So, you were just completing orders?'

'Yes, I was,' reaching for oil and vinegar, setting them on the table.

'So, you didn't happen to call in at Seaside on the way here?'

'No, like I said. Why? Why are you asking this now?'

'Well, it's only that Belle says she saw you there, half an hour before it supposedly happened. When you didn't answer my calls?'

He goes back to the icebox, brings out some mayonnaise. He hasn't looked me in the eye yet.

'I wasn't in Seaside, Grace,' he says, realising no one eats mayonnaise with spaghetti, putting it back, reaching for a beer. 'Belle must be confused. You know how she is.'

Finally, Eli stops fiddling, sets down his bottle and comes across to place his heavy hands on my shoulders, saying, 'Look, I'm sorry I wasn't here when it happened. I'm sorry I took so long to get your message that day. I hate that I wasn't here for you. But I'm here now. I will be in future.'

I let him press my head into his chest and stroke my hair, but something feels off – the safe harbour shaky. So, after dinner, after Tilly's bath, I wait until she's asleep and Eli's in the shower before creeping out to his car. I take Officer Danny a coffee first, soon to switch with Officer Dolores for the night shift, as a cover for being outside in the freezing Northwest night, then pretend to need something from Eli's glovebox.

I know there's a built-in GPS he uses to find his way to new sites and appointments – it also records routes and mileage unless you tell it not to. It's the same in my car, one advantage of 'his and hers' hybrids – well, what else would Mr and Mrs Eco-energy drive? It's supposed to track fuel consumption and log road congestion, and you can send the information, digitally, to the parent company for analysis. I turn mine off when I go on my swimming expeditions so Eli won't see them and frown.

It takes just a second to click into the log for the day of the incident, but to my surprise it's blank. Completely blank. As if he never went anywhere at all that day. Now what would the police think, if they saw this? If someone familiar enough with these cars were to check. Perhaps they are and they can't. Maybe they need a warrant or something and they don't have grounds for one? But how far would Olsen's eyebrows slide up under her bangs if she looked at this big, blank expanse of *nothing suspicious, nothing to explain, nothing to see here*, nothing except what I'm thinking – what are you hiding in the middle of it?

What I'm thinking now about my Eli is that my solid as oak, 'I cannot tell a lie', Abraham Lincoln-channelling husband is lying.

BEVERLEY JONES

'Lying by omission is still lying, Laura,' Ms Perkins the solicitor said, more than once. 'Pretending you were somewhere else won't make the police believe it – they'll just think you're lying about everything else too.'

'I'm not,' I insisted. I was.

And Elias? He should have been smarter about it at least, I think, as I click into the menu and erase the whole month, then close the car door and wave goodnight to Officer Danny.

Eleven

Playing Dress-up

The season is finally turning soft and brown underfoot, and, as I pop some barbecue pulled pork into the oven, I'm getting used to darkness tucking us in straight after dinner. It's been fifteen days since the incident, with no further news on my pervert intruder. Thankfully, Officer Danny was called off 'mommy-watch', as Tilly was calling it, three days ago, which is just as well as I hated being under constant scrutiny.

Speaking of surveillance, Eli hasn't noticed the missing mileage report from the Prius's dashboard record yet, or if he has, hasn't said anything about it. I know I should probably have just asked him about it right away – come right out and said, 'Why did you delete all the travel information on the day I was almost attacked and murdered, Eli?' Isn't that what wives and husbands are supposed to do? Confront issues? Keep no secrets? Be honest with each other?

But I can hardly claim to have been completely honest

with him all these years, can I? And I keep thinking, what if I do ask him outright and he says he doesn't know anything about it, that it must be a glitch? Because that *could* be true. Almost anything could. Sometimes you just can't ask a direct question when so much hangs on it. When it seems so much like an accusation. And the longer I've left it, the harder it's become.

So, over the last two weeks I've tried to put it all behind me, give him the benefit of the doubt, keep myself busy, starting with the specs for a remodelling job on a moth-balled fish cannery, butterflying into a boutique hotel near Garibaldi. Andreas Poliakoff, who was also in the running for the job from Lawrence-Hannigan, got mugged last week, out jogging, and fell down some steps. He's had to withdraw, which is bad for him but good for me. One man's shattered femur is another woman's gold-clad commission. *Don't look a gift horse in the mouth*, as Mum would say.

I've also been up to the city to buy a cocktail dress for the awards ceremony, always a difficult balance. Black is so formal, a bright colour too 'look at me' bold, anything quirky, a desperate attempt to pretend you're ten years younger and down with the hipster dolls. I've settled for my own take on retro blandness, a sheath dress in 'morning mist' with a 'hint of seafoam' stole. Hopefully I'll blend elegantly into the arrangement of winter white tablecloths like a cream chocolate wallflower.

Elias will look awkward and amazing at the same time, as if someone forced a bear into a dinner jacket, but what a bear and what tailoring! Tilly will be with Anoushka that night but she's already working through sartorial considerations of her own as Noushki's college mate Nell is apparently a whiz at 'upcycling' old clothes. She's offered to whip up a bespoke Halloween costume for us, and it's for outsourcing things like this that our 'town assistant' (not nanny) comes into her own.

It was such a stroke of luck that Noushki was interning at Bright Brothers during her summer vacation two years ago. She ended up entertaining Tilly with den building in the staff lounge while I delivered a last-minute presentation, which has come in handy since for babysitting and little crafting details like costumes. While Grace might dutifully toe the line, passing off ready-mixed cookie dough as her own for bake sales, Laura is not sticking pins and needles in anything to make dress-up outfits, unless it's her own eyes.

Anoushka, being from Salem, the witch capital of New England, cheerfully lets everyone know that Lookout Beach's annual Halloween effort is a C plus at best, though it's already impossible to go ten yards without snagging your head on fake cobwebs and dangling paper skeletons. The $18 organic pumpkins are waist high in the market, ready to be mutilated, and every public space reeks of cinnamon spice.

Usually, after traipsing the length of Main Street, beset by superheroes and fairy princesses, MK and I round off Halloween with a few much-needed shots of Lookout Beach Distillery's finest whiskey at her place. She gets crates of the stuff on special for Walter's construction clients. With Tils rosy and limp with insulin shock from the candy, and Eli doing bedtime, MK breaks out a spliff and we lurk on her backyard lawn chairs. Very occasionally I allow Grace a couple of puffs, a kid sneaking a drag away from parents' prying eyes.

This won't happen this year, though, with Walter finally allowed home. A private nurse, who looks unfortunately like Kathy Bates in the film *Misery*, helped him out of a car two days ago and will be calling back every other day to check on him. At MK's request, we've given them a couple of days to settle in, and now, with dinner on, we're ready to trek dutifully next door bearing grapes and sympathy.

It seems we're welcome when Walter offers a cheery, 'Hey guys,' from his feet-up position on the La-Z-Boy, though there's no ignoring the stubbly patch on his head where they shaved it to insert a tube to drain the pressure from his brain, or so he delights in telling us. It's a start-ling Frankenstein monster's rumple in the flesh, creating a pin-tuck effect I'm worried Tilly might find a bit 'gross' or scary. But she merely takes a long, forensic look before proclaiming, 'Cool, Walter,' then thanking him for scaring away our burglar.

Other than this early Halloween make-up effect, Walter looks remarkably unscathed but MK has warned us he's on a cocktail of pills, is 'whacked out' for around eight-een hours a day and mustn't get overexcited. While we try to think of non-agitating things to say, Tilly disappears into the kitchen to find treats for Oprah, back from the sitter and in tail-and-lick overdrive. Meanwhile, Mary-Kate, barefaced in sweatpants and plaid shirt that might be from JCPenney, fusses around arranging cushions. I don't recognise the woman fidgeting before me – I didn't know she even owned any 'cosy clothes' that weren't from Lululemon or Anthropologie. When she offers us a plate of what might be homemade cookies, I'm tempted to grab her collar and demand, *Who are you and what have you done with my friend?*

Following her into the kitchen, when the self-confessed 'takeout queen' announces she has to 'check on some pot-roast', it occurs to me that I should have offered to bring something over. To be neighbourly. Offered her a tray of Tillamook Jack mac and cheese at least. But the kitchen table is already laden with cling-filmed offerings; Maria Weathers's vegan casserole in pride of place, alongside a four-pint pot of Petra's mother's homemade chicken soup and a basket of twenty cupcakes with Belle's signature swan-wing tops.

'Sorry,' I apologise, annoyed with myself for letting Grace slack. 'Looks like I've missed the rush,' relieved when she puts her finger to her lips and beckons me out-side, retrieving a sneaky Lucky Strike from her pocket. 'I come bearing other gifts, though,' I wink, pulling a small bottle of tequila from my purse as the kitchen door closes and she lights the cigarette. 'How are you holding up?'

By way of answer, she takes the bottle, twists off the top and takes a slug. Listening to make sure the sound of excited barking and eight-year-old laughter stays at the far end of the kitchen, I throw back a sneaky gulp too. God, it's good. Hot and sharp. I've missed this with her.

'Do you ever wish you could have been a better person?' asks MK, as I refuse a second swig. 'I mean, do you ever think things could have been different if you weren't such a selfish, entitled bitch?'

'Steady on!' I grin.

'Not you, obviously, I mean me. You're the exact oppo-site of a selfish bitch, hon.'

Don't be so sure, I think, but don't interrupt.

'You're a great wife and mom, and you help make homes that are good for this overheating planet as well as bringing your old friend secret tequila. Me, on the other hand, what have I ever done except spend money and try to have fun for a living? What use am I to the world?'

'Well, you've kept me sane for six years so, at the very least, you've saved a perfect mom's life,' I suggest.

'Really?' Her eyes brighten for a second as she takes a greedy pull on the Lucky Strike.

'Hell, yes. How exactly would I have the energy for all this working mommy-wifey, good-deed doing if I didn't have you to burn off a little steam with,' reminding her of the last CBD oil conference in Portland when we stayed in a suite she paid for because she wouldn't hear of me putting it on my credit card, along with the margaritas and three bottles of $100 champagne that ended up on her room bill.

'Well, there is that, I guess. That's kind of public service,' she smiles.

'It is. Obviously, everyone stops and takes stock when something awful like this happens but is something else up? Are you that worried about Walter?'

'I dunno, Grace. I see him sitting in there and know all he's ever done is look after me and bankroll my "lifestyle", and what have I given him back? He wanted kids, you know? I never did. I'm forty next year. What if it's just the two of us from now on, in this house, him sick and confused. And it's my fault.'

'It's not your fault,' I say. 'And Walter will keep getting better. It's early days. Brain injuries take time.'

Baby steps, I think but don't say.

'That's what the doctors say,' says MK. 'But how much time and how many tests? You know that Annie Wilkes nurse who comes over costs $500 a visit?'

'But you have insurance, right?'

'Sure, some but . . . not enough, not for ever, if . . .'

'What about Walter's business, though? I always thought you two were, you know, set for life?'

'Well, that's what I thought. Except things have been tighter the last few years. People don't want old-fashioned throw-'em-up starter homes any more. They want what you're selling, baby, eco-conscious, sustainable housing. Walter's been telling me to rein in my spending for a while. I didn't realise how bad it was getting until my car payments bounced. Remember when I told you it was in the shop last month? It was in the repo yard. We fought about that right before he left for Bend, and I was so mad with him. He'd started talking about maybe needing to sell this house. There's some money left but not a lot, probably not enough, if . . . if . . .' she breaks off.

'Jesus, MK, I had no idea. I'm so sorry,' grabbing her hand because what else can I do?

'Don't be, it's karma,' she says, blinking her eyes dry. 'My karma and my fault. Walter came back from Bend early to try and make things up with me but then he went over to yours and . . . I mean, I'm not sorry he stopped that sick son of a bitch from, well, you know. I don't blame you in any way, hon. But if I'd been . . . if I hadn't been such a selfish bitch, he'd have stayed up there and this wouldn't have happened.'

'You can't think like that, MK,' I insist. 'They'll get the guy. He's the one to blame.'

'Yeah, yeah, of course.'

'Take it one step at a time. Walter's already doing well. There's time to start over.' Or at least I think there is. There's always time. You just have to commit to it. To wanting it. 'I'm here,' I add. 'I can help you. Anything you need.'

'You're an angel.'

Then Oprah's heavy body skids into the door behind us, the night filling with Tilly's raucous laughter.

'Time to give you both some quiet, I think,' giving her hand a last squeeze.

'Sure, just gimme a sec,' stubbing out the cigarette, popping a Tic Tac from her sweatpants pocket into her mouth.

Once I've peeled Tilly away from hugging the dazed dog, Elias gives me a grateful smile as I offer a cheery flourish of, 'OK, kids, supper time, let's go,' and a whey-faced Walter makes us promise to come back in a few days.

'He's not so good, is he?' Elias mutters, once Tils has been sent upstairs to change.

'I don't think so, no. How did he seem while I was out back?' pulling the barbecue pork out of the oven.

'OK at first but then . . . it seemed like something was missing in his face. Like he was only pretending he knew me.'

'MK says he has periods of confusion.'

'I wonder if he'll ever remember what happened that day?'

We both look at the almost invisible pale patch on the wooden floor for a moment too long, before Eli reaches for the tacos and puts them on the table.

Then I'm thinking of the blank day I created in Eli's

112

dashboard computer again, the nagging little itch that he was hiding something, one way or another, resurfacing.

'I think I left my phone charger in the car,' I find myself saying, while Eli sets the table, as I swipe his keys from the bowl and I head out to the yard. Moving swiftly, I jump into Eli's driving seat and call up the Prius's mileage log for the last two weeks. I'm not sure what I'm looking for, monumentally relieved to see there are no more missing days. There are no strange journeys logged to anywhere I don't recognise either, except for one trip to Seaside, logged last Tuesday, to somewhere called the Buccaneer Diner. The sort of diner Elias would never normally be seen in . . .

Dashing back to supper as Tilly calls, 'Hurry up, Mom, I'm starving,' through the open door, I watch my oblivious husband ruffle our daughter's head as she plonks down at the kitchen table, before moving into the warm circle of light at the table with them. I share out the sloppy pork with a tight smile as my mind whispers once more, *Ask him, Laura. Go on, just do it*, but all Grace says is, 'Who's for extra sauce?' The coward inside me is still silent. Because what if I don't like the truth? What if it changes him and then me and then us? For ever?

Right now, one of us at this table has to remain who they say they are, even if it can't be me.

Twelve

Ebb and Flow

I'm in my winter wetsuit, heading down the slough at the back of the Project towards the briny pull of the sea. I've dropped Tilly and Seb at school and now this clean, green ravine is all mine for the next few hours. Picking my way down, I spy one of the eagles, eyeing me loftily from a bough before it flaps into flight. I think the rangers might be up there today, carrying out their checks in the conservation area. Something has startled the big male but no one can see me, up there or down here, except the birds.

I'm carrying my battered kayak, the one I found washed up on Shell Beach last year and realised was seaworthy, along the sandy bed of the slough. Elias doesn't know I keep it tucked under the overhang of rocks beneath the Project with a spare paddle. I hide a cheap suit here too, so there's no damp neoprene around to spark his curiosity. He doesn't know that I slip through the wooden fence at the foot of the Project to the water, sliding one plank of the perimeter fence aside where I eased out a nail. The only other way in and out of this slit in the rocks is by the sea itself.

Luckily, the tide is low and light today, I've checked, but you still have to be careful. The currents beyond the sea stacks are treacherous with wanderlust and will drag you onto the banks guarded by Terrible Tilly in the blink of an eye. It's OK if you hug the shoreline, if you're strong and experienced, and it's the only way to get the relief I crave when my head is ticking enough to make my teeth tingle.

I sit near the water, stretching into the second skin of my suit before sliding the kayak through the frondy green shallows. Once past the rocks, it's only a couple of minutes solid pulling to Cannon Cove, though a workout not many people could do or would want to. You have to go in diagonally to any rip currents at the last headland, if you don't want to end up waving to Terrible Tilly from far too close up. Once beached, you can walk the whole length of the deserted, craggy bay that soon becomes Ecola State Park.

There are trails dipping through the mossy, old growth rainforest there, from the well-kept car park to the north, but most tourists content themselves with the short-hike selfie spots on the other side. Between here and there, there's no way to access the bluffs and I love the feeling of total invisibility, the illusion of tranquillity, even though, if the Pacific rim tsunami ever strikes, this is one of the many paths it will forge inland, up these shallow fingers of streams, between the rolling rock headlands. Tilly always traces the routes along the information boards at the beach heads with her finger, to see which parts will stick up from the flood water. She calculates where she could run to in time, only imagining what that wave would look like, because you simply don't get the sweeping tidal ranges here like you do on the Bristol Channel, the vast swathes of sand and mud that appear as the sea retreats almost to the horizon before roaring back twice as fast.

Breathing in time with my paddles, I try not to remember how I explained the massive tides of the Severn Estuary to Priss once, back when I thought she might care. How, in 1607, a tsunami hit the coast at a staggering height of twenty-five feet, sweeping four miles inland in north Devon, Pembrokeshire and Glamorganshire, and fourteen miles in the Somerset levels. Woodcuts of the era show people in peaked hats and bonnets clinging to the tops of trees as sheep float away, though it was hard to believe the sea could surge so cruelly on the day Priss and I ambled past the dipping bridge in the close and green evening.

We'd just passed the swimsuited kids splashing in the lazy river and were lying out on the large, flat rock we'd always called the sacrifice stone further up the bank. She wasn't really listening, though, as we fell into a sticky silence, until I plucked up the courage to ask, 'Do you miss London, Priss?'

'Nah, not really. I mean, there's more to do, if you can afford it. But I guess it's no big thing, to leave behind the shitty neighbours yelling and the traffic stink.'

'Do you miss your friends, though?'

'I miss one friend, Josie. She was cool. She was into the stuff I was into. She'd have liked this place.'

'Really?'

'Yeah, the weirdness of it all, you know?'

'Weird?' I raised myself up on my arm. 'Weird?' The most ordinary, chocolate-box town in boring land?

'Yeah, you know, all these creepy cottages and those sand dunes. That sound the wind makes across them in the nights. All these stories you've got about ghosts and dead people. It's like something out of a horror movie.'

'It isn't really,' I countered, suddenly defensive.

'Sure it is, you said so yourself. The Cap Cock and all that,' the closest she could get to winding her English tongue around the Welsh consonants. *'Don't say his name, don't stay to eat. Don't close your eyes, la, la, la, la,'* she parroted Liam. 'This must be the actual place, right? Where they sacrificed all those girls in olden days. Kinda pervy, all that black magic. I mean, always the naked virgins getting sacrificed?'

I'd forgotten I'd told Priss that story a few weeks back, adding a few spontaneous satanic embellishments of my own that were never in Dad's book. 'Shame you can't find the inn anymore,' she said, 'the New Inn's foundations. It must have been right around here,' shivering, though it was seventy degrees in the shade. 'Wonder how he tricked them inside, if he even bothered to show them up to their rooms. If it was me, I'd have done it right away, slit their throats outside, because of the blood. I wonder if he used an axe or a butcher knife.'

'I don't really know,' I answered.

'I bet it was a butcher knife, easy one, two, three,' sitting up beside me, miming slitting my throat with a twist of her hand, laughing when I winced. 'You're a bit of a baby really, aren't you, Lolly Pop? You like stories about pirates and curses and ghosts but you're all mouth and no trousers. Not like Josie – she was hard as nails. Not scared of anything. She was the best with the Ouija board, the tarot cards. This would be a brilliant place to set them up. At night it'd be well creepy.

'*We summon you, oh Red Cap,*' she chanted, raising her arms in supplication, 'save us from the fucking boredom of Gwyn Mawr. Bring us cute boys who want to get it on with us, because Lolly will need to *pop* her cherry in a few months when she's legal.'

As I focus on the swells, I remember how annoyed I was when Priss mentioned my birthday that day. Normally, I loved the fact it fell on 4 November, slap-bang between Halloween and Bonfire Night, which meant a whole week of ghost stories and dressing up, presents, then fireworks – the extra-long autumn instalment of *The Laura Llewellyn Show*, just for me.

That day at the river, I was definitely thinking of ways not to invite Priss to any party Silas, Liam and I would plan that year, knowing she'd only spoil it, so I'm not exactly sure when I'd changed my mind, when I first thought about my grand scheme. Though I knew I could pull it off, when I'd put it into action a few weeks later, not at all daunted when Silas dismissed my suggestion with, 'It's a bit stupid, Lolly. We're too old for that dress-up shit now.'

'Oh, come on, you boring bugger,' I laughed, lying on his bed, rolling my eyes. 'It's Halloween soon, we have to dress up one last time this year, do some cool shots for our art projects, yeah? We'll do a theme, the Cap Goch,' as if I'd just plucked the idea out of the air, 'we'll make it a pastiche on devil worship. We'll make it a black mass set-up. We'll tie it in to classic horror movies like *Rosemary's Baby* and make a Devil's Pact to pass our GCSE's. It'll be a laugh. Just think of Mrs Cadogan's face when she sees our end of term portfolios. She'll shit a brick,' I insisted. 'Priss can bring her tarot stuff. We'll do fortunes. She can get some good weed and Liam will bring whisky.'

'She won't go for it,' Silas sighed.

'Course she will,' I pressed, wearing him down, remembering that summer day by the river, her gory fascination with the Cap Goch tale. 'She will if *you* ask her.'

It was an implicit challenge but he didn't rise to it. We'd never spoken about that single bedroom kiss since it had happened in the spring. He hadn't kissed me again.

'Priss is nothing but a pain in my fucking neck,' he snapped back. 'In fact, I'd like to wring it. She's too much hassle these days. Always hanging around.'

'Come on,' I begged, 'it'll be part of my birthday present,' and eventually he'd agreed. Then I'd got him to invite Liam, told him what to bring in his rucksack, not to forget his knife, the rope, the red ribbons.

We never celebrated my birthday that year, of course, nor really acknowledged it for years afterwards. Now, when Eli makes a big deal of it, I somehow manage to smile at the 'surprise' cake he's made with Tilly, the oyster dinner at Lemon Soul he's arranged, at another thoughtful gift of jewellery. Thankfully, this year, my birthday falls on the awards night so I'm more than happy to let that double as a celebration. For now, today is all mine and I focus on the salt heave of the Pacific as I ditch the kayak on the shore.

Slipping into the salt chop, I let the water cleanse me, arms thrashing over my head, the sound covering everything, though the peace never lasts. Eventually I have to leave, go back to the role I embody in a life that spools out under my feet every day, just so, my cage of cashmere polished hardwood.

Don't misunderstand me. I love my husband. I love my daughter. It's the day-to-day confinement I find so hard, straitened in the suit of Grace Jensen I've stitched for myself, which I sometimes long to rip my way out of, except for their love tying me inside, and that's the hardest bond of all, isn't it? Half of me is out here in the water, striking out – the other on shore holding tight to the anchor chain. One day one of us will have to win the struggle, but for today, I have to turn around and head for home.

When I finally get back to the Project, salty and stiff, I peel off my wetsuit to luxuriate in the new, smoky-glassed rainfall shower. The water was connected to the recovery tanks under the roof last week, the bathroom wet area completed. The walls are up in the rest of the rooms and the first countertops are in the kitchen. It's taking shape, it's becoming a home, ours to fill with fresh stories of happy families.

But I'm far from happy when I hear the intercom buzz and see Det. Olsen's distorted fisheye stare in the door camera display.

'Can you give me a minute, please? I just need to dress,' I mutter into the speaker.

'Been swimming?' she asks, clocking my wet hair as I call her in, a minute later.

'No, just freshening up.'

'You've been busy,' she nods at the renovations.

'Yes, the work's back on schedule. We hope to move in early in the spring.'

'How lovely, though a little out in the backwoods for my

taste. Don't you get freaked out, in the middle of all these, well, woods? It's kinda *Blair Witch*, isn't it? Especially at night.'

'Only to a city girl, maybe,' knowing I shouldn't say this, as it will probably irk her, the city and the girl part, but politeness has its limits. 'I'm used to it. And it's a quiet place to work. No interruptions,' nodding at the pile of sketches on the draughtingboard.

She picks up the hint and nods, 'Sure, no nosey neighbours. A good place for, you know, romantic assignations as well, I imagine. No prying eyes.'

Assignations? The word seems prim on her lips, a Grace Jensen word, more appropriate than the more-trendy hook-up or fuck-buddy in use now. Either way, she's back to me and Walter again, despite my denials at the boating dock. She's starting to grate on my nerves, as I say, like a good citizen. 'What can I do for you today, Detective? Do you have any news on the investigation?'

'No news exactly. Just a few more questions.'

'I assumed as much, guessing you weren't here to tell me you caught the pervert who broke into my house?'

'We haven't identified any suspects, no. We looked at some of the witness reports again, at a senior review meeting yesterday, and cross-referenced them with police reports for the weeks before Mr Lennon's assault. I noticed that one of the rangers, the conservation team monitoring the eagles' roost, reported a black Prius driving around here a few weeks ago. She notes it on two occasions, travelling from town to the ridge but turning here. It was parked outside one time, for two hours.

'She made a note of it because she was concerned it

was those environmental protestors that papered your car with flyers, maybe looking to cause more mischief. The night the car was parked here was August fourteen. Were you here that night? *Working* perhaps?' She means in my 'assignation'-friendly sex pad.

'August fourteen,' I echo. 'I don't know,' stretching my mind back, 'I'll have to check my diary.'

She nods as I go to the desk and call up my day planner, relieved when I see a full day blocked off. I don't need an alibi but I do have one this time, pointing to the screen saying, 'Oh, that's right, I was in Portland with Elias and Tilly. It was the aikido intermediate skills display.'

'You're sure? Because Ranger Morgan says a light was on in here that night. From around eight until ten p.m.'

'Well, you can ask about thirty people if we were there when Tilly got her certificate on stage. Then we stayed the night in the Willamette house, so I don't see how we could have been here from eight o'clock, unless we had a super-sonic jet and flew back from the Pearl. You know, even Eli isn't that rich.'

She ignores the barb. 'Could it have been a contractor, perhaps? Working overtime on the building?'

'No, the work was on hold then, for some glass to come in from Portland.'

'Does anyone else have a key, though? Perhaps working unofficially, stopped by to check on something?'

'No, we have electronic keypad entry, a six-digit code, and Elias supervises all the work himself. The contractors don't have it.'

'Does anyone else?'

'No.'

'Hmm, and you haven't noticed any intrusion on the site? Any trespass?'

Have I? I wonder. *Have I noticed anything strange?*

'No, I can't say I have,' I answer, as if giving it serious thought. 'I mean, the fence rings the property. The access track is the only way up. It's pretty secure. Do you have licence plates for this car you mentioned? I could ask Elias if it's anything to do with the Bright Brothers' team?'

'No,' says Olsen, as if the failure of the world to be anything but vague is more than she can bear, 'unfortunately the ranger wasn't close enough to make out a plate, just the suspected model. Do you know anyone who drives a black Prius?'

I snort, 'This is Lookout Beach, about fifty people I should think.'

'Yes, indeed. Gotta manage that carbon footprint.'

'Quite.'

'OK, well if you think of anything, or anyone, give us a call.'

She pauses at the foot of the steps and adds, 'If you see anything suspicious. Anyone hanging around. Call my number. Lock up tight, now.'

Surprised, I take the card, maybe she's changing her mind about the whole 'you're a cheating slut' stance and, after she leaves, I can't help but scan the gallery in a new light. The ranger must be wrong. No one could have been in here that night, maybe she confused the evenings. Still, I go to my everyday purse and check the inside flap pocket, just for reassurance. I want to know the Glock is there, to feel its lean, hard shape. I hold it in my hands, test its weight, cool on my fingers, palm the grip.

'Just aim slow, breathe out as you pull the trigger,' I hear May, my old dorm-mate, coaxing that Saturday afternoon out in the backwoods. May grew up in Washington State, which, like Oregon, permits 'open carry' of firearms. Her afternoons on the shooting range were very different daddy–daughter bonding sessions to the folk tales and chocolate biscuits of my youth, but she was serious about safety. 'Not a toy, Grace,' she would say. 'Store it safely, check the chamber. Rounds kept separate.'

I never quite got used to it, never stopped thinking of a gun as a movie prop, but I hung onto it for some reason. A sense of security or simply theatricality? Could I use it if I had to? Could I draw it out? Point it at someone in fear or self-defence? An intruder, maybe? Perhaps someone who promised, long ago, to do to me exactly what he did to Priss? I hope I never have to find out.

Thirteen

Trick or Treat?

The witching hour is on its way, the whole town now orange, black and shades of demonic All Hallows' Eve. It's not ideal timing, now that I've been told I might have a stalker, every black Prius that hums by sparking an electric twitch of alarm. As the milky Oregon mist bowls in from the bay my nerves tingle, but it's not just the mystery car that's set my teeth to grind and click, it's the inability to escape the in-your-face excitement of this time of year.

Can't blame the Americans for their Halloween fervour, I suppose. We brought it with us, the first settlers, our Puritan legacy of witchcraft and hindleg-hopping goats that entice you to do evil in the crucible of shame. All those stories clinging to the rotten planks of the old world, the ships that spewed out homesteaders, huddling together in the dark night of the soul in this heathen land, pushing back the devils of the old tribes. Now their descendants enact a week-long sugar homage to things that go bump in the night, people whose usual nightmares include corn syrup, hydrogenated fats and food additive Yellow 5.

And me? I'm just struggling to stop the smell of wood-smoke transporting me back to Gwyn Mawr, that butter-tinged moon sailing over crooked rooftops, skipping the frost-furred streets eager for Silas to come out to play, or in later years, get together to watch a sneaked copy of a slasher flick, battling demons from the safety of our mum-supervised homes.

I'm in the kitchen, fending off the ghosts of two decades past with only a wooden spoon and a packet of cookie dough mix I've pretended to make from scratch, when Tilly arrives home through the yard door, yelling, 'Look what I got for Halloween show-and-tell, Mom. Come and see.'

'After supper, hon,' I grin, as Seb waves his way inside, closely followed by Belle, who slumps against the counter asking, 'You got a tramadol, hon? My head is splitting.'

'Try my purse,' I nod, hands sticky with dough, 'the middle pocket. Then could you maybe roll this out for me? You know how I suck at it,' as I head to the downstairs cloakroom to wash my hands, the sink full of organic veggies waiting to be de-soiled and made into a black bat (beef) pie.

'We aim to serve,' she calls to my back.

'See my new book, Mom?' insists Tilly at the foot of the stairs. 'It has pirates and everything,' waving a bat-tered hardback that smells alarmingly like old bedrooms in January. I hope it doesn't have mildew, not with Seb's asthma.

'In a minute, honey,' I wave, as a car beeps out front and

Anoushka throws the front door open. I swear, sometimes my house is like a circus.

'Hi Anoushka, I thought you were in the city today, working on your thesis?' I say to my impossibly young and chirpy assistant.

'Meant to be, but me and Nell decided to get some research inspiration for our theses, down at the arts centre in Nehalem. And I think I left my notebook here on Wednesday, after I brought Tilly home from Otters.'

Hovering by the front door, I spot, with a stomach lurch, a black Prius idling in front of the house. But it's not a Prius, just a beat-up green Ford, towards which Anoushka yells, 'Two minutes, Nell,' at the woman waving out of the window. She dashes past me and grabs an A5 notebook from the coffee table in the den, before grinning, 'Oh, and don't forget this,' handing me a bag of black satin and lace with a pointy hat, in a separate holdall.

'Thank God! I was going to ask Eli to come grab Tilly's costume tomorrow,' I say, gratefully. 'Let me know how much I owe you. Do you want to stay for dinner? Nell can come too.'

'Thanks, but we have to drop some of her Native American animal masks off at the gift shop in Cannon Beach before it closes. We've just come from the bookstore on Main; they're stocking her stuff too and some of my gift boxes with the dreamcatcher motifs.'

Just what the world needs, I think, *more faux authentic souvenirs from eager art students*, but keep the words inside my mouth as Mum's voice says, *Sarcasm is the lowest form of wit.*

'Don't forget, Mrs J,' continues Anoushka, 'I have a

tutor meeting on Thursday, a paper to rewrite. Sorry again to miss all the Halloween fun, but you'll be OK with Belle and the gang, right?'

'Of course,' I nod, realising Anoushka might actually be avoiding staying here with us, since the incident in September. On one hand she's been pretty much her usual glitter-and-puppies self, but has been only too glad to sit for Tils up in the city while finding several excuses not to sleep in the spare room like she sometimes did. The town moms were also a little noncommittal when I told them our usual open-house party would be running on Halloween night. Christ knows who'll eat all the sugar crap I've prepared if no one turns up this year, but I can't worry about that now, as Anoushka calls, 'Catch you soon!', throwing a grizzled 'Ahoy, Captain!' to Tilly before disappearing down the yard.

'I've greased the trays, cut the cookies and put the oven on,' nods Belle, as I re-enter the kitchen, and, for a moment, she reminds me of my mother, comfortingly organised and inherently practical. Her ex-husband must have been a complete arsehole to leave her but *finders keepers*, as Mum would say, she's mine now. Belle and Grace are we, two upscale, cinnamon-scented, cookie-wrangling earth-moms. There are worse things to be, I suppose.

'Want to drink chai and talk about Halloween until the cookies are done?' I ask, disappointed when Belle says, 'Sorry, G, I need to get home. Seb has to practise his show-and-tell. He doesn't have Tilly's natural performance skills.'

'She gets that from me,' I quip, as she waves their way out.

Sitting down at the counter at last, sipping a wincingly sweet Pinot Gris that's in favour here, I survey my steamy domain, the steak marinating in the glass dish, the cookies browning in the oven. Black plush bats roost in the kitchen nooks and more flock in the living room.

Halloween was never this big a deal in Gwyn Mawr, confined to a few fake cobwebs or plastic jack-o'-lanterns in windows, the local shop wheeling out a tray of rubber spiders. The church would hold a fancy-dress competition but, if you were a tween or teenager, the annual Surf Club Disco at the Anchor was pretty much your only option. When I turned up early at Silas's house, that 31 October long ago, I was surprised to see Priss already there, sprawled with the boys in the living room, watching *Buffy the Vampire Slayer*.

'Let me come to the disco, Silas,' pleaded Abi, bouncing in dressed, as chance would have it, like Buffy herself, in a plaid miniskirt, brandishing a fake stake. 'Let me come to the *proper* party. I want to come with Lolly and you and hear Lolly's ghost stories again.'

'Bugger off, creep,' muttered Silas, waiting impatiently for his dad to stop nattering with the vicar and give us a lift.

'Next year, Abi,' I smiled, knowing Mr Cracknell was never going to let his still thirteen-year-old daughter out of the house dressed like that. Sure enough, there was an awkward slanging match when he was ready, with *change now or stay behind* instructions that sent Abi storming off to her room. Just as well, as the surf disco was merely our cover story to provide us with alibis for our parents. We didn't think we'd need the real kind as we looped around the Anchor's lounge, groaning at the cheesy skeleton decorations and paddling pool of ducking apples laid on by the club parents.

Some girls from our year were there, Willa and Dawn and a few borderline slutty witches, and we made sure they saw us, throwing out a couple of 'heys' and 'cool outfits' as we circled the room, then waving at Coach Turner before slipping out the side door by the stacks of beer crates.

We headed straight for the Norman castle as planned, leaning like a storybook relic into a great, glowing moon. Priss had pulled out the vodka before we'd even skipped across the stepping stones, spanning the shallow river at the castle's broken stone back, and the fields were black slicks of water after almost a week of gusty rain. The sky above was tossed with stars as the wind picked up and the alcohol was passed back and forth, warming us against the frigid air.

No one had worn fancy dress in the end, unless you count Priss's 'like, they're meant to be *ironic*' stripy green and black tights, but we were all black-clad, dodging into the shadows cast by our torches, footpads up to no good. By the time we reached the riverbank and the sacrifice stone, we were tipsy and ready to get high.

Priss seemed high enough already, though, babbling about how, back in London, they'd always done this and that creepy Ouija thing for Halloween. How she and her mother had once snuck in on a séance at the Ten Bells, Spitalfields, where Jack the Ripper had reportedly lurked. It was the first time she'd spoken about her mother.

'She was really into spiritualism and stuff. I tried to talk to her, once or twice, you know, in spirit, with the board, but she's never answered,' Priss said, 'not so far, anyway.'

With no answer of our own, we laid out the blanket gathered from the cottage next to the sacrifice stone and set out the candles we'd brought on the flat rock, one at each of its corners. Silas used his knife to trim the wicks and Priss used his lighter to do the honours with the weed. Silas didn't seem that keen on taking a puff, though, even though it was supposed to be 'Kev's best gangja mash'. But Liam, sitting on the stone with Priss, was taking long drags, prompting Silas, hovering, stamping his feet to keep warm, to warn, 'Slow down, mate, or you'll pass out.'

To my surprise, Liam snapped back, coughing, 'What the fuck's it to do with you, *mate*? You're my wife now, are you?'

'You're the wife, if anyone is, Liam, *mate*,' laughed Priss, shoving him with her elbow, rolling her eyes.

'Fuck off, Pippi Longstocking,' he hit back, so unlike Liam, easy going, eager to please Liam, with the pristine manners my mum always praised, that I stopped and stared. That was the first time I noticed the sharpness between them that night, the cut of the words they were aiming at each other. I assumed Liam was still annoyed with Priss because she'd said one of his portfolio pieces lacked perspective, in art club that Friday, and Silas had agreed it could do with more depth of shading. But I didn't mention that tension to Detective Inspector Maureen, in the interview room three days later, when the police had already been questioning us for twenty-four hours.

We were under caution by then, being kept in separate interview rooms while search warrants were issued for our houses. Because, soon after the police had called at our homes to tell us Priss Hartford was missing, Liam had told them everything. He'd told them about our visits to the cottage that summer, the first searches revealing an empty whisky bottle, weed traces on plastic wrappers, all our fingerprints on everything and the pentagram carved on the fireplace. But, soon enough, all DI Maureen was interested in was the 'chain of events' by the thick, fast water of the Ogmore river, the last place Liam said he'd seen Priss alive.

'So, the four of you left the Surf Club disco together?' said DI Maureen, though it wasn't really a question by then. 'There's no point in lying now, Laura. Some of the other kids have told us you did. So, whose idea was it to go to the spot by the dipping bridge? Whose idea was it to take the photographs?'

I almost crumbled then, when she mentioned them, even though I'd half expected her to all along. Until that moment, I'd been hoping that, by some miracle, the roll of film we'd shot that night at the sacrifice stone might have gone unnoticed, and, please God, Mrs Cadogan might not have shat even more bricks than predicted in the school's darkroom.

I tried to explain that it was Priss who'd happily suggested posing for the pictures, when the grainy six-by-fours were laid on the table in front of me.

'Really?' said DI Maureen, hamster cheeks blowing out in a sigh. 'Because Liam O'Rourke says it was all your idea. Yours and Silas's – to go to the river and take the photos.'

'It was just a silly game for Halloween,' I muttered.

'Silly?' She looked baffled, and how could I explain that Priss, drunk and glazed with pot, had offered to play the 'sacrifice' even before I could suggest it. That she'd jumped up from the blanket next to Liam as they bickered, to rifle Silas's rucksack, pulling out Abi's old red hair ribbons, the ones I'd told Silas to bring, along with the rope from his dad's shed.

'Oh props, how very theatrical,' she'd grinned. 'Didn't know you were fans of the theatre, boys,' making a limp wrist gesture.

'I'm not fucking gay, all right,' snapped Liam, jumping to his feet, fists clenched, though he was glaring at Silas not Priss.

'Course not, bet you get laid every Wednesday night by a different surf bunny,' Priss shot back, pulling out the ribbons, tying them around her neck. 'Look, this will be like the blood, right? How they used to tie them around the sacrifice's neck, the virgins? Symbolism and all that, to represent how the Cap Cock slit his visitors' throats. Liam, you be the devil worshipper. Put your hood up, like a cowl. Get Silas's knife and point it over me. Come on, Laura, Miss Pissy Pants Pirate. Get me in the best light. That's what we're doing here tonight, right? Why we're here, freezing our tits off? Homework for your super-cool photography club?'

She sneered as she asked, 'What's that song you sang, Liam? Sing it again so we can summon the Red Cock. How did it go? *Don't say his name . . . Don't go to sleep . . .* we'll say it three times, like in the *Candyman* movie, and he'll appear for us.'

That's when Liam said, 'I'm not doing this. I don't want to play stupid games any more,' and got to his feet.

'Don't worry, big boy. I'm not going to ask you to actually shag me or anything,' laughed Priss. 'Unless you really

133

want to. That's what those guys did, right? Had their horny way with the virgin before they killed her. What about you, Silas? You up for some consummation?'

'Fuck you,' said Liam, suddenly. 'I'm going home,' and before we could stop him, he was stomping back down the path through the woods, alone. If he'd stayed, perhaps things would've been different.

Instead, Silas said, 'This is fucking stupid, Laura. Let's just all go home and drink at mine until my dad comes back, yeah? It's fucking freezing out here.'

He was right. Even in my woolly gloves and hoody layers I was trembling, but we couldn't abandon the evening so soon, not before I'd convinced Priss to take her clothes off as I'd planned. I can still see the outline of her black bra and knickers against her white skin, the iron tang of blood overpowering the scent of baking cookies, as the oven timer pings me back to the present of my perfect kitchen. I'm unable to summon a candy-sweet mommy smile, even when bat-eared Tilly bounces in pleading to taste one. Instead I pour another glass of Pinot and down it in one.

Fourteen

Stay on the Road

I know I'm in trouble the next day, not just because I'm fighting a hangover from the wine I finished in the yard last night, but because Mrs Babcock meets me at the school gates with the exact same expression on her face she had when Tilly initiated a cupcake food fight on the fourth of July. With a complaint or helpful parenting 'suggestion' obviously coming my way, I tug my coat collar up against the damp sea breeze and force on my best smile as she says, 'Mrs Jensen, I wonder if I could have a quick word? I know we encourage the kids to bring in spooky stuff for Halloween, and I'm honestly made up when one of our kids brings in a good old-fashioned book but, well, I'm not sure this particular one is age-appropriate.'

She looks excessively sorrowful as she hands me my dad's book, *Fairy and Folk Tales of the South Wales Coast.* It's not *my* book, of course, I realise that even as I try to hinge my mouth shut. It's not the original one I read when I was younger than Tilly, but the waxed cover with the pen-drawn figures screams familiarity as an invisible fist punches me in the gut.

'Are you OK, Mrs Jensen?' enquires Mrs Babcock, perhaps mistaking my reaction for parental outrage. 'I mean, some of the stories are nice, but some are rather . . . mature. And the gender roles are, well, a little reductive for the girls. I just thought I should mention it in case . . . I mean, I'm sure you've checked the reading material?'

Because what mom in this Woke and sensitive era doesn't read every single line of every piece of written word that could warp their precious child's brain?

'Where did this come from?' I manage eventually, ignoring the now swirling drizzle as Mrs Babcock pulls up her anorak hood.

'Sorry, Mom,' says Tilly, detaching herself from her teacher's side. 'It's from the book sale yesterday – I *tried* to show you last night!'

So she had but, after dinner, books had been forgotten when we'd played pirate attack around the tent in the den, with Elias as King of the Cannibals.

'Ah, I see, well that makes sense,' says Mrs Babcock, relieved. 'I assumed you'd bought it for her. I know you and Tilly are our gold-star readers. Some of the stories are quite nice, but one or two, they're . . .' she leans in and whispers, 'there's a murder in one. It talks about throats being cut . . . the subject matter . . .'

'Yes. Yes, of course,' I mutter, better to be seen as a careless vetter of reading material than a corruptor of youth. 'Clearly, I should have done a proper check. I'm very sorry, Mrs Babcock. The children weren't unduly upset, were they?'

'Of course not,' gushes Mrs Babcock, 'the kids are fine and it sure is lovely to look at the history of other cultures, you being from Wales and all. Though we couldn't say the Welsh words properly, could we, Tilly? Maybe we need a lesson from you on the pronunciation?' she laughs. 'But maybe we'll stick to some of the nicer tales for now.'

'Yes, sure. I'm sorry, Mrs Babcock, I'll sort this out.'

'Oh, no harm done,' she's grateful for my reasonableness and suddenly eager to get out of the soggy chill. 'Tilly got an A in her show and tell, by the way. Good job, Tilly!'

As I load Tilly into the car, the book on the seat next to me, my daughter's already talking nineteen to the dozen about what a baby Mrs Babcock is, how the book is not scary and girls can be both princesses and pirates if they want to, so I have a minute to calm myself. That won't be long enough, though, not to put my childhood back in the box where the book should be, five hundred miles away in a cottage attic.

I can't panic. I won't let the spit of vomit in my mouth become a heave. I make approving noises and then ask Tils, light as air, 'Where exactly did you say you got this book, hon?'

She heaves a theatrical sigh at silly Mommy before repeating, 'At the bookshop charity sale, Mom! I *told* you already. Remember I said I got some cool stuff? And look, this writer has the exact same name as Grampy Lew. You're from Wales. These are stories from there, right? Mrs Babcock couldn't say the words and couldn't say Llewellyn.'

While Grace tries to smile at Tilly's improved pronunciation, my shoulders slump as I ask, 'But how did you find it, Tils? Where was it exactly? Did someone at the store give it to you?'

'No, Mom, it was in the two-dollar tub, don't you listen? Why? I can read it, can't I? Just because Mrs Babcock thinks we should be reading stupid stuff. I'm not a baby like Mrs big old, wobble-belly, Babcock.'

She giggles and I should reprimand her, but my tongue is still stuck to the roof of my mouth as I stare at the cover in my hands, at the wailing woman in a flowing dress, her mouth a wide O, the pirate at the prow of his boat, cutlass raised. I hold it up to my nose, inhaling the smell of olde English disappointments, basements and damp shelves. When I force myself to look at the title page it doesn't say, *For Laura, love from Dad*, but I know all the other words that will be inside.

How can it be here? Only a few dozen copies were ever printed by a small publisher. How could one find its way across the ocean and into a store in this teeny, homespun town? Someone is playing a game with me, I know that now. But who and how? What are the rules? And what is the endgame?

When a fist bangs on the misted driver's window, the word 'Fuck' escapes my mouth before I can imprison it, but it's only Belle, her halo of rain-frizzed hair instantly familiar through the glass. Ignoring Tilly's fly-catching look at my F-bomb, I hit the button to open the window where Belle's blabbering something about Seb getting a B in the show and tell, interrupting her with, 'Belle, how in God's name did you let Tilly pick up this book? Seriously, what were you thinking?'

I immediately feel bad. She looks like I've just slapped

her, which I suppose I have. Slapping Belle would be a bit like kicking a baby sea otter, but it's too late now.

'Gee, what's wrong, hon?' she frowns, taking the book from my hand. 'Is that one from the second-hand sale? We called there yesterday on the way home, remember?'

'I know that. But it's hardly a young kids' book, is it? Was it in the kids' section? Where did it come from?'

'What? I dunno. I'm sorry. Is there something wrong with it?'

'Enough gore and gender stereotypes to get Mrs Babcock's panties in a bunch, apparently.'

'Hee, hee, panties in a bunch,' laughs Tilly, but stops when I shoot her the knock-it-off stare I've learned from Det. Olsen.

'Where did she pick it up from, then?'

'Er, I'm not sure,' fumbles my friend. 'There was a tub filled with a bunch of stuff. It all looked like fairy tales. Seb got one on *Ghostly Tales of New England*.'

'Oh, that's fine then, as long as you checked what Seb was buying.'

'Oh Jeez, isn't it age appropriate?' she looks horrified. 'Has Mrs Babs had a conniption, Tilly?'

Tilly doesn't answer, looking at me like I've lost my mind. First, I've done the bad curse-word thing, now I'm being mean to Belle, lovely old, flowers and cupcakes Belle, who is meant to be my bestie. As Grace bites her tongue, Laura tastes blood.

'I'm sorry, B,' I apologise, and I am. 'It's not your fault. I should've checked it myself. Apparently, there was a bit of a commotion at show and tell, that's all.'

'Did you get in trouble, Tilly hon?'

'No, Belle,' says Tilly. 'Mom's just being weird,' rolling her eyes at Seb, his bubble glasses make his eyes seem twice as large as usual.

'I'm sorry, guys. I guess I *am* being weird today. Long day. Can I give you a ride home?'

Both are fuzzed with beads of rain, but Belle declines as they need to stop by the optometrists near the school to get Seb's new glasses.

'Catch you Tuesday, then? Any time after five,' I offer as a peace pipe.

'Sure,' smiles Belle, though I can see she's still hurt.

'Can we please go home now, Mom?' asks Tilly, squirming in her seat when I tell her I just need to make a quick stop at the bookstore first. 'You're not going to give Mr Milton a hard time too, are you?' She looks alarmed as I cruise down Main Street and indicate left. She means the store owner who looks like Richard Attenborough in *Miracle on 34th Street*, a bearded, twinkling, ribbed sweater of a man no one could give a hard time to.

'No of course not,' I reply. 'Just stay here for two minutes, OK?' as I pull up at the faux cottage with its white-stepped porch. I'll be able to see her in the car from the big window.

'Hi, Mr Milton,' I try for a smile, the book tucked under my arm as I shake off the rain. 'A drizzly one tonight.'

'Sure is, honey,' says Santa Milton, hanging a skeleton in the window display. 'And what can I do for you today?'

'Actually, I'm wondering if you know who donated this?'

He takes a long look at the book I offer, opens the cover then closes it with a, 'No darlin', can't say I do. Did you get it here?'

'Tilly picked it up last night, from one of the two-dollar bins.'

'Hmm, well, we had a bunch of stuff in from Portland yesterday, but I don't think it's out yet, except for some *Sleepy Hollow* stuff for Halloween.'

'Could this have come from that batch?'

'Oh, maybe, though I'd probably put that in the history or folk section. I could ask Agatha if she knows. Agatha?'

He summons his ancient sister, who slides silently out from behind a rack of travel books as if rising from the pages of a ghost story herself, long grey hair in swathes around her head, clad in flowing layers of white, with a silver locket the size of a soup spoon sitting below her bony clavicles.

'Grace, honey, nice to see you again,' she smiles. 'Where's the pirate queen?'

'In the car. Say, Aggie, have you seen this book before?'

She takes one quick look and shakes her head. 'No, do you want to sell it? Looks interesting.'

'She doesn't want to sell it, Agatha, she thinks *we* sold it to *her*.'

'No, we didn't.'

'You're sure?' he frowns.

'Sure I'm sure, Albie. I know every book in this store.'

I don't doubt her for a second but say, 'Are you positive? Because Tilly and Belle picked it up yesterday, from the two-dollar bin.'

'Well, maybe,' says Mr Milton. 'You can just put the money in the cup there – that money goes to the tidepool protection fund.'

'But people shouldn't put books in there without my say-so,' huffs Aggie.

'So, someone could have put it in there? Donated it?' I check.

'Yes, but they shouldn't have,' repeats Aggie. 'I mean, we have to know what's in our store.'

'Yes, of course. You didn't see anyone in here, though, did you? Who might have donated it without knowing the rules?'

Her eyes narrow. 'Why? Is there a problem?'

'No, no, not at all, it's just,' I improvise, 'I think this might be a first edition. I should give the guy his book back or put some more cash in the collection at least.'

'Didn't see any guys in here yesterday, darlin',' says Mr Milton with a shake of his head.

'Yes, we did,' says Agatha immediately. 'You remember? That tall guy, from out of town.'

'Now how would you know if he was from out of town?'

''Cause he was dressed out of town and talked out of town.'

'Did he buy anything?' I interrupt, sensing a sibling dispute brewing. 'Maybe there's a name on the credit card receipt or something?'

'He was looking at the architecture books but he didn't buy anything,' says Agatha, glaring at her brother.

'What did he look like?'

'Well you know, real tall, beard, how the young guys look now. City leather jacket too. Actually, he was asking about the house on Shore Road, if you'll be selling soon? He was asking about your beach house too. Everyone is just dying to see it finished, Grace. Might you have an open house one day, you know, just so we can take a look around?'

'Maybe. Yes. Thanks, Aggie.'

As I step outside the store, my throat constricts to the size of a penny. Suddenly the Northwest night is filled with pumpkin grins and watchful eyes, none of them kind. Is there a tall man with a beard in the dark recess by the closed coffee shop across the street? There, lighting a cigarette? A risky enough choice in this smoke-free town. Something an out-of-towner would do? But the flare of the lighter is lost in the wet whoosh of a passing bus, and when it's gone the street shows only shadows again.

'Get in, Mom,' complains Tilly, yanking the door handle, then, 'Are you OK? Are you mad at me?' when she sees my face.

'No, honey. Forget it.'

But I don't give the book back to her. I don't want it in the house. I don't want Elias to see it. He might find it more of a coincidence that it bears my father's name than Tilly does, so I take the volume and shove it under the car seat.

Fifteen

Guilty Party

Today I'm on my way to Astoria, the river mouth town dwarfed by its vast, steel-boned bridge. Usually this trip is a fun, family jaunt, fuelled by sing-songs and Gummy Bears, the subject of many of Tilly's 'What I Did on My Summer Vacation' essays, because this is where John Jacob Astor, the USA's first millionaire, staked a claim to the fur trade on the mighty Columbia River.

As far as Tilly is concerned, it's also the site of our annual *Goonies* movie pilgrimage she has yet to grow out of. Back on wet Sunday afternoons in Gwyn Mawr, it was me, Silas and Liam joining in with the Hollywood kids searching for pirate treasure in the eighties classic, shouting the catchphrase, 'Hey, you guys!', watching out for the villainous Fratelli brothers while scoffing chocolate fingers. Imagine my surprise when Elias took me down to Cannon Beach for the first time and there was Haystack Rock, the famous sea stack straight out of the movie. I'm used to it now, although I spent a year deliberately not looking at it.

Tilly loves the Oregon Film Museum in the old county jail, full of memorabilia, where you can see the bullet holes in the Fratellis' car, parked outside. If she was with me today, we'd drive up to the hilltop Astoria Column, the stone tower with a wrought iron balcony you can launch little balsawood planes off, that you buy in the gift shop. Then she'd recite tidbits from the journey of intrepid Lewis and Clark, at the place where they finally spotted the Pacific Ocean. She likes the parts about the dysentery and starvation best. She thinks death and desperation are glamorous, like all kids who love stories but have never known hunger or fear on their gilded little journeys.

And how will mine end now? In this far-flung corner of the world, at this treacherous confluence of water and forests? Where it seems I have been tracked down in my hiding place. After Tilly skipped off to school this morning, I jumped straight into the car and headed up the coast, driving north to chase a ghost. Because I need to conjure Silas's face somewhere other than in my dreams today. Because I can't do that at my home, and I couldn't keep any photos of him after what happened, I was too afraid to. They would've given me away one day if I had, I'm sure. They always do, don't they? Keepsakes, charms, trophies? Bleed connections from other lives into the present, set traps.

'Who's this?' Elias would've asked, a photograph fluttering from the leaves of a book, the back flap of a photo album. 'You've never mentioned him.'

As the close ranks of pines slide along beside my wheels, I wonder if Silas has changed over the years. But of course he has. No one is formed and whole at fifteen, the world yet to mould and break every bone and sinew, and Silas was frozen in time even beyond my memories. Spending half your life in prison will see to that.

That's why he can't be out here, looking for me, toying with me, ready to take revenge. This isn't a story in a book, like the *Count of Monte Cristo*, where he's escaped through a spoon-dug tunnel, shrugging off vitamin D deficiency and the psychological damage of incarceration with a haircut and a shave, to enact retribution. Even if he could have found me, or sent someone to seek me out, why break into my house with props and equipment then wait so long to strike?

'*Whatever I did to her, I'll do to you,*' I heard him snarl, as they dragged him away from the dock after the sentencing, putting my hands over my ears, screwing my eyes shut. '*Do you hear me, you bitch? You lying bitch!*'

Today I have to look him in the eye the only way I can, just to reassure myself he's still where he belongs. I've wanted to for so long, since straight after the incident at the house in September, just to reassure myself there's no way the two things could be linked. I've longed to look him up online, like I used to in the lonely years before I met Elias, every time I had the urge to revisit what we had been. But since the wedding, I've stopped myself, like I did this morning, because that would've felt like picking the stitches out of the past yet again, beckoning him here through the ether to violate this successful re-versioning of Laura Llewellyn into Grace Jensen.

Also, I'd wanted to be very careful. Until I'd really known what was happening with the intruder, I didn't want the police, should they suddenly request permission to pry into my life, my communications, to start asking who the boy in the old South Wales mugshots was. Even if it was all dead and done, they would've thought it worth looking into, surely? Trying to identify the man who might want to hurt me, and then I could never have kept it from Eli.

I was determined to cover my tracks, not to be careless like I had been when I'd allowed DI Maureen to get the upper hand, when she'd asked, 'What's this, Laura?' holding up the bloody jumper in the plastic evidence bag. 'We found it in your washing machine.' That's when I realised I'd set the quick-wash programme but, in my hurry to shower as soon as I'd got back from the riverbank, hadn't made sure the sticky start button had engaged.

'Pretty little girls don't do so well in prison,' warned DC no-first-name Davies at that point, when the pretending had worn down to a point he wanted to push home. 'Pretty little rich girls like you get eaten alive.'

'That's enough,' said DI Maureen, pretending to scold him, pretending to be the good cop for once. 'This is not about scaring you, Laura. It's about the reality of what happens next, if you don't tell the truth. He's right, though. You don't want to go to a young offenders' institution, do you? No literature lovers there, no A levels. No Oxford exam. Fifteen is too young to throw away your life. It's your choice.'

But just like then, I have no choice now, as I pull up in Astoria, bypassing the art deco storefronts of Main Street, heading straight for the pier-studded waterfront. Inside the warm fug of the retro internet café with the old-style arcade games Tilly loves, I order a Stumptown

Americano and look for a seat. The staff here change every few months, so it's never the same rangy, edgy brunette or man-bunned dude at the counter, and I'm as good as anonymous when I log on to one of the old-fashioned PCs, installed as some sort of post-ironic statement about smartphone dependency, and start typing.

When I'm sure the two teenage lads, no doubt calling up some porn in the corner, aren't looking at my screen, I take a swig of coffee, and Google *Silas Cracknell – Trial*. And there they are, the same, as they ever were. The headlines:

Teen Torture Killer in Court

Occult Murder Rocks Seaside Village

Black Mass Mutilation

Devil Killer Sentenced

Priscilla Killer Was Hooked on Sick Films

Disturbing Mind of a Teenage Monster

That's Silas now. No longer *my* Silas. A killer.

His arrest photograph, released to the press after the sentencing, glares out at me, accusing, stubborn. Further down, I click on the one of him from the Surf Club fundraiser, me and Liam on either side, though everything below my pirate hat is a splodge of pixels now, Liam's grin and plug ears smudged away, ghosts in the news narrative. *Whatever happened to Liam?* I wonder. The boy who told the truth, or the little of it he knew. Mum said he went back to Belfast with his mother, but for me he'll always be this. We all will. The images are like a punch in the throat. My airway closes.

I don't read the words of the articles because I know what they say. Instead, I force myself to make a new search, just to be sure, tapping in the words and changing the combinations three or four times. It's merely a precaution, to reassure myself, so I'm not in any way ready when a fresh hit comes up and the new headlines scream:

Teen Torture Killer Released from Jail

Satanic Cult Teen Gets New Life

Let Him Rot, say friends of Occult Killer's Victim

As I scroll, three smaller pieces of down-page moral outrage pop up, all general, because these articles can't reveal where Silas is now, or what he looks like. There's such a thing as 'time served' for child offenders, as rehabilitation; he's paid his debt in the eyes of the law, though clearly that will never be enough for those remaining in Gwyn Mawr.

'They should have thrown away the key,' says 'unnamed resident', and there's a quote from Priss's father, 'her life was stolen while he gets to live his'. He's holding a picture of his daughter up to the camera, his face brittle and pinched, hers forever sealed in the grainy pixels of a youthful smile.

I have to concentrate hard to make my vision un-fuzz as I squint at the newsprint to find what I'm looking for – the date on the paper's search box telling me Silas was released almost eighteen months ago. Greyness creeps up through my eyes when I realise he's been out in the world for a year and a half. All that time I've been here, acting as if everything is normal, kayaking and baking cookies, designing mid-century-modern interiors, building a huge house and a small girl, erecting a life.

Is that possible? How could I not have known? Why didn't I feel it? The change in air pressure out under the wide skies? The closed, red places under my skin? The ticking in my head increasing in volume until I have to rest it on the clammy keyboard to not pass out. For all these years, the only reason I've been able to push on is because I knew it was all contained back there, staunched, unable to infect anyone.

Of course I'd known it would happen one day, that they'd release him, but they were supposed to warn us. A few years back, Mum had been informed by the Crown Prosecution Service that they'd extended his sentence, on psychiatric and welfare grounds, so this shouldn't have been possible. But that hardly matters now, as I click off the screen, opening my eyes to erase the words burned onto my closed lids.

Avoiding the concerned look on the Goth-girl server's face, I grab my purse and head out onto the water's edge, leaning over the iron rail, drinking in the salty air. The mist floats over the idling Columbia today, birds pick in the mudflats among the rotting timbers of lost pierheads as my coffee returns in an acid rush, exploding onto the riverbank below. Then I'm empty inside, leaning against the railing, wiping my mouth with my sleeve as the out-raged gulls flap windward.

When the hand falls on my shoulder, I start back like a prizefighter, arm pulled into a sea-strengthened curve

150

with a fist at the end. I'm ready now, to get the first hit in, at least that might give me a chance to step back for a moment, to explain to Silas how sorry I am, before he finishes things. But the man at my elbow has already withdrawn, out of range.

'Sorry, I didn't mean to startle you,' he apologises, looking and sounding nothing like Silas, frowning when he smells the vomit, sees the brown spittle on my sleeve. 'It's Grace Jensen, isn't it? Jesus, are you OK?'

'Who are you?' I demand, taking another step back, rummaging to find the zip of the pocket in my purse with the gun inside. This tall man with a beard and leather jacket may not be anyone I recognise but that doesn't mean he's not the one, the avenger, the player of games and leaver of books, someone in action on Silas's behalf or because of him. And the voice is somehow familiar.

'Mrs Jensen, are you all right? Do you need me to call someone?' he asks, concerned now.

'Who are you?' I stutter, my hand finding the zipper, but something is wrong. I can't feel the cool nose of the gun against my sweat-slick fingers.

'I'm Neil Morrow. I didn't mean to scare you. I've left several messages on your answerphone, five actually, but you haven't called me back. I'm from *Crib* magazine.'

Then I remember the voice on the answering machine at the Willamette house, the night of Tilly's birthday, the reporter with the maybe mid-Atlantic accent who asked me to call him back. It's true he's left several more messages since, but I've deleted every one.

'You haven't returned any of my calls,' he repeats. 'I was hoping we could have a chat.'

'What about?'

'The awards, of course. They're less than a week away now. Elias is up for an impressive gong.'

Of course, the awards. The soundbite. Trying to place the accent I ask, 'How did you know I was here?'

'I didn't,' he explains. 'I was up here on another story. I saw you across the street. I was taking a call, charging the car, and spotted you coming out.'

He gestures to the dust-streaked, black electric hybrid, Astoria being one of the first towns to have public charging posts, and I notice the odd roll of his voice when he says *car*.

'Where are you from?' I demand, my hand still searching for the gun. The bag is not that big.

'I told you, *Crib* magazine.'

'No, I mean, you're not American.'

'No, you can pick up on the accent, huh?' he grins. 'One ex-pat to another? I'm still a little bit Newcastle, right? Though I've been out here a while. *Way-ay, man*, a Geordie boy and all that. You know we have that in common. I read one of your mother's books at college but I wasn't good enough to study under her, or read architecture as it turned out. Now I write about other people's buildings and designs. I was hoping to do a "Geordie girl" done good piece, out here, you know, in the other Great North.'

'How do you know about my time in Newcastle?' I demand.

'Your bio mentioned it, when you won the newcomer award a few years back. Bree, my editor, wrote it; it said you were from Newcastle originally and I made the connection with your mum. Collins was your maiden name, right?'

Not quite, though it's true Mum used to teach under her maiden name in Newcastle. I used it for uni too, just in case, and for my Bright Brothers profile the magazine would have looked up. It wasn't an official alias, just some camouflage.

'Out here they think all Brits who don't sound like the Queen sound alike, right?' he laughs, taking my silence for assent. 'But what is that, a bit of Welsh in there?'

He can't know, surely? Where I'm really from? Is that what he wants, my real story? To expose what I've made here, from the blood and flood back there?

'With the awards coming up, this would be a companion piece to the profile on your husband,' he insists, hurrying on with his story pitch, 'the power couple, you know. We're a long way from the "great woman behind a great man" thing now. You're a rising star in your own right. When he gets up on stage next week, you'll be with him. We want a double feature. You must have so much to say, the journey you've made. And your beach house – a real milestone in sustainable eco-architecture. I'm sure everyone wants to know the inside story, how you've sourced the materials and so on.'

'I'm sorry,' I mutter, taking a stab at regaining my composure. 'I don't really want to steal my husband's thunder. This is his moment.'

'Yes, of course, but your beach house will be finished in the spring. That'll make some waves. You've been involved in that all the way, right? The design, the environmental build? You've got some great features, used fully sustainable methods, sourced locally?'

'Yes, it's all my project.'

'So, you might be up there yourself next year. I'd love to have a look around, have you talk me through it all. I mean, once it's complete everyone will be asking for a tour.'

Then I remember what Aggie said at the bookstore, about the tall guy in his out-of-town leather jacket, with his out-of-town voice, asking questions about me.

'I'm sorry,' I fumble for my car keys. 'I can't talk to you now. I have an appointment.'

'Yes, of course. I didn't mean to ambush you.'

He fishes in his jacket pocket and passes me a card. 'You know, I'm sorry about jumping on you like this. After that thing that happened at your house a few weeks back, I wasn't thinking.'

So he knows about that, though they seem to have kept the details out of the city news, apart from a couple of little pieces on a break-in at a 'prominent architects' home' the week afterwards.

'Such a creepy thing to happen,' he mock shivers. 'Have they caught the guy yet? Any idea what it's all about?'

'No,' I admit. 'No arrests have been made.'

'No leads? In your position I'd have to ask if the police are doing their job properly. Is it true there was a knife and a rope?'

'I can't talk now,' I repeat, hoping my seasick legs will be strong enough to carry me away.

'No, anyway I suppose that would make anyone edgy, and you obviously value your privacy. Call me when you feel up to it, any time. I'm working out of a little office in Seaside right now, it's a temporary place, above a café. But if you give me a call, I can drive down to Lookout Beach.

Don't wait too long, though, there are deadlines for these things.'

'What?' I snap, head jerking up as I read the card he's just handed me.

'I just mean, you need to get in first, to control the narrative.'

'What narrative?'

'That's what I want to explore.'

He's smiling as I stumble away, forcing one foot in front of the other. I don't look back to see if he's following but I'm shaking by the time I get to my car, lock myself inside and pull open my purse.

I rifle through all the pockets, practically turn it upside down, the tissues and painkillers, juice box, lipstick, hair-bands, sunscreen, pouring onto the passenger seat beside me. But I already know it's pointless, as I check the rear-view for signs of Neil Morrow or anyone else. The bag is empty and the gun is gone.

Sixteen

The Secret Season

I'm back on the main highway, forcing myself to breathe away the crush in my chest. By instinct, I don't loop back southwards, towards Lookout Beach. Instead, I let myself be carried by the traffic across the Astoria bridge, streaming along its humped steel back, over the shimmering mouth of the Columbia, into the wild.

I check my rear-view mirror every ten seconds, as I leave Oregon and slide into Washington State on the other side, to see if anyone is following me. Morrow was driving a Prius, just like the car Det. Olsen said was seen at the Project in August, and now it seems he's very interested in me. He was hiding something, I'm sure of it. I sensed another angle under his so-called backslapping article. But there's no sign of him as I head through the tree-thickening landscape, along the giant's yawn of the bay, cruising the north edge of the vast estuary basin before I see the sign for Dismal Nitch.

Realising where I am, I pull over just in time to hurl the

last spittle of my Americano into the grass by the picnic bench where we usually stop with Tilly – the exact spot where Lewis, Clark and their entourage almost died before the end of their trail. It's not so dismal today, a neat little rest area stippled with sunlight, a jaunty information panel and a panorama of blustering sky and sea. But if you walk a few minutes along the water's edge you can still imagine yourself the only person in this empty land, the edge of the wilderness where people come to lose themselves.

I sit on a blackened hunk of wood from a forgotten mooring post, trying to scour my brain of the ticking that rattles my skull, imagining myself vanishing into the ragged teeth of the trees. Because I don't know how to deal with this. To breathe like this. Not any more.

How hard would it be to disappear out here, to hide? Bigfoot seems to have managed it for decades, despite the odd shaky photo and camper sighting Oregon has built an industry around. Hell, D. B. Cooper, the USA's most famous fugitive, managed it in the 1970s, after parachuting from an aeroplane he'd hijacked with thousands of payoff dollars in his backpack. No trace of him was ever found, so how difficult would it be to empty my bank account and vanish with my own bag of cash, keep driving north, past Willapa Bay and into Olympic National Park?

I could get a job on a logging station, or bussing tables, as they call it, in a diner, spend my afternoons beachcombing, staying at campsites where travellers are always welcome to use the restrooms and beady-eyed dogs bark at the North Star. Because if this man is somehow here for me, if he has been sent by Silas after all these years, maybe it's finally time for me to let go of the chain I've been gripping and float away with the riptide.

As if the ocean has read my thoughts, an empty bottle of Von Ebert's Pilsner bobs by, reminding me of the messages in bottles we once consigned to the sea in Gwyn Mawr, an annual Surf Club ritual organised before anyone thought twice about tossing stuff into the plastic-choking ocean. Most of us just wrote our names and addresses on the cards inside, in the hope some kid in Bangladesh or Brazil would one day send us a letter back. Silas being Silas, wrote just five words on his. *I know where you live.*

'Imagine their faces,' he'd grinned. 'It'll be so creepy. Like a *Twilight Zone* episode. It'll be the coolest joke.' The sort of joke that made it easy for the newspapers to write all those things about him later.

Has Silas sent me a message in a bottle now, disguised as a red ribbon, a knife and handcuffs? Or has he just shared his story with Neil Morrow, who wants to pick out the scabs and tear them open, just like DI Maureen did, when she refused to believe my account of what happened on the riverbank that Halloween.

'You're trying to tell me Priss Hartford took her clothes off willingly, on a freezing October night, to pose for some school art project?' she insisted. 'That she set up the scene with the rope and the knife herself? How stupid do you think I am?'

'It's the truth,' I yelled, because after Liam abandoned the party, Priss really was the one who said, 'It's just the three of us now, then. Are we gonna get naked and have this sacrifice orgy or what?'

She really was laughing when she pointed to the

rust-stained iron ring fixed in the sacrifice stone's side, nothing more than an old mooring point for a boat, saying, 'This is where they tied them, right? The virgins? Gimme your knife, Silas. Let's make this look good.'

It all happened very quickly after that. I remember Silas had put his knife down on the sacrifice stone, after trimming the candle wicks for us, but he snatched it up then, meaning, I imagine, to follow Liam's exit from the riverbank gathering that had started to go wrong. But Priss lunged for the knife a second after and she caught the blade, opening up a long slice of her palm, creating what would later be called a 'classic defensive wound'.

'Priss, Jesus!' recoiled Silas, at the deep slash seeping blood, dropping the knife to pull off his sweater to staunch it, just as we'd learned as good little sharks at Surf Club's first aid training. But she pulled away, arms flailing, spraying droplets of blood on the leaves, on him, crowing, 'Fuck off, Nurse Cracknell,' seeming to not feel it. 'Think I've never cut myself before?'

Then she pulled off her black hoody, her chunky biker boots, tights and denim skirt, while we stood there, watching her, unsure what to do. Standing in her black cotton underwear under the moonlight, clad in silky teenage skin, I remember thinking she looked like a creature from a folk story, ethereal, ghostly, cursed, until we saw the blood really flowing from her hand and the lattice of silver scars and healing gritty lines across her stomach, breasts and upper arms.

'What the fuck, Priss?' whispered Silas, as if he'd never seen them before, never seen her naked, when of course he must have.

'Look, this'll look cool, won't it?' insisted Priss, her eyes glazed with vodka, pausing only to throw up a little bit at her feet, then wipe her mouth with the back of her bloody hand. 'And the blood is real, not a movie prop effect. We should have a video camera to capture this. Eat your heart out John Carpenter – our *Halloween* movie is much better than your tired shit. What will Mrs Cadogan say about this? She'd better at least give us an A for commitment.'

She spun around then, like she was in the grip of some Mayday rite, whirling white and red. 'Come on, trick or treat?' she offered, smearing the red between her black bra and knickers, across her throat. She took the rope and looped it around her wrists, fumbling to tie it through the iron ring at the end, before laying herself out, limp and languid like a maiden ready for slaughter. I had the camera around my neck, poised to take the pictures I'd planned when I'd originally thought I'd need to coax her to get undressed.

'Take your picture, Lolly Pop,' she demanded, lying back, a parody of seduction, her throat exposed, ribboned in red. 'Or are you just going to gawp? Like what you see, Silas? What do you say? Wanna do the ritual rape part, for fun? I bet Pissy Pants here would like to watch. You can just pretend, fake it, if, you know, I'm not your type.'

I didn't tell DI Maureen that last part, or that this was the moment I started snapping shots with the Nikon. I didn't tell her how I was still hoping, as per my original plan, to develop the photos on the sly the next day, in the school darkroom, share them around among everyone we knew and everyone we didn't. That sober, I hoped Priss would know the humiliation she'd visited on me with that pirate photo. Long before selfies were weaponised and slut-shaming existed, it was only fair, because in my own teenage story I was the wronged and righteous maiden, the brave heroine, while Priss was the villain, the slutty temptress who would get her comeuppance and me, the guy.

You could see what the jury thought, though, seeing Priss lying there, eyes closed, bloodied like a corpse, apparently not even breathing. Even though I insisted she was only *pretending* to be dead the prosecution had other ideas. They said I was lying to protect Silas, that he was obsessed with the Red Cap story, had even invented his own elements, the disturbing ritual sacrifices and the summoning of Cap Goch that was never in the original folklore.

'Had Silas Cracknell become withdrawn, that autumn before Halloween?' asked Mr Kamal. 'Did he show any signs of dark thoughts that summer?'

Dark thoughts. Does The X-Files *count as occult?* I wanted to ask.

'Did he ever talk about death? Was he obsessed with horror movies and TV shows?' he persisted.

And how could I explain that, just because Silas watched genre shows and films like *The Exorcist* and *Rosemary's Baby,* that he wasn't into all that demon stuff. He wasn't a sicko. He was just really into the cinematography, the 'dark visual language of the era's paranoia' as he called it.

But they still kept saying he was obsessed with the occult, that he'd planned the photoshoot and brought the red ribbons, the rope, taken the shots. How could I explain that Silas was simply tired of Priss's bullshit and just wanted to go home. I couldn't say, in front of strangers, in front of my mum and dad sitting on the front bench at court, that

Priss had yelled at him, 'That's it. Run after your boy-friend Liam, leave us girls to our fun. Maybe Lolly Pop would like to fuck me instead, since you haven't risen to the challenge so far? Was that the plan all along, get us down here, watch us get it on? You know you could have just asked if you wanted lesbo porno photos?'

Priss was slurring heavily by then, as she looped the rope tighter around her wrists, holding them up, laughing, 'Kinky, or what? But I bet you won't come near me, will you, Silas? I'm not the right sort for you any more.'

'I told you, you stupid bitch,' yelled Silas. 'Just because I don't want to fuck your skank hole doesn't mean I'm gay.'

'Right, if you say so. But what do you think, Lolly Pop? Does he like dick, do you reckon?'

I wasn't really sure what they were talking about by then, the vodka kicking in, making everything slow and fuzzy. What I did realise was that they'd clearly had a fight, they'd broken up, my heart ringing with relief that things could go back to how they were, as Silas raged, 'I don't need this. I don't need any of this. I'm off.'

'Don't go,' I insisted. 'Help me get her dressed, get her back home. She's obviously wasted.'

'Why? So we can finish off your stupid photo project and act like we're all still twelve years old? Grow up, Laura,' he snapped as he stomped away.

'So, you just followed him home because you were bored and too cold to stay at the riverbank party?' asked Mr Morley, Silas's defence barrister.

'It wasn't a party,' I mumbled, 'it was just teasing and stuff,' because I couldn't use words like skank and fuck and talk about porn in front of him, not with Priss's father there in the upper court balcony, his lips clenched, his hands gripping the rail in front of him.

'Either way, you left your friend in the woods, undressed and drunk, alone. Nice friends,' he remarked as I nodded, even though I'd known, even half full of vodka, that I couldn't go with Silas and leave Priss there like that. Even if she wasn't too stoned to dress and head for home, she'd never find her way through the woods and back to the castle in the dark.

So, after that came the part I've never told anyone, that, as Silas disappeared into the trees, I went to help Priss. Because that's what decent people do, angry as I was, a little afraid of the scars on her flesh that spoke of self-harm and self-hatred. No wonder she'd never taken off that T-shirt of hers. She needed help, clearly, more than I could give, she just didn't want it. She wouldn't let me near her.

'You sad little cow,' she laughed. 'Run after him if you want but don't you see he's strung you along?'

She was trying to stagger to her feet but failing, the ropes tangled around her wrists, the length snagging on her left foot.

'Priss, just shut up, why don't you?' I yelled. 'Come on, let's just go home.'

But as I reached for the rope to untangle her feet, she kicked out at me, catching me in the gut, sending me backwards onto my backside, landing on the muddy river-bank, winded.

'Fuck you,' she spat. 'Pissy bloody Lolly Pop,' as I struggled to my feet. 'Hah, now you look like you've shat yourself,' as I tried to brush the mud from my jeans. 'No wonder Silas thinks you're a big baby. You need a nappy and a big fucking dolly to suck your thumb with, as you ain't sucking anything else. You should be the virgin sacrifice. Except no one would want to fuck someone so ugly with no tits. Silas says your tits are like fried eggs on a saucer, though I bet he's never even tried to cop a feel.'

'Silas would never say that,' I screamed, suddenly a black hurricane of rage. 'He doesn't talk about me like that. Not everything's about fucking and sucking, you stupid London slag. He loves me!'

'Aw, baby little Lolly Pop. You mean you love him. You know, I told him that, that you were in love with him, ages ago. You know what he said, as I got on my knees and unzipped his fly? *She'll get over it.*'

The worst thing was I knew she was right. I didn't really love Silas. I loved the idea of what we had been and wanted him to want it too. He didn't though, not enough. And my fury for him almost equalled my fury for her.

And that's when it happened, something broke inside me and started bleeding, rising up into my throat black and sticky. It flowed through me as I pounced on her and shoved her backwards, looped the rope around her wrists and tied a knot, a tight Surf Club, seacraft knot we rarely ever used but had all learned. She was too stunned to react, until she realised I'd actually tied the end of the rope off through the metal loop set in the sacrifice stone.

'What the hell?' she slurred. 'Untie me now and I'll kick your arse.'

'Try it,' I yelled. 'See how fucking sexy you are when you freeze to death. Stay here all night, see if I care. And just you wait until everyone at school sees these photos.'

'Laura, come on. I was just playing,' she yelled, a start

of panic in her voice, 'just because he likes you better.' And I liked it, seeing her squirm, God help me, watching her sliding her legs off the stone and bumping her arse to the ground, her hands still tied above her head, pleading, 'Come on, Laura, it's not funny.'

She sounded scared as I ran from the riverbank into the wicked night, sloshing across the stepping stones by the Norman castle, half submerged now, pounding back along the dune path to my house. The light was on in Silas's living room but I didn't want Mr Cracknell to come to the door and ask why I'd left the party when Silas would've already made some excuse. My house was in darkness, Mum and Dad at my grandfather's for dinner, so I let myself in, tossed Silas's camera on the armchair and punched the stuffing out of the settee in a rage.

It was only after I'd collapsed to the floor and caught my breath that I texted Mum to say the disco was crap, I'd come home early. Seeing her, *OK, love you, home soon xxx*, made me realise what I'd done, how horrified she'd be if she knew, and just how much trouble I'd be in as soon as Priss wriggled loose.

In seconds, I was running back, coatless, to the riverbank, legs like lead, wading across the stepping stones now a full six inches under the thrashing water. Perhaps twenty-five minutes had passed since I'd fled the sacrifice stone but when I got back to the riverbank two things had changed. The river had risen by two feet with the incoming autumn tide and Priss was dead.

Watching the water at Dismal Nitch, I know how she must have felt in her last moments, unable to free herself, what the court heard from the prosecution – 'official cause of death, drowning' – I've lived it in the nightmares I've had for years, of water rushing up into my nose and throat, lungs burning, waking retching, saying, *I'm sorry, Priss, I'm so sorry.* I've sat for hours, my head in my hands, until the sound of the waves has blended with the tick-tick-tock in my head.

Seventeen

Coming Clean

When I eventually get back to the Shore Street house from Dismal Nitch, mascara corrected, lipstick reapplied, Eli is waiting for me in the kitchen, full of questions. 'Where've you been?' he demands. 'I was worried about you when you weren't at the school pickup.'

Oh Jesus, I stop dead in the doorway. How can I have forgotten that Belle, the twenty-four-hour child taxi service, was working one of her occasional shifts at the coffee shop today and I'd offered to pick up the kids?

'Where's Tilly?' I panic, only to be answered by feet on the stairs and a sulky girl in a pirate hat demanding, 'Where were you, Mom? Mrs Babcock had to call Daddy to give me a ride.'

'I'm sorry, hon,' I rush to her, 'Mommy got her days mixed up. Are you OK?'

'Sure I am,' she huffs, squirming away from my embrace, 'it was just lame, having to play chequers with Mrs Babcock until Daddy came, that's all.'

'Luckily, I knocked off early and was already on my way home,' says Eli. 'Seb's here too. Tilly, baby, go get washed up, we're ordering pizza tonight.'

'Yay!' yells Terrible Tilly.

'Yay!' comes Bosun Seb's voice from the den.

'So? Where were you, Grace?' asks Elias, as she thunders back upstairs. 'I called three times.'

By way of answer, my phone in my jeans pocket offers three consecutive chirps, alerting me to a cluster of messages, arriving late.

'I was driving from Astoria,' I explain, pulling it out of my pocket with a wad of tissue, a business card coming out too. 'I was sourcing some tiles and slates. I must have been in the blackout area with no signal.'

But Eli isn't interested in my excuses. His face darkens as he picks up the card I've tossed on the table and asks, 'Grace, why do you have this?'

'It's a reporter's business card. I bumped into him in Astoria. He's from *Crib* magazine.'

'What did he say?' asks Elias, face wooden, like his tree-trunk posture.

'What?'

'Neil Morrow? Was he hassling you? What did he want?'

'Nothing, a feature to follow the awards next week. The usual thing.'

'What feature? What did he say, for God's sake, tell me?'

'Why?' I ask, clocking his stance now. 'Why are you so upset?'

'I'm not upset . . .' He makes an effort to relax his huge hands, that are biting into the back of the chair. 'I'm concerned. Was he harassing you? What did he say? Did he say something about me?'

'What do you think he said?' I ask, because Elias is never anxious or cryptic. 'And why didn't you tell me you've been meeting him in Seaside?' Surprising myself, because, looking at the business card again, I realise Morrow said he has an office there, where Seb said he saw Uncle Eli the day of the incident. The address on his business card is the same as the one for the Buccaneer Diner Eli had visited when I checked the car's data log.

'I don't know what you mean,' says Eli, hackles up, and that's how I know he knows exactly what I mean.

'So, you didn't meet him up in Seaside, the day I almost got murdered? And you didn't lie about being there, to me and to the police, and then erase your car's info reports?'

At that he sits, the vintage Ercol chair creaking worryingly as he falls into it and I ask, 'Eli, what exactly is going on?'

'I should have told you before,' he says eventually. 'That I met with Morrow, the day of the incident and once again since.'

I sit down too, waiting for the worst to come, because it will come now. Then I suspect I have worse to share with him.

'That's why Belle saw me that day,' he admits, like he's ready to confess a terrible crime. 'It was stupid, really. I would've told you but, with everything that happened later, it didn't seem to matter, and I didn't want to upset you even more.'

'For God's sake, Eli. What is it? What have you done?'

'Nothing,' he shouts, then checks himself with the kids nearby. 'I haven't done anything, that's just it, but try

telling Neil Morrow that. He's doing a story, some sort of
exposé. He thinks the sourcing for the Project is suspect,
that the foundations and shell have been made from some
redwood reserves, illegally felled up in Olympia.'

'What? You're kidding?'

'Yeah. No, I mean, it's bull-crap. I know it is. I check all
the papers, the permits, I do the site visits. I know every
inch of everything. But he says the suppliers are a shell
company, linked to the logging pollution damaging the
oyster beds across Willapa Bay and they've been faking
permits across the state. He says I must have known, and
if not, why not? He's been threatening to out the company
and it would ruin us, Grace. It would destroy our reputa-
tion, even being linked to a scam like that. Imagine the
contracts we'd lose, the clients. No matter that we haven't
done one damn thing wrong.'

'Do you think it's true?' I ask. 'About the sourcing, the
timber?'

'I don't know. I mean, it's possible to fake anything if
enough people are taking kickbacks. I've met with him to
try and keep him on side, trying to show him we're in the
clear. I thought maybe it'd worked, but if he's harassing
you then he must still be on the scent. Son of a bitch!'

I almost laugh then, because Eli is a bit ridiculous
when he swears, and because of the oysters. Oysters, for
fuck's sake. And redwoods. And permits. Is that what
Neil Morrow wants, the next eco-scandal story? Jesus, I'd
thought for a moment he was no better than a hitman, a
harbinger of revenge come to finish me off in person or in
print. But if he isn't the one with the ribbons and rape kit,
who the hell is?

'I didn't want to upset you. I know you love that house,' says Eli, taking my hand in his bear paw, squeezing it. 'It's rumour, honey. This guy doesn't have anything but we might have to be ready for some bad press.'

'But why lie to the police, Eli? That looks bad.'

'I know, but I thought if I told them I was meeting a reporter they'd find out why and that would look even worse.'

'Why?'

'Because Morrow says our good old neighbour, Walter, is one of the directors of the shell company, that's why. If the police linked me to Morrow, I was afraid they'd think I had a reason to hurt Walter, that we'd had a fight. A full police investigation with me as a suspect would be even worse for us.'

'Yes, but Morrow would also be your alibi for the incident. If you were in Seaside, you couldn't have hurt Walter here.'

'I know that now. I didn't know exactly what had happened then, did I? Not the timing. And I was so close by.'

'But Eli,' I say, 'why didn't you tell me? You might have made everything worse.'

'I hated not telling you,' he puts his head in my hands. 'I hated feeling I had to hide things from you. That's the one thing we have in this marriage, honey. Honesty.'

Not like his mom and dad, he means. Not like his mother who had affairs behind his father's back and made Eli and his brother Alex lie for her. Not like good old Mommy who hid vodka bottles in wardrobes until they rotted her liver.

Not like Laura, the stranger in his house.

How can I tell him now, what I was thinking of telling him earlier, even some of it? How can I explain everything that led up to Priss's bound hands? Would he believe I'd tried desperately to untie her in the icy water, her face paler than ever, slumped forward into the lapping tide. That I'd knelt beside her, hands around her neck, tugging, trying to get her head to stay above the rising river, putting my mouth on hers, huffing, one, two, three, to breathe air back into her lungs like on a hundred beach drills.

Could I make him see that I struggled to untie my steadfast knot, still chaining her hands to the stone, as my fingers turned solid and icy? That I had nothing to cut the rope with, had to let her go as the water lapped at my waist, struggling to breathe from the chill, her head dipping back down into the flood?

How could I explain I lost all decency then, heated by a sense of self preservation and denial so strong it powered me only in hot flight? That I left her there, picking up Silas's sweater starting to float at the edge of the sandy bank, tossing it and my own sopping clothes into the washing machine as I heard Mum and Dad arriving home, diving straight into the shower.

What sort of person would lie and say, when asked, that their evening had been 'fine'? Would lie awake listening to the Cyhireath batter the cottage walls, feverishly terrified of what they'd done until the inevitable phone call came later, and Dad's voice in the hall said, 'No, she isn't here, Ben,' then, 'Wake up, Laura. Priss Hartford hasn't come home tonight.'

What sort of girl would say she had no idea where Priss was, when the police called to ask some questions the next morning, telling them that she and her friends had left her at the Surf Club party? Surely only a villain would then sit still and silent, kept home from school complaining of flu, while the same police searched for the missing girl supposed to be her friend?

I remember how Silas called at the back gate of the house that lunchtime, to check on me, he said, and no doubt to talk about the night before, only for Mum to turn him away saying I was ill in bed. Later that day, he would text me, texts the police found afterwards, just two of them – *We need to talk!!* And, *Destroy those photos!!*

That's when I remembered the camera, the Nikon I'd already grabbed from the sofa after the police had left at 9 a.m., whisking it away to my room to hide it. When I eventually opened the back flap, to remove the old-fashioned reel of film, expose it to the light and consign the Cap Goch images to the dark, I realised the chamber was empty.

Flying down the stairs, I asked my mum where my project film was, only to be told that Dad, taking his weekly sixth form study group that day, had taken it into school to get it developed for me, since I wasn't going to class. He knew I'd want to work on my projects with Silas over the weekend.

There's no way to describe the primal fear that exploded inside me at those words, the heat in my chest and feet that had nothing to do with the fever I'd only half faked. I would've run in my slippers, over the frosted fields and into the tiny darkroom then and there, to pluck it from Mrs Cadogan's in-tray, destroy the images that would rise spectre-like from the chemicals to point fingers at me.

But somehow the police were already knocking on the

front door again, voices asking if Mum and I would mind coming with them to the station for some 'routine enquiries'. Because, though they didn't tell us until much later, they'd found Priss's body just half an hour earlier.

'Did you leave Priss Hartford with Silas Cracknell that night?' asked Detective Inspector Maureen, as the hours passed into days and the police searches expanded into our homes.

'No, we left together,' I kept on insisting, once I'd had to admit I'd been to the riverbank.

Apart from that untruth, I didn't lie exactly, just told a story that omitted my final part in it. 'I can't explain what happened after we left her, or who hurt her.' I repeated my denials, as Mum, Dad and Ms Perkins the solicitor nodded in resigned agreement. 'I can't tell you what I don't know.'

But the police were sure I did know or that I suspected what Silas must have done, whether I was present or not. Because he was the real suspect. Priss's blood was on *his* sweater, even though it was found in my pantry. That was the physical evidence they needed to tie him to her death, the crucial forensic link.

'Is this Silas Cracknell's knife? With a blade identical to the ones believed to have caused Priss Hartford's injuries?' Mr Kamal asked in court, presenting Silas's knife as Exhibit 21. 'Did you see him using it that night?'

They said it had been found in Silas's jeans pocket, though I thought he'd dropped it on the sandy bank when Priss cut herself. They simply didn't believe him when he told them he'd left Priss by the river with me, alive and well.

Because they had a motive.

'Are you familiar with these drawings?' DI Maureen had asked, showing me an A3 book with pages and pages of sketches depicting the scene at the riverbank, drawn out in red, black and white pencil. 'You don't recognise them?' frowning at the taut white limbs on the sacrifice on the stone, the red O of Priss's mouth open in a scream, the hooded figure standing over her with the knife.

'Strange, because it seems Silas Cracknell drew these in the weeks *before* Halloween. Now, to me, they look like fantasies of what he wanted to do to that girl, maybe even a practice run, drawn up in a storyboard, like the horror movies he's so interested in. Silas testing out what he intended to do when he got Priss Hartford drunk and helpless.

'Were you there at the riverbank that night when he killed her? Did you watch? You do realise that if you were there and let her die, it's a manslaughter charge at the very least.'

I didn't understand. I'd never seen that sketch pad before or known Silas to draw images like that. I shook my head, exhausted from the sleepless days of questioning, accusations, repetition and insistence, unbalanced by the story she was weaving with only echoes of the truth.

'Priss's father has told us that his daughter complained Silas Cracknell was obsessed with her,' she insisted. 'Was this a sick fantasy of his, because she wouldn't sleep with him? When he was finished with her, did he make sure she drowned so she couldn't tell anyone what he'd done?' demanded DI Maureen. 'Did he hold her head under the water or just sit there and watch it happen as she struggled?'

Sitting in that pregnant, ticking, interview room I didn't know any more. Had Priss really refused to sleep with him?

Had I misread the signals between them? Had Silas drawn those bloody images on the pages? Could he possibly have waited until I'd run away, then seen an opportunity to enact these fantasies, to hurt her, even drown her, in the time it took for me to change my mind and discover that she was dead?

My Silas would never have done that. But was he my Silas any more? Did I know him at all?

I supposed there'd been time, just, if he hadn't gone home, had waited nearby or walked back to the sacrifice stone when he saw me running away, made good on his threat to wring her neck. To the police, the window of opportunity was much larger – they were adamant that, even if I didn't see him hurt Priss, he must have returned to the riverbank. The prosecution later told the jury there was a fresh wound on Priss's thigh that looked like someone might have tried to carve something there.

I don't remember seeing that, but she was half under water when I returned. It was getting harder to know what the whole truth might be. Maybe, in a cold, throbbing place inside, I just wanted it to not be all my fault.

'Laura,' DI Maureen said eventually, removing her glasses, rubbing her raw red eyes. 'It's quite simple. One of you is going to prison for this. Which of you do you think it should be?'

That's when Dad pleaded with me, 'You have to tell the truth now, Laura. No matter how bad it is. I'll always love you but you have to tell the truth. I know you care about him but you can't protect him for ever.'

So, when DI Maureen asked, for the twentieth time, 'Let's assume you didn't actively take part in this killing.

Did Silas Cracknell ask you to hide the camera for him after that night? We know he ordered you to destroy those photos later, by text. Did he ask you to wash the bloody sweater for him?'

With no way to explain, I answered the only way I could, to save myself:

'Yes, he did,' I said. 'He did.'

So Silas was charged and I was called as a witness. And there our lives parted.

As I eat dinner with my family, making the smallest of talk I can squeeze around the pizza slices we're munching straight from the box, I'm only waiting until Eli takes Seb home and Tilly is changing for bed, before I can do what I've been waiting to do since I left Astoria – call my mum.

When she answers with, 'Hello, love. I was just about to call you,' I forgo all pleasantries to ask, 'Why didn't you tell me, Mum? Why didn't you tell me Silas was out of prison?'

There's silence on the line then, vibrating with the moment that's been gestating for more than half a lifetime, as I shiver in the backyard under a bowl of smoked-out stars. Eventually she clears her throat and says, 'I'm sorry, love. We had a letter from the solicitor a while back. Remember Ms Perkins? She's Mrs Reilly now, but she kept our details on file in case of any developments. Silas was released eighteen months ago and she assured me he was to be settled in South Wales and wasn't a threat to you. We didn't say anything because . . . Well, we were going to tell you in person, when we came out last spring . . . we were waiting for the right moment but it never came up and then, well, we waited too long.'

'Jesus, Mum,' I whisper-hiss, keeping an eye on the yellow rectangle of light behind Tilly's closed curtains. 'The moment never came up? What moment did you need, especially after what he said he'd do to me if he ever got out? You haven't forgotten that, have you?'

The threat he spat with outrage as they led him out, that she could only have taken as a confession: *I'm a killer now, so just remember, Laura, whatever I did to her, one day I'll do to you.*

'Of course I haven't forgotten,' she says, infinitely patient.

'I mean, you do know what this could mean,' I cut her off, 'if he ever finds out where I am? For God's sake, how could you not tell me?'

'Gracie, listen to me,' sternly now, 'stay calm, love. He can't hurt you.'

'Really? Don't be so sure. Don't be so sure he can't find out where I am, or speak to someone who can.'

'It's too late for that. It's all OK. You're safe.'

'Safe? Are you insane? What if he's found out where I am and is coming after me?'

'He can't, love. He's dead,' she says.

Then I drop my phone.

Eighteen

Lone Women

So it's Halloween at last, and this year it appears the trick is most definitely on me. The news that Silas is dead has washed me away from myself like the tsunami no one can outrun, but Grace keeps a smile plastered on her face as she walks the length of Main Street with Tilly, Seb and friends as if everything's normal.

Tonight, Ashley Weathers and her *Go Mom!* Maria are both dressed as Elsa from *Frozen*, Ashley's long, white wig pulled around her face to hide the slight droop of her eye from her cliffside fall. Then there's the usual moms: Gilly as Mary Poppins, to match her daughter Petra's parrot umbrella costume (inventive), while Jack's two moms sport matching Rey 'Jedi' outfits to his Finn ensemble (trying too hard). Belle and I have both settled for the lazy option of black outfit, cute cat ears and drawn-on whiskers, not a bad fit for Tilly's Gothic witch, though I think my girl's feeling a bit passé this season, among the Hollywood trendies, including Seb's surprising Thor outfit.

179

'What can I say?' smirks Belle. 'He spotted it at the JCPenney and I'd left it too late to make anything good.'

We amble onwards, with Silas not coming for me, though someone else must be. And I need to tell the police everything now, or my suspicions at least, that someone from my old hometown has carried a grudge across the ocean tied with red ribbons and bound in a children's book.

But how? That's all I've thought about today.

While I laid the Halloween table, putting salted 'skin' chips and marshmallow 'eyeball' bites in bowls, pouring Vampire Blood (Kool-Aid) into pitchers, the smug pumpkin Eli carved with Tilly sat on the counter mocking me with its uneven grin. Because we both know it's really too late now, that there's no time to see Silas just once more, to talk, to tell him I'm so sorry I turned out to be such a bad friend. Mum's voice smashed through any chance of that after I'd picked up my phone from the backyard gravel, with her words, 'He died three months after his release, love.

'Mrs Reilly said he'd been set up in a rented room by the probation service,' she'd continued, 'since his mother wouldn't take him back. I heard she'd moved up north, years ago. He had a job in a warehouse arranged for him but his probation officer found him dead a few months later. It was an overdose.'

'Did it . . . was it . . . ?' I couldn't form the words.

'Apparently it was heroin. An *accident*,' she emphasised. 'I'm sorry, love,' reading my silence, 'I suppose there was no good way to tell you. I wanted to, when we came out, but you were so happy. I didn't think you'd find out. How did you?'

'I was just looking online, at the old pictures, and the headlines came up,' I said eventually.

'It's not your fault,' she'd said, because she doesn't know the truth. 'None of it was. Things got out of hand after you went to the river. You couldn't have known what Silas had planned. You didn't kill that poor girl and you didn't send Silas to prison. He did that to himself.'

Now, the smiling citizens of Lookout Beach laugh and toss candy to swirling Elsa and cackling Tilly, as I wonder how much longer this torture will last. Eli was meant to come with us tonight but had to stay and work on some kinks in the Slabtown project, which at least means I haven't had to look him in the eye and lie for a few hours. I kept grinning through the 'open house' too, for the wanderers who turned up for free food and voyeur value. I caught Maria Weathers staring at the hardwood floor more than once. How long now until I can curl myself into a ball under the bed covers and weep the tears I've fermented for seventeen years? The tears I'll weep for the boy he was, not the man he became. Once they start, they might wash me away with the storm and that might be a relief.

'Look, Mom, look,' grins Tilly, as we pass a stall selling spider-shaped cookies and spooky gifts, 'glittery demon dolls. Can I get one?'

'Sure, honey,' smiles Grace, as Lolly chokes on her own shiny, black-eyed demons.

When the moms and kids finally wander off, to knock on the last few doors of lower Shore Street, Belle and I shepherd our sugar-high pair back along the sandy path towards home.

'Thank God that's over for another year,' she smiles,

as the kids play tag in the scrubby trees and I manage a laugh.

'What? I thought you loved all this, *Super Mom*?'

'Well, usually, but things have been creepy enough this fall already, haven't they?'

'Yes, yes they have.'

'I thought they'd have caught the guy by now, you know. Your pervert. Arrested someone.'

'Yeah,' I mutter, 'me too,' as the mist bowls in and Belle's eyes rake the shrubs along our route in a way that makes me nervous.

'What?' I ask. 'B, are you still upset about that? That guy is long gone,' glad I sound like I mean it.

'Yeah, sure, except we still don't know why he picked your house, G. We don't know that he won't come back. What if my house is next, or MK's?'

'I hardly think . . .' I begin, glancing at the rectangle of light through the trees that marks MK's bedroom window up ahead.

'You know, I haven't wanted to scare you,' cuts in Belle, 'but I'm pretty sure I saw someone out here yesterday, hanging around, and last week Seb said he saw a man smoking a cigarette across the street, over by the beach. When I asked Seb what the man was doing, he said nothing, just watching. Who smokes around here? Well, apart from MK. And there's nothing out here to watch except us and the birds, is there?'

A twig cracks and our heads snap sideways before Tilly bursts from a bush, witch's cape thrown wide.

'Tils, don't do that!' I laugh, but Belle doesn't.

'Look, B,' I offer, 'if you're that spooked tell the police. Come stay with us tonight, you and Seb.'

She seems to be considering it as we reach the yard door of her cottage and Seb bounces up onto the porch like Thor on springs. That kid will have a serious sugar hangover tomorrow and carob balls won't cut it. But then Belle freezes like a dog on point, nose in the air, staring at the bushes that run between her house and mine.

'What now?' I ask.

'Look,' she says quietly, 'someone's there.'

'Where?' I'm about to laugh. She's left the porch light on to guide us back and the area hides few secret spots, but, as I follow her raised finger, the leaves resolve in my night vision into the outline of a figure. *So, this is it*, I think, oddly detached, *this is the moment triggered weeks back when I entered my kitchen, now ready to hit home.* I'm about to say, *It's OK, Belle, whoever he is, he's not here for you*, but I don't get the chance as she yells, 'Seb, Tilly, stay on the porch!' and pushes me behind her.

The kids freeze at the tone in gentle Belle's voice, as do I, even as she shouts, 'I can see you, asshole! Get the fuck out of those bushes right now!'

The bushes don't move and, for a moment, I wonder if we're mistaken, seeing shapes in the paranoid darkness the way you might see the benevolent face of Jesus in a slice of toast. I start to walk over, to disturb the wavering outline, show it to be just branches and folly, but Belle grabs my wrist and hisses, 'Don't move.'

She's rummaging in her purse for what I imagine are her keys, to let us into the house, but when her hand comes up she's holding a gun. My gun. The Glock. The one I couldn't find in Astoria, and have been wracking my brains over, searching the house to see if maybe I'd forgotten that I'd moved it from my purse. With everything going on I just hadn't been able to bring myself to ask Eli if he took it. Surely he'd have said something if he'd found it? But here it is, in Belle's hands.

'This is your last chance,' says the woman next to me, seemingly inches taller and wider than the friend I know, with a new voice of hammered steel. 'Get your ass out of those trees or I'll shoot a hole in you the size of the Seattle Great Wheel.'

The kids huddling on the porch, mouths agape, both shout, 'Mom!' as I recover enough to say, 'Belle, what the . . . Jesus . . . No one is there, please, just . . .'

'I'm going to count to three,' she orders, no further explanation needed, 'one . . .'

On the two she cocks the slide. I remember that satisfying click from my tin-can practice, twice as loud now in the crisp, waiting night. Long before she can say three, a guilty shape detaches itself from the shrubbery.

'Jesus, love, OK, OK, don't shoot,' says a familiar voice, as the shape throws its hands in the air. 'I'm sorry, it's me, Mrs Jensen.'

'Don't come any further,' says Belle, still steel, still with her finger on the trigger, until I shout, 'For God's sake, don't shoot. I know him, he's a reporter,' recognising the panicked face of Neil Morrow.

'Yeah, really?' she sneers. 'If you're a reporter let's see your identification, boy.' She doesn't lower the gun and, for a moment, I think it's all going to go horribly wrong, as Morrow reaches slowly into his pocket and pulls out a card.

'Toss it over here,' orders Terminator Belle, and he does

as he's told, babbling, 'Jesus, Mrs Jensen, make her put the gun down. You know me. I'm sorry, I didn't mean to spook you. I was just hoping for a chat.'

'A chat?' sneers Belle again, motioning me to pick up the ID, looking at it for a long time before spitting, '*Crib*? Seriously? What the fuck are you doing lurking in the bushes, Mr Morrow? Researching a feature on landscaping trends?'

'No, I . . . look, I was just hoping to speak to you and Mrs Jensen. I thought I'd catch you at home, nice and easy, no formalities.'

Formalities? It's my turn to sniff at the trembling man trying to overturn mine and Elias's life, but by the look of alarm in his eyes he's not faking his fear. I raise my hand and place it on Belle's arm. 'He's telling the truth, B,' I say, 'he's doing a feature on Eli, before the awards ceremony. We already met in Astoria.'

She looks from the grainy, laminate ID to her rabbit in the gunsights and back to me. Something clicks off in her eyes and she lowers the gun, slowly.

No one speaks for a few moments. What is there to say?

Eventually Morrow mutters, 'Jesus, ladies, now I know why they're calling for gun control,' pulling a packet of cigarettes from his pocket.

He attempts a laugh but it's the wrong thing to do, as Belle raises the gun again.

'Why? Because you think it's wrong for people, *lone* women with young *children*, to be able defend themselves against prowlers creeping around their backyards in the middle of the night? This is Oregon and this gun is licensed, Mr Morrow. You're trespassing on my property. You have no business in my yard, unless, of course, you've been here before for other reasons and you're back to finish what you started. Did you pay a call on my neighbour here, two months back, and beat the shit out of our friend Walter because he interrupted your fun?'

'No, you mean the Walter Lennon thing? Jesus, no,' he freezes with his lighter in his hand. 'I'm not a pervert, love. Look, I'm sorry. I wanted a story, an exclusive, that's all, and Mrs Jensen wouldn't speak to me or return my calls.'

'Then that means she doesn't want to talk to you, asshole, and neither do I. When women say no, they mean no, or have you missed the whole MeToo movement, shit for brains? So, I'll tell you what, you won't tell anyone about this little altercation and we won't tell your editor or the police that you're creeping around, harassing us, lurking in gardens and making us vulnerable women fear for our safety. How does that sound?'

Morrow's mouth falls open but he's quick to agree.

'Off you go then,' says Belle, lowering the gun at last, as Morrow backs away and Tilly runs down the steps from the porch, a flurry of black polyester cape and cobwebs, to land a mighty rabbit punch in his stomach.

'Take that, creepo!' she yells, as he doubles up.

'You people are mental,' he wheezes, breath in hot starts before he retreats, bent in two, towards the street.

Standing there, no one is quite sure what to do, until Seb yells, 'You kick ass, Mom!' his eyes huge behind his glasses.

It's the sight of a speccy Thor air-punching with a Norse god plastic hammer that does it. We burst out laughing.

Once the kids are inside with mugs of hot chocolate,

we break the 'nothing important has just happened' air of Halloween japes and retreat, as adults do, to the kitchen.

'Jesus, Belle? You stole my gun?' I whisper, shutting the door as she turns the radio on to some twangy folk station.

'I know, I'm so sorry. I was so on edge after that home invasion at yours, I thought I'd seen someone sneaking around, then there was this black car down the street a while back. I saw that reporter guy in the bookstore the other night, you know, hanging around, asking about you. I thought . . . I thought maybe he'd followed us home.'

'You could have told the police,' I mutter, realising it's my hands that are trembling from the adrenaline when she's the one who almost shot a man.

'I told Olsen a few days ago and she just shrugged it off like I was some hysterical housewife,' says Belle, passing me a steady glass of brandy. 'When I saw the gun that night, in your kitchen, when I looked in your purse for headache pills, I'd been spooked at the store and, well, it was a spur of the moment thing. I mean, I knew you wouldn't use it, probably didn't even know how to. It wasn't even loaded.'

'Of course it wasn't loaded,' I interrupt, tossing back my shot, thinking of my friend May's instructions, *It's not a toy. Rounds kept separate.* 'I'm not crazy enough to have a loaded gun in my purse with kids around. The rounds were in my change wallet.'

'And what good would that do you if Mr Sex Fiend came back, huh?'

'I figured it was a good bluff at least.'

'You're sweet, Grace, hon, but when it comes to assholes, a loaded gun is best. Sometimes you have to take matters into your own hands. You run or you stand, you know.' Then she clicks the slide open and shows me the three rounds inside.

'Jesus, how do you have those?'

'You can buy them at a gun store, hon. God bless the second amendment, right?'

'You're taking this very calmly but you pulled a loaded gun on Morrow!'

She empties the chamber with a click, pauses, says, 'Yes I did. Maybe you'd better have this back,' looking at her watch. 'To be continued?'

She's right of course, it's getting late. When we go into the living room, Seb and Tilly are already sugar-doped out on the sofa. It's no easy task to wake a grumpy witch and get her home.

'Belle was so cool, wasn't she, Mom?' she mutters as she undresses. 'Do you think that reporter man will tell the police on her?'

'I don't think so, hon.'

'I don't think so either. I bet he pooped his pants.'

'Exactly. Look, we'll talk about this tomorrow. I don't think we should tell Daddy about Belle and the gun just yet, OK? He'll be *real* mad with her.'

'Sure, secret,' she yawns, giving me the pinky-swear, finger-lock sign I've seen her giving Seb as she burrows under the blankets.

When her breathing slows, I head for the kitchen on a mission to regulate mine. Right now, a pint of Pinot seems not only desirable but essential for my continued existence. One of MK's grassy spliffs would hit the sweet spot too, or some of the CBD herbal 'relaxation drops' still tucked inside the last box of freebies she gave me, stashed in the bathroom closet. But I need a clearish head, rummaging in the cooler for alcohol, finding a passable vintage and cracking it open.

I pour a glass right away and take a long swallow, but when I turn around, ready to down the rest more slowly in the den, I realise I'm not alone. Someone is waiting for me in the corner of the lamplit kitchen.

'Hi, Lolly Pop,' says a voice. 'It's been forever. Pour me one too, will you? We've got a lot to talk about.'

Nineteen

My Silas

The voice that stretches across the gloom is one I almost recognise, the first phrase spoken with a slight Anglo-American inflection, but by the time it insists, 'Go on, top me up,' it's more familiar, the years rolling back leaving me high and dry. It's not just because the ticking in my head has reached 100 decibels but because the person walking towards me has changed almost beyond recognition in seventeen years, except for the same bright green eyes, always so attentive, waiting for my next words.

'No glasses today. You recognise me now, don't you?' pleased but also hurt I've been so slow on the uptake, that such a small thing could stop me seeing who was behind those lenses.

'Oh, come on,' chides my visitor. 'The bar of the Portland Hyatt, at the CBD conference? You and MK drinking those expensive passionfruit things? MK introduced us.'

So she had, to the slim blonde in the rooftop bar,

sheltered behind the Jackie O sunglasses when I got back from the bathroom. MK had said, this is so and so, I didn't pay any attention to the name, 'a new seller – one of my twenty-first-century Avon ladies, ding-dong!' The woman who'd smiled but declined when MK asked her to stay for a drink.

'Now you remember,' she nods. 'It wasn't like I was in disguise or anything. I just had a hangover from drinking with MK the night before you came up. I knew you'd be there, had this idea of a big reunion, whipping off my glasses, saying, *Hey Lolly* . . . but once I'd had a good old bender and girl-chat with MK, it seemed clear your so-called best friend knew nothing about you, about your past, where you come from.

'And you looked right through me, *Grace*. I guess I've changed. Lost half my body weight, grown a few inches, and the hair . . .' she twirls a razor-straight, blonde tress not unlike mine. 'You look the same, though, apart from the expensive haircut and the smell of real money. Nice redesign job, sleek, minimalist, like your work. Like your new beach house. *I* can see you, though, underneath.'

They never looked alike, I think, even now there's so little resemblance it seems like a mistake. But I keep seeing the scared eyes of the red-headed girl she used to be, feeling the heat of her skin as she clung to me, warm snot running onto my shoulder, pleading, 'Please don't let me go!'

I saved her life. Plucked her from the riptide of Ogmore Bay. It's Abigail, Silas's little sister.

'So, you're surprised, right?' she grins, taking the wine bottle from my hand.

That's one word for it, the ticking in my head unable to drown out the thunder of blood behind my eyes.

'OK, Lolly, relax,' she smiles, pulling out a chair from the table, steering me into it. 'Don't worry, I know Eli isn't here, so I won't be a sudden spectre from the past at the dinner table, all Macbeth-like, or anything. Come sit down. Let me get you a drink of water.' She moves to the cupboard like she's at home, like she knows where everything is, sets some water in front of me and puts a wine glass for herself opposite mine on the table.

'How did you find me?' I ask, at last.

'That's a great question,' as she settles in, pouring herself some Pinot. 'It's quite a story. Almost as good as your tales used to be, remember? Your stories with maidens and heroes, quests and . . .' she pauses for dramatic effect, '*betrayals*. Disappearances in this one, too. You disappeared after Silas went to prison for murder, didn't you? Poof! Gone. I can't say I blamed you, but we were left behind and it wasn't easy going back to school after that, I can tell you, everyone so sympathetic, so careful around me, like I might break.'

I remember only too well how it was, the looks, the whispers, except in my case everyone was looking at me as if they hoped I *would* break. How can I forget Silas's mother, yelling on the court steps, 'Why are you lying, Laura? Why won't you help him?' Then there was stone-faced, calm-voiced Mr Jones, my head of year, sitting in our lamplit kitchen with my parents, explaining how the school felt there was 'no tenable way' for me to resume my studies '*because of the impact on the student body*'.

'It was impossible to escape the whispers,' continues Abi,

'even though *I* wasn't the one in the dock. I still had to face the silences when I entered a room, the way no one came to call afterwards, everyone at church making such a virtue of pretending God would forgive everything, because to err is human but they could only forgive from a distance.

'Mum gave in and moved in the end, after Dad finally checked out. We had nothing much to live on by then, as we'd spent most of our savings on Silas's legal fees, and Dad's life insurance wouldn't pay out for a suicide. Poor Dad. He was so angry at God for taking his son, his precious son, when he felt he'd been such a good Christian all his life. I was the one who found him, you know, in the Mill Barn four months later. Swinging to and fro.'

She makes a gesture like a pendulum with her forefinger that turns my stomach. 'I would've liked to have been able to talk to you about it all afterwards,' she sighs. 'We had so much to talk about, didn't we? But you were long gone and I was alone with the ghosts of my parents who were hardly there to begin with.

'I wanted so badly to hear some news of you. I asked everyone I could think of but no one would say. I was still little more than a kid, just turned fourteen so it was hard to find out anything on my own, but I was patient. Over the years I kept looking for you in newspapers, Googled you endlessly. Since they never named you, I guessed maybe you wouldn't need to change yours, so I tried keyword searches on your mum, your dad, under art and architects. I felt sure you'd resurface. But it wasn't like it is now with social media.'

She takes several long swallows from her glass, drains then refills it, leaning back in her chair for a long story.

'Well, we were living with Gramps at the farm in Abergavenny by then. The Gwyn Mawr house had been on the market for ever – no one wanted to live in the Cult Murderer's house. Once I was old enough, had saved up some money, I passed my driving test and got crafty. After my A levels, I drove back down to visit your grandfather, Mr Llewellyn; what a lovely old guy he was. As you know he stayed put, in his house in Cornelly, just ten miles up the road.'

Of course I knew. Mum and Dad had asked him to relocate to the northeast with us but he hadn't wanted to leave behind everything he knew, or the home he'd shared with my gran for forty-five years before she passed away. His was the generation that stayed close to home, fronted up, kept calm and carried on. He couldn't understand why we were running away.

'He didn't know me, of course,' continues Abi. 'I told him I was a student, researching a local history project. He couldn't wait to tell me all about the good old days, about Island Farm, the prisoner-of-war camp, "the British Great Escape", remember? He came into school that time to tell us about it? He was careful, though, never talked about you, nothing in the house to give you away. But I went back a few times over the years, for other "stories", had a few cuppas, and it was easy enough to search when I went upstairs to the loo or he was putting the kettle on.'

I screw myself down inside, to hear her talking about my grandfather like this, of him telling her the tales he used to lavish on me. I hadn't heard his voice much in the years before I left England and hardly at all since my move here. Dad called regularly at the beginning. Grandpa even came up to Newcastle on the train twice, but he hated the eight-hour journey. Soon our contact had dwindled to routine phone calls on birthdays and at Christmas. He must have been lonely and Abi used that against him. Against me.

To rinse the bitter tang of resentment from my mouth I down my own inch of Pinot, as Abi continues.

'Well, after he moved into that nursing home and his mind started to wander a bit it was a lot easier. His care worker, Claudia, remembered me from my "research" trips to his house, the Welsh toffee I took him, which she stuffed her face with, and she asked the nurses to let me keep visiting, even though I wasn't family,' so pleased with herself now, she can't stay in her seat.

Jumping to her feet she starts a lap of my kitchen, tracing her fingers along the hardwood surfaces like a prospective buyer.

'He was confused by then, kept asking where his little granddaughter was and why his boy only came to visit a couple of times a year,' she says, picking up a dolphin sculpture Tilly brought home a few days ago, smoothing the awkward clay lines with her thumb. 'It kept me going, somehow. That link to you. That family tie. I felt he was more like my grandfather, *our* grandfather, than my own. I'd call Claudia to check he was up to a visit and, when she told me he'd passed away, I was devastated I'd missed the funeral, because surely you or your parents would have come back for it.

'The old cow in charge of the care home would never give me your grandad's family contact details, *data protection* and all that, so I just told Claudia I'd love to be able to send sympathy flowers to Mike and Christine and she passed them right along.'

She's standing in front of the picture window now, squinting at the blacked-out invisible sea beyond the scrub, and I wish she'd come away from that yawning glass eye that could reveal her to anyone standing outside. But I can't find my voice to ask her to sit down.

'Imagine how excited I was, to finally find out where you were hiding,' she grins, picking up the photograph of me and Eli at the Space Needle from the low sideboard. 'Newcastle was a goddamn long way but I drove up and checked it out. I could see you weren't at home with your mum and dad any more, but ten years had passed and I could hardly expect you to be. So, I pretended to be a student on an open-day visit and found your mum's office. It wasn't hard to sneak in while everyone was milling around. On her desk, in a frame, was a cutting from some trendy design magazine called *Crib*, one of Grace Jensen winning an award for student architect of the year. Your hair was different. A bit like this,' she rubs at my shorter bob behind the photo glass, 'but it was you. At Bright Brothers in Portland, Oregon.'

So it came down to that damn article, published the year after the photograph she's caressing was taken, twelve months after Elias and I got engaged. When he asked me to marry him, at the top of the Seattle Space Needle that day, down on one knee with a ring, like a good gentleman, the idea of Grace Jensen was born, the clapping of the cooing sightseers affirming what a beautiful couple we'd make. And with the 360-degree panorama of the new world spinning out below my tower of steel and glass, I'd thought I was free, safe, until now.

'So I'd found you,' says Abi, hugging the frame to her chest. 'It seemed like a sign. A portent. A decade on, a new season for us all. It wasn't hard after that, to track you down, to get the Bright Brothers' newsletters emailed to me, subscribe to the e-version of *Portland Life* magazine that had a bit on your wedding in it. Maria Weathers's *Go Moms!* webpage is such a mine of information on Lookout Beach too.

'It let me get to know you, but it was just too far to pop over and say, *Hi Lolly! Surprise!* I mean, it's an eight-hundred-pound return flight to Seattle and then a four-hour drive, for God's sake. But I was patient. I wanted to call you, so many times, but I didn't know what to say without being able to look you in the eye. I had to wait until I could afford a flight and I wanted you to be proud of me when I did, before we could set things straight. So here I am.'

'Set things straight?' I parrot. My head is cartwheeling to keep up with this woman standing in my kitchen, spinning our history with her words, weaving Laura and Grace's bones back together. 'So that's what this is? You've come to settle a score?'

She looks baffled when she plops back into her seat, sets the photo between us, says, 'Don't be obtuse, Lolly. You think I'm here to hurt you? Aren't you listening? We're friends. We're more like family. You saved my life, remember, that day in the bay? Do you think I'd ever forget that? I'm here to be your friend again. I want to repay you.'

'By breaking into my house with rope and a knife?' I snap, my fist clenched around my now empty wine glass, because that's what this comes down to, after all.

'Ah, that's . . .' Abi's mouth twists into a shape I can't decipher as she refills our glasses, 'that's complicated. But you mustn't think I'd let anything happen to you. Not after I saved your life in return – it's the least I could do. And I wanted you to know from me, in person.'

'Saved my life, I don't understand.'

'I *saw* you that night, Lolly,' she explains, 'by the river, on Halloween. I wanted to be part of your game, remember? I wanted to come to the *real* party. But even if Dad hadn't got his knickers in a twist about my whoreish *Buffy the Vampire Slayer* kilt, Silas would never have let me come along. He never let me be involved in anything you guys did. Not the annoying younger sister, the fat, ginger whinger,' her mouth twisting into an echo of childhood hurt.

'He'd even moan at you for sitting with me, remember? For telling me your stories while you waited for him to get showered after practice, couldn't even let me have that one little bit of you. Remember how he used to sneer at me, say "Fuck off, chubbo, go play with the little girls," slam the bedroom door in my face?

'He tried to keep me out of everything,' her mouth assuming the exact same sulky line it used to when Silas would banish her from our presence, 'but the walls in that mouldering cottage were only thin plaster, there were other ways to be one of your gang. You never knew it but I used to lie with my ear against the partition lath for hours, listening to your chats from my room. That place was rotting from the ground up, so I poked a hole by the wooden joist so I could see you doing your art projects and everything else.

'I heard you talking in there. I saw him kiss you, the stupid prick!' the venom in her voice startles me. 'Then I heard you talking about Priss and knew you were going to do a Cap Goch theme for Halloween. So I snuck out from the stupid kids' apple bobbing party at Suzy Lewis's house just across the fields, as soon as Mum started sneaking cider punch with Mrs Lewis. She never even noticed I was gone, while I saw it all from my hiding spot in the bushes. I saw Priss stripping for you like the stupid slut she was, then you two fighting. I saw you leave her . . . tied up, half naked.'

She swirls the dregs of her glass around, knocks them back, pours some more, as she insists, 'Of course, I knew you hadn't really *meant* to hurt her, you just hadn't realised it was the "super tide" that night, twelve feet and rising, a full moon, the water flying up the estuary. I meant to untie her when you stormed off, I really did, but she wasn't nice, Lolly. *Little weird creepy girl*, she always called me, when she'd sneak over and fawn over Silas, call me a fat cow, only good for creeping and peeping.

'The tide was coming up fast, but it was only by her legs and waist at first. She wanted me to cut her loose so I picked up the knife Silas had dropped. I was going to cut the ropes, honestly, until she said she was going to call the police, tell them you'd assaulted her and kidnapped her and they'd send you to jail. She said you were a sad, useless bitch and Silas and her would run away together, and I knew that, if you thought that, it would break your heart.'

'But I already knew they were a thing, Silas and Priss,' I say, because what else can I say? It had seemed so obvious at the time.

'They weren't a thing, Lolly. I should know,' Abi sighs, 'I watched them all the time in that room. She was into him, yes, but he wasn't really into her. Liam, bless him, hated that bitch because of it. He wanted Silas too, you knew that, right? He was hoping Silas would want him in time, that they would "come out" together, and Silas knew it.'

'Abi, I don't know what . . . ?' I interrupt, because I don't know why she's telling me this, when it doesn't change anything. But she throws up a hand commanding, 'Just let me finish, OK? It would've been all right in the end, I think. I mean, they were friends and Silas wasn't a gay basher, but Priss spoiled it all, like she spoiled everything. She came around early that Halloween, when Liam and Silas were in his room. She'd let herself in the back door and crept upstairs, to make them jump, I suppose, but she saw them sitting on the bed. She saw Liam trying to kiss Silas and him laughing it off.

'She pretended to think it was hilarious but only because she was jealous, because she thought Silas wanted her. He didn't though. He didn't want her, he didn't really want you, he didn't want Liam. He was only ever into himself and his moody, broody artwork.'

She stares at me now, to see how I'm taking all this, and all I want to do is press my hands over my ears to make her stop saying these things. But I don't, because I hear Liam at the riverbank yelling over the din in my head, 'I'm not gay,' then Priss asking if Silas liked cock. Though it should be mine to remember, this story Abi's telling of everything I somehow managed not to see, has the toll of truth and it's my turn to jump to my feet, walk away from the pool of light at the table so she can't see my face.

'Anyway, I meant to cut Priss free, but she wouldn't shut up,' says Abi, her eyes following my turned back as I try to focus, 'she just kept yelling at me. In the end, I got really mad, just lost it and shoved the knife in her thigh a couple of times to make her shut up. I think it was just an instinct, but then she lost it too, thrashing in the water. I wanted her to stop yelling. The water was coming up by her chest and I pushed her head under just to make her shut up. I only did it for, like, maybe twenty seconds.

'Lolly, look at me,' she says calmly, but I can't turn, can't face what she's just said. 'She deserved it, right? She stopped struggling really quickly and I realised she wasn't breathing any more. Then I heard someone coming and hid, but I saw it was you, saw your face, what you thought you'd done. When I watched you run away the second time I ran away too, back to the party, told Mum I felt sick, I'd got soaked apple bobbing.

'I thought you'd go to the police that night, or the next morning at least, but when you didn't it meant we had a secret between us, one only we could share, and I could protect you like I'd always wanted to. That's what friends do, right? Save each other? That's what family do.'

Save each other, I think, as finally I turn to find her looking at me, waiting for me to acknowledge the right-eousness of her statement.

'But . . .' I stutter, as she reads my mind and rushes towards me, grabs my hands, insisting, 'I was going to tell Silas she was dead that night, I really was. I knew he wouldn't care about helping me out but I thought he'd want to help you if you were in trouble. But do you know what happened?' She draws me back to my chair, seeing that, if I don't sit, I might fall. 'He was in his room, drunk, listening to some whiny indie music as usual, and he yelled at me to fuck off. *You fucking girls*, he said, though I tried to say you needed him. All he said was, *She can go fuck herself, along with the rest of you.*

'So, the next day, I got his knife out of my jacket and put it back in his jeans pocket. I'd been wearing my winter gloves that night and I used kitchen gloves that morning, so no fingerprints! I knew how to dispose of key evidence to my advantage. I learned something from all those *X-Files* episodes he always had on repeat. Clever, huh? Not bad for a silly little fat kid.'

She's not wrong, and perhaps part of me should respect her for the attention to detail I'd so woefully lacked. But I can't congratulate her on her cleverness, not while I still feel the dumb weight of Priss's head, heavy against my hands, the ice of her lips as I try to huff the life back into her, no longer able to convince myself that there was a chance Silas had gone back to the riverbank that night like Mr Kamal had suggested.

'But what about the drawings?' I ask. 'He drew it all out, remember, the Cap Goch sacrifice scenes? I saw them. They used them as evidence of premeditation. He'd planned it. On some level he was obsessed with her.'

'You can stop deluding yourself now, Lolly,' Abi sighs. 'That was their story, not his. They were *my* drawings. My story. My comic book tale. Silas wasn't the only artist in the family. I was a lot more talented and I practised hard because I wanted to be an illustrator and a writer like you. *I* drew the Red Cap story the week before, to keep myself occupied, to share in it, because I knew what you were planning. It was my way of being in the gang. Afterwards, when they found her body and the police turned up, it wasn't difficult to hide the sketchbook under Silas's bed to make sure they didn't suspect you.'

'But, Abi . . .' I'm at a loss that none of it was true, not even the so-called motive that convinced the jury and gave me a shard of doubt. 'You could have just stayed quiet. Things might never have gone as far as a trial in the first place, if you had. You made people think your own brother was a killer. Why?'

'Other than the fact he was a massive arsehole, you mean?' that sulky line of her mouth back again. 'Look, Lolly, he was a total prick to you, wasn't he? Even though he knew you were seriously into him. Flicking that stupid fringe out of his eyes at Surf Club, sneering, all mean and moody, to get the attention of the girls when you were right there. You know he got it on with Willa Pritchard, right? That bimbo you used to eat lunch with? Even though he knew you were her friend. And he was an arsehole with Priss. He didn't care about her so he didn't see the harm in letting her give him a couple of blow jobs for fun, even though he must have known you'd notice something was going on. He never stopped to think how it would make you feel. That's not gentlemanly, is it, not the behaviour of Captain Carruthers, like in your stories, remember? I loved them the best.'

How could I forget? Childish Captain Carruthers, the model man from the tales I'd concocted in my notebooks and shared with her to pass the time, the bold and right-eous buccaneer, the illustrations that looked like Silas.

'Silas knew you cared for him,' she says sorrowfully.

'He kissed you and made you think it meant something. He let Liam think maybe he had a chance too, because it made him feel powerful and flattered. He was just so fucking arrogant, the firstborn son. God, it made me sick. How he thought the sun shone out of his arse. That he could do what he wanted. Treat us all like rubbish. I suppose I hoped it would wash the shine off him a bit. If he was out of the way, Mum and Dad might realise I existed too. If he wasn't there convincing everyone I was stupid, telling me to shut up, ripping up my drawings to light his bloody spliffs, eating all the brownies Mum made for church and blaming it on fat old me so I got grounded – ha, bloody, ha! With him in the doghouse for a change, maybe I could show I was clever too, could go to Oxbridge, that I wouldn't always be fat and freckly and useless.

'I didn't think he'd go down for so long, not for actual *murder*. I just wanted him to get some of the blame, to point the police away from you. I mean, you ran because you knew how it would look, that they wouldn't believe you didn't mean to hurt her, not after that sacrifice set-up. But it was partly because, deep inside, you knew they couldn't prove anything. All that changed with the sweater, though, didn't it? You lied to save yourself, said Silas asked you to hide it for him, covered in her blood and his DNA. And then there was the camera, that he asked you to hide it. They were never going to believe that he left her alive after that. No one would.'

Now all I can see, flickering like a grainy old movie across the picture window behind Abi, is Mrs Cadogan, our art teacher, tearful in the witness box in a strangling blouse and rigid jacket. I hear her explaining how she took the roll of film my dad had dropped off in my pigeonhole for processing, as a favour for a model student. How she readied the chemicals for developing but had no idea what she was looking at, as the grey turned red and black and horrifying in the blood-red light of the darkroom.

'I wish I'd never done that,' she'd said. 'I'll never not see them now, will I? What he did to that poor girl. I knew it wasn't Laura who'd done it. It could only be that Silas Cracknell. He always made me uneasy. I should have known. The signs were there all along.'

'So, exactly what is this now, Abi?' I muster my voice, meeting her eye at last. 'Is this you trying to set things straight? Because it's a little late, now that Silas has killed himself.'

'He didn't kill himself, Lolly,' she says, rocking back in her chair. 'He became a drug user in prison. I've heard you can get anything in there these days. I went to visit him once or twice after I turned eighteen, without Mum knowing, and you could see he was tanked up on something, just kept going on about how you'd lied and he was innocent and I had to help him get a solicitor for an appeal. He guessed I'd done the drawings, kept ordering me to own up, like that was ever going to happen, so I never went back.

'We didn't hear anything from him for years, until he phoned the farm from some halfway house in Newport when he got out. Mum flat-out refused to see him and I was living with a guy called Simon, in a flat in Abergavenny, and didn't want Silas to know. I suspected he only wanted money, so I agreed to meet him somewhere neutral, a café in Cardiff, and I was right. He said I owed him, fifteen years plus interest, and we must have loads of cash from the sale of the cottage and it was his right. He called me creepy girl, Lolly. He kept asking about you, if I knew where you were. He hadn't changed.'

She pauses, trying to swallow her obvious anger as she says, 'I told him to bugger off, that I'd tell his probation officer he was hassling me, but he tracked me down anyway. I mean, it wasn't hard. Mum was still living at the farm after Grampy had passed away. Silas followed me – it was only a hop on the train from Newport, and there was a break-in at Simon's place.

'I didn't tell Simon but I knew it was Silas, and sure enough, the next day he left a message to meet me again. He didn't even try to hide the fact he'd stolen our stuff, some earphones and a cash box, said he was just debt collecting. But the worst thing was that he'd taken my portfolio and found the cutting of you, plus six years' worth of Bright Brothers' research. Careless of me really, I should have protected you better.

'He said you were minted and you should pay him for the years you stole, and if not, he was going to take it to the papers, get them to talk to you about what happened that night, make you tell the truth. I think he really thought he could get a retrial. It was bullshit but I couldn't risk him finding you, messing your life up. Not that he could have afforded to turn up on your doorstep, even if he wasn't a convicted murderer – American immigration tends to frown on that sort of thing. But this is the digital age; he could still expose you, ring the press, cause a scandal. You know those gossip mags. Even send someone to track you down for a story.'

My heart thumps as she confirms my worst fears. What I'd always held inside me, parcelled up, ready to be torn open on the day Silas was freed. He'd wanted me to pay and it was only what I deserved, but he'd made the mistake of thinking his little sister would be a good little girl with the desire to do the same.

'Of course, I told him what he wanted to hear,' Abi continues, 'that I'd help him. He wanted me to go back to his squalid room because he had a curfew, and he needed cash to score again before we could work on the big *revenge plan*,' making air quotes around the words. 'We dodged the other residents and the warden guy, and I snuck into the flat, let him get his fix. Then, when he was out of it on the sofa, I gave him an extra shot of brown. It was easy enough to leave without anyone seeing me. I took the file on you and tossed it in a skip. No one looks too deeply into these things, not when an ex-con addict ODs. It was for the best. He'd only have done it himself inside a year, anyway.'

She raises her glass in a toast, sloshing back the last gulps of wine, a gesture for a job well done, but, noting my silence, tips her head to one side in a gesture that is suddenly purely her brother, flicking her blonde fringe out of her eyes.

'Hmm, I can see you're not ready to be grateful yet. It's OK, Lolly. It's a lot to take in. I understand.'

'But I don't,' I say eventually, taking the photo of me and Eli from her hands, placing it face down on the table. Because I can't find the words to acknowledge what she's just admitted in front of him, that she killed her brother for me. 'If you wanted us to be friends again, why the little game? Why the ribbon, the rope in my kitchen? And what happened to Walter?'

'Ah, we'll get to that, but not tonight. Maybe you should ask your friend MK about it first. Ask her about Doug Tindall. Then we can wrap this up and move on,' cool and business-like now, making me want to lunge across the table, grab her by her newly dyed hair and scream *Tell me, you bitch, tell me everything*. But the sound of a car snaps my head towards the front of the house.

'That's probably Eli,' she says, getting to her feet, the almost inaudible electric engine cutting out. 'I should vamoose, let you gather your thoughts before you introduce us. It'll be easier than you think once you've calmed down.'

She gets up and heads to the front door, as I hear his heavy crunch on the gravel. 'I'll call by the beach house tomorrow evening, about seven-thirty. We still have a lot to discuss, going forward,' then, as an afterthought, 'You probably want this back now,' holding out what is obviously a copy of our spare key, the one that used to be hidden in the birdfeeder out back.

'Nice ears, by the way,' she grins, as she leaves through the back door and Elias comes in the front, calling out, 'I'm home.'

Twenty

Creeping and Peeping

'Hey,' Eli grins, opening the door, as somehow I re-arrange my face into a smile. Leaning into his usual 'hi honey' hug as if everything is ordinary, I realise he smells like car leather and raincoat wax and nights when the world has not ended. 'Meatballs for dinner tomorrow?' he asks, releasing me to start unpacking tomatoes, garlic and onions from a brown bag. 'I called by the farm store in Cannon Beach,' putting a paper wrap of minced beef into the fridge as I steady myself against the countertop. It's his Friday night speciality. Old-school, blue-collar food that his dad taught him to make.

'You look tired,' he says, and I am, so bone tired now, because everything Abi has said in the last half hour weighs more than enough for one lifetime. I'm surprised he can't see my spine bending under the load.

But he merely asks, 'How'd the trick or treating go?' glancing at the uncharacteristic mess of the dining table still covered in paper cups and bowls of soggy chips from the open house earlier.

'We were late back,' I manage to reply. 'The Terrible is crashed out upstairs. There's some eggplant pasta bake in the oven for supper.'

And even as he nods his approval, I know that somehow, tomorrow, after he's cooked his comfort food, after Tilly has finished Otter Club, indoors now in the bitter-edged evenings, I'll have to find a way to drive to the Project for an appointment with a woman who has already killed two people. Just thinking about it makes me want to vomit out all the words I've already absorbed from Abi's mouth tonight, gyroscoping in my stomach making me seasick, heartsick, as I wonder exactly what she meant when she said, 'going forward'.

'Needed a pick-me-up, huh?' grins Eli, looking at the bottle of wine and *two* glasses on the table.

'Yeah, me and Belle had a nightcap after all the Halloween fun.'

'Nice. I'll take a shower then we can have supper. Nice whiskers by the way, kinda sexy,' and I realise I haven't cleaned off my trick-or-treat face yet, or removed the cat ears from my hair.

'OK,' I nod, rubbing at the face crayon with a snatched wet wipe. 'Though I might just pop next door to say hi to MK first.'

'At this hour?'

I check my watch, it's only 9 p.m., but Lookout Beach is early to bed and early to rise. 'I'll only be a minute. She likes Halloween,' I lie. 'She might be feeling a bit left out this year. I saved her a bat cookie.'

'OK. Want me to walk you to the door?'

Bless his heart, my kind, caring Eli, my solid, chivalrous husband, I married the character from my own story, didn't I? I married Captain Carruthers, minus the cocked hat, offering to escort me all of twenty feet. But I don't deserve his kindness. I'm not the honest maiden, the one he thought he married. I never was.

Moments later, and I'm standing outside MK's yard door, head against the wind-blistered wood, trying to breathe. There're so many questions, but for now the one I have to ask most urgently is 'Who is Doug Tindall?', the man Abi mentioned, and I can't wait until tomorrow. My head will split right down the middle in the dark hours before dawn if I don't do it now.

As I approach the door, I think maybe MK really has gone to bed, seeing the windows dark. But after my second knock, I hear the chain being deactivated and her face appears in the mean crack behind it.

'It's me. Sorry to call so late.'

'It's OK, I'm up,' she says. 'For a moment I thought you were another reporter. Some guy's shoved three cards in the mailbox this week – persistent little shit.'

The odour of dog chews and bourbon greets me as I follow her back to the sofa, where Oprah lifts her head and wags hello. I spy two of Neil Morrow's business cards on the living-room table among a litter of candy wrappers. Climbing back under her blanket MK asks, 'Want a drink?' adding, 'Sorry about the mess.'

When people say this, they usually mean they haven't got around to doing the 'guest ready' mega-blitz and the floor needs a quick vacuum, but this room resembles an overturned dumpster, half-eaten takeaway cartons,

211

discarded sweaters everywhere. Oprah's slobbery fur friends are scattered on Walter's La-Z-Boy and it smells of desperation and something I know only too well, regret.

'I meant to clean up in here,' she grimaces, seeing my face, 'after I settled Walter for the night, but he's had a bad day and Nurse Ratched is down to three days a week now.'

'It's fine, hon,' I mutter, knowing I should have called before, offered to help out, but the pleasantries will have to wait.

'What is it?' she asks, reading a Pacific low approaching on my face. 'Has something else happened?'

'MK, I don't know if this will make any sense to you, but I need to ask you something important. Who is Doug Tindall?'

Her face crumples then, folds in like an origami interpretation of surrender before she says, 'So they've caught him, have they? Or he's given himself up? I knew it was only a matter of time.'

She rises without warning and, for a moment, I think she's going to leave me there, but merely returns from the kitchen with a glass saying, 'Go on, have a drink. You'll need it.'

'MK, what's going on?' I ask, not touching the bourbon, my head already swimming.

'I knew he'd crack first,' she shakes her head. 'He wanted to turn himself in right away but I begged him not to. Jesus, everything was such a mess. How could I let Doug tell the truth? I thought maybe it would all just die down if we kept our mouths shut, but now you know who he is it's obviously all over. Was it the police who told you? Are they on their way? Was it the fingerprints or something? He said he had gloves on but you never know. He could have touched something.'

'What are you talking about, MK?' I almost shout, 'Who is Doug Tindall?'

'He's the guy I was having an affair with. Yeah, you can judge me, I deserve it. It started out as a stupid one-night stand when he was doing a bit of security consultation for the conference hotel in Portland. We got talking at the bar, got trashed, ended up in my room.'

She leans back, pulls up her legs and crosses them, clearly reading my mind and the words *What the hell were you thinking of?* flashing there in neon like the *Keep Portland Weird* sign.

'Nothing was supposed to come of it,' she sighs, 'but then we started, you know, texting each other, *sexting*. So childish, right? I think it was just the thrill of it. Things were not great with Walter, he was away all the time and I was bored. You're gonna be mad at me so I might as well just tell you right now. I wanted to meet again at the hotel but Doug wouldn't let me keep paying and a cop's salary's hardly generous. His six-year-old daughter stays with him two weekends a month, when she's not with her mom in Salem, and he didn't want the neighbours to see him bringing a woman to his apartment. Well, I'm too old for dive hotels and I didn't want to bring him here, so . . .'

'What does any of this—' I interrupt but she cuts me off.

'So, we went to the beach house, your beach house, just once, to screw around, when I knew you'd be in the city for Tilly's aikido thing. We met out of town and he drove us up.'

I remember Olsen's words then, when she'd called by the Project that afternoon, 'Nice little place for an assignation . . . the ranger saw a dark Prius . . .'

'But how did you get in?' I ask. 'Through the security gate and main door?'

'Grace, baby, I've been there with you, like, half a dozen times. When you've shown me the developments. I've seen you use the gate code and pin-pad entry. I'm sorry.'

'But I don't understand what any of this has to do with—'

'Let me tell it in my own time, OK? Well, we didn't see each other for a while after that because his daughter was staying at the end of summer vacation. But he'd come to the hotel when I was in town and we'd text and pretend like we were, you know, strangers in the hotel bar, getting a kick out of it. Then we started sharing fantasies. At first, it was like, he was an undercover cop looking for a sexy girl on a warrant. God it was stupid, all that *You're in big trouble, Miss. How can I convince you not to arrest me, Officer?* stuff, but it was so hot. I had the best sex of my life in the downstairs washrooms. Then it was, *I'm the lone woman and maybe you're the sex stalker with handcuffs who'd follow me to my room.*'

'MK, I'm not sure I really want to know . . .'

'No, I know. Just listen,' her cheeks flushing scarlet in the half light. 'It was all talk. I mean, I never meant to . . . well, I mentioned this one "home alone" fantasy one time, about being at home and an intruder coming in, finding the housewife all alone, tying her up, but she's really horny and gets into it. Like a classic porno setup, rape-not-rape fantasy.

'And Doug played along, and I was asking what he would tie me up with and I was in control of it all. Then he had a fight with his daughter's mom and she came to take her home and he wanted to come up here. But I saw the workmen at the beach house fitting that glass panelling and I knew Walter would be in Bend. I was mad, after we fought that day about the car being repossessed, my "insane" spending. I thought, fuck it. I gave him the address. And, well, you know the rest.'

'Not really,' I say, baffled. 'You mean, you invited this guy over here. How did he end up in my house?'

'Well, that's the funny part. Though not funny ha-ha. I'd texted him the zip code, but you know how the GPS sends people to the wrong places round here? It wasn't Belle's art supplies or your swatches that went to the wrong house. It was Doug.'

'He called at the wrong house?'

'Yeah,' she laughs, a hollow sound. 'So that's how it happened, my old friend. I was upstairs waiting in this dumb negligee thing, waiting for my twenty-eight-year-old toy-boy to arrive, and he was setting up his kinky kit next door. You were supposed to be in the city that night but Doug said he found the door unlocked, thought it was part of the thing, the "intruder" game.'

'He didn't check?'

'Well, this is the good part. I'd shown him the feature on this place in *House Beautiful*, from last year. The snarky, *is mid-century modern "passé-d its prime"* piece? It had a picture of the outside of the house. He didn't know there are two identical houses back to back. He had no reason to think he wasn't in the right place.

'It would've been OK if Walter hadn't reappeared. Good old Walter goes to investigate a prowler and finds a great big bearded guy in your house with a knife. Then they slug it out and Walt goes down. It's an accident but Doug panics – there's no way in hell he's going to be able to explain himself so he runs like hell. Then you enter the little party. All this, while I'm fingering myself on the king-size, oblivious.'

She laughs again, devoid of all pleasure. 'First thing I know, there's the sound of a siren and Doug is calling me from the 7-Eleven out on Pine, asking what the fuck is going on and who that guy was. You would laugh, right, if it wasn't so messed up?'

'Jesus,' I manage to mutter, not remotely tempted to chuckle.

'I know, I know. You can't say anything I haven't already said to myself. Doug wanted to turn himself in but I persuaded him to wait. I told him he'd lose his job and access to his daughter if anyone knew he'd been involved in a violent attack. Luckily, he used my work number that day, the one I use for the Extraordinary Oils orders, and I get dozens of client calls on it, so I could have explained it away. We deleted all the sex stuff from our other phones and just stayed quiet. I mean, they weren't looking at me or him. Walter was the victim, wrong place, wrong time. They were looking at you. I know it was shitty but I was scared.'

'They thought maybe Walter and me were having an affair,' I say slowly, taking a slug of the bourbon after all, 'and that Eli stumbled on us. They kept asking how he got in if I didn't let him in.'

'I know, I know. And I would never have let that get any further, I swear to you, Grace. If they'd tried to pin anything on Eli, I would've told them everything. I kept expecting them to call and say they'd linked Doug with me, or to ask to look at my phone records, and then it would've been over anyway. But, as time went on, nothing happened and it got harder to come clean. And I didn't want Walter to know. I was so ashamed.'

That I understand. But, if it makes a sort of twisted sense, what about the red ribbon Tindall brought with the knife and handcuffs? That can't just be a coincidence.

'Jesus, MK,' I tread carefully, 'a knife, handcuffs, ribbons? It's a bit hardcore.'

'I know, I don't know what got into him. A fucking knife? I'd have been happy with some *Fifty Shades* velvet ties and a blindfold or whatever, but he said he was trying to play the part and some girl had told him it was hot, what the girls like. Maybe he is a closet perv after all but he's not a sex attacker. So that's my sordid story. All because I wanted some excitement. My husband is lying back there with brain trauma and Doug is going to jail because of me.'

As she sniffs back the tears, I recall that night in the yard, when we smoked the sneaky cigarette. 'Do you think things could have been different if you hadn't been such a selfish bitch?' she'd asked me. Now she looks relieved that she's been able to confess to someone, at last. But that urge can be dangerous for everyone involved. Some tales can't be told.

'Doug's not going to jail, not yet anyway,' I say after a moment.

'But if you're here, how do you know his name?'

This is the difficult part. I can't tell her about Abi. I want to ask her if she knows her from Portland but I can't, not yet.

'The police didn't tell me,' I say slowly. 'I don't think they have any idea what happened. They told me a car had been seen up at the Project but that's all they have.'

'So how *do* you know about Doug?'

'Could someone up in Portland, at the Hyatt, have seen you with Doug? Someone you work with, put two and two together?' I deflect.

'I don't think so, though we have a bunch of regular home sellers who move the beauty stock through their book groups or mom and baby groups. Everyone's in the bar all day, so someone could have seen us talking, but why would anyone care? Why, has someone said something?'

'No, someone just left me a phone message asking if Doug Tindall was a client of yours.' It's not a good explanation but she seems to buy it, whistling through her teeth and adding, 'That's weird. But they can't know about any of this, as long as Doug has stayed quiet. So,' she asks stoically, sitting up straighter in the chair, expecting the worst, 'will you tell the police?'

'I don't know. I hope I won't need to,' my mind spinning.

'And Walter?'

'I think he's suffered enough, don't you?'

'Thank you. Thank you, honey,' she sobs, hurling herself off the sofa now, sending Oprah flopping with annoyance onto the rug as she hugs me. 'You're such a good friend. I wish I could be more like you, as kind and good as you are.'

No, you don't, I think, holding her tightly because I have to hold something, someone, right now, or I will fall from the deck of the good ship Grace Jensen into the unending sea and never surface. The ticking in my head threatens to shatter what remains of my mask of normality, as we part with promises to speak soon and keep in touch.

'It feels so good to tell you,' she sniffs in the doorway, 'to not have to lie any more, to you at least. Tell Belle to come around soon and we'll do margaritas, yeah? I haven't seen her this evening. She's been stopping by every night, bless her heart, just to check on me. But,' she laughs with real warmth at last, 'if she brings one more bag of those carob ball monstrosities, I might have to strangle her.'

Belle's had a demanding day, I want to say, thinking of her pointing a gun at Neil Morrow, but that already seems like a lifetime ago and I can't worry about that now. I need to be alone, to think. And to find out what Abigail has planned for me.

Twenty-one

'Don't say his name . . .'

By 5 p.m. the following evening, my cheeks are cramping with enforced cheer as I chew Eli's meatball pasta with a sandpaper mouth.

'How was Otters, baby girl?' he asks Tilly, 'being mommy' tonight, serving us from the vintage tureen that belonged to his dad.

'Cool, Dad, we did Eskimo rolls with the club kayaks,' she nods, drowning her pasta in shaved parmesan. Let someone else worry about cholesterol and evil dairy overdose tonight, Grace doesn't have the energy to make her usual protest and Lolly has other things on her mind. Tilly is talking for everyone, anyway, adding, 'Ashley and me did races and I won two out of three.'

'How did Seb get on with his paddling?' Eli asks, ever attentive to the current affairs between besties.

'He wasn't there,' she frowns. 'He was supposed to be my partner but he bailed on me. Could we teach Noushki and Nell to kayak next spring, Mom?' she mumbles, through a full mouth. 'You're a cool teacher and Nell says she's up for it. I think I need more crew if Seb is going to not show up all the time. He can still be my bosun, just from the shore. I know his asthma makes him wheezy but he could have Snapchatted us so I didn't have to partner Debbie Cole. She always has boogers in her nose.'

As Elias guffaws, I realise I haven't heard from Belle today either, but I don't have time to call over to check on her because, as soon as we've cleared the plates away, I have to make my exit.

'I just need to pop next door to arrange something for the Thanksgiving bake sale,' I tell Elias, loading the dishwasher.

'So soon?' he frowns.

'Yes,' because I always help Belle with the cake stall. 'I'm collecting her from the coffee shop first.'

'OK, honey. Bring me a bear claw if there are any left.'

'Sure, honey,' I wave.

All is well. Nothing to see here; grateful, as I start the car, that Belle's house is in darkness, to support my lie.

When I get to the Project there's no sign of a car near the drive but, as I head towards the gate, Abi detaches herself from the shadows and consults her watch.

'I was wondering if you'd come,' she smiles.

'Why wouldn't I come, Abi?' trying to keep my face neutral. 'Like you said, we've got a lot to talk about,' because I've decided the only way to play this is to make her think I'm as glad to see her as she is to see me.

'Now this is swanky, Lolly Pop,' she whistles, as we climb the stairs into the gallery and she takes a slow turn of the room. I wince to hear that name on her lips, the violation of her being here in Grace's immaculately clean and engineered world. The past is a stain carried by her feet, her breath. Her fingertips, trailing the hardwood furniture, are a contaminant, a ghost of rot. I feel it seep into my pores, enter my lungs, waking the bones of an old, complicated world and a younger, more complicated girl.

'You've done so well for yourself,' she beams. 'You look so good too, so polished. You, who turned her nose up at tinted lip balm, spent half her life in a wetsuit. I've missed that, you know, the sea, the surf. Not much of that in Abergavenny. I've missed talking to you, all our stories. You must too.'

Like a hole in the head, Lolly wants to snap, but Grace is becoming sharper around the edges, even if no one sees it yet, and I let her do the talking.

'It seems like another lifetime,' I respond carefully.

'But we had some good times, didn't we? When Silas didn't spoil everything. I liked to pretend that you were my sister, you know. Brothers are rubbish. Silas was rubbish anyway,' a smile of nostalgia breaks across her face as she adds, 'It was a good place to grow up. But this is great too. What a place you've found. What a summer I've had. I want to live here for ever.'

'So, you've been out here a while, then? Since August?' I ask, using polite small talk to create the illusion of interest as I switch on a lamp and we sit at the coffee table.

'I've been here a bit longer than that, Lolly,' she replies, flopping onto the new easy chair. 'I wanted to find out about you first, your life. I didn't want to scare you by popping up out of nowhere. I wanted to be friends with your friends, feel my way in. That's how I *accidentally* met MK.'

'In Portland?'

'That's right. You know, everyone drinks like fish in the hotel bars there. You can pretend to be anyone. Me and MK had a good chat over some canapés and a vat of Stoli and she signed me up for home selling on the spot. God! That woman can drink. Speaking of drink,' she pulls some vodka from her purse, 'want a little tot? I know I was never allowed to, back then, at the cottage with you guys, but, here,' she hands me the bottle. 'Find glasses for us. I think we should toast.'

'But, Abi, I don't understand,' my voice still curious and calm as I liberate some tumblers from the sideboard. 'How did you know about Doug Tindall?'

'She told you, then? Naughty Mary-Kate and her dirty little secret. OK, so I saw MK a couple of times up at the Hyatt and we'd shoot the breeze. She told me about her life in Lookout Beach, about her friend, the brilliant architect. And I mingled with the other guests and watched them flirting, her and Doug, in the bar. The barman told me his name, that he was a cop doing private security. I knew they went up to a room together that night and they weren't playing Scrabble, right?'

She throws back her first tot of vodka and motions for a refill. I nurse mine. There's too much stuff burning a hole in my throat already.

'I saw them once or twice after that, in the bar,' she explains, 'not sitting together, pretending not to know each other. He was watching her every move, though, she being all coy. It was obvious they were texting each other, casting glances, getting a kick out of it. This one time, she was over in the restaurant with some clients and I went and sat next to him at the bar and just started chatting, flirting.

'I saw something flash up on his phone on the bar, a bit of a dirty message about "tying me up", and made a joke of it. He was so embarrassed, but tipsy, and I felt like playing a game. I told him I had a friend who liked role-play, and the one thing that really got her going was being tied up by a pretend stalker with a knife, with red ribbons like a doll. I didn't say MK's name but I said, *like a really cool friend*, working for Extraordinary Oils, a wild child. I looked over a couple of times and let him see me looking at her.

'To be fair the poor guy was blushing like crazy but I told him it was a fantasy we'd talked about and I thought it was hot. I just had this idea that he might try it with her one night, use the props, and she'd mention the red ribbon and stuff to you and it'd be a game. You might get the hint. It would start you thinking and you'd know I'd found you. Because best friends share their secrets, right?

'Except MK didn't tell you anything about Doug the cop. Not besties after all, then? It backfired a bit when the stupid bugger got the wrong house. I'm sorry, Lolly, that was just bad luck. Imagine how I felt when I saw him coming up the yard.'

'You were there?' Grace manages to sound surprised.

'Yeah, I was upstairs. I popped in for a couple of visits. I wanted to see if you had kept keepsakes of us, photos of your childhood, a journal like you said you used to keep at home, the books we used to love, your dad's book even. I thought you'd at least read those stories to Tilly, they're her heritage.'

And I remember, once or twice, pulling his book out of my schoolbag, if I'd taken it to class to copy the drawings, Abi poring wide eyed over the pages at their kitchen table while Silas had his hands full with the post-swim cheese on toast. She'd liked it so much I'd given her one of Dad's spare copies, always lying around the house, as a birthday present that year. From then on she'd carried it in her own kitbag.

'But you don't write stories any more, do you, Lolly?' Abi sighs, gesturing for more vodka as the tale unfolds. 'There are none of yours in the whole house, no journals or notebooks. Tilly doesn't even know her mom used to write brilliant ones. Of course, that day, when Walter arrived, I could hardly hang around for the police to arrive. I'd only just legged it when your car came down the street.'

Such a quiet street, I think to myself, such an upmarket neighbourhood in the safest little bolthole south of Seattle. At least that explains why Doug Tindall was able to walk into my house. Why there was no breaking and entering.

I take a shot of the vodka after all, saying, 'You've been busy then, Abi,' with something like a smile. 'So, what have you learned about me now? And what do we do before your extended holiday ends?'

'Ends?' says Abi in surprise, knocking back a vodka in one. 'I'm not on holiday. I'm staying.'

'But, don't you have a job? Someone back home? What about this Simon guy you're living with? And your mum?'

'Simon? That's over,' she laughs. 'He wasn't ever going to be "the one", not like Eli is your one. I had a few boy-friends at college but none of them really clicked for me. I just never had enough to say to them. I'm footloose and fancy free and all ready for Lookout Beach.'

'I don't understand,' I say, trying to keep my face calm, because how can a thirty-year-old woman have no attachments, no job, no family of her own. No ties.

'Well, we're not all like you, Lolly.' She turns slowly from the view of the black sea behind me, beyond the windows, as the Cyhireath whistles against the glass, low and leering. 'I had to look after Mum after Dad died, it was expected. I finished school up in Abergavenny, then I was at the local college studying graphic design. I'd wanted to go to one of the London art schools but who was going to pay for that?

'Mum wasn't good with money. She'd finally sold the Gwyn Mawr house, for a lot less than it was worth, but Grampy convinced her to invest in some new dairy equipment and a farm shop that never paid off. When he realised the extent of the debt he'd buried us under, he keeled over in the milking shed. Mum was never the same after Gwyn Mawr but after that she was a wreck.

'I'd been working in a bookshop in town since college, to make ends meet, and eventually Simon, one of the trade reps, took a shine to me. I showed him some of the stories I'd been writing and a friend of his published them. They were a bit of a minor Welsh hit, inspired by your stories, of course – a twenty-first-century folk-tale collection you could say. I did all the illustrations too. I was saving up and waiting for my moment, to show you this myself.'

She reaches down then, pulls a hardbacked book out of her bag and holds it out to me, like a child awaiting approval. I don't take it, but sit there absorbing the cover, the drawing of a girl who looks a lot like me, like I used to, with long hair flowing. The author name is A. E. Marshall.

'I'll leave it here,' she says, putting it down on the coffee table between us. 'Take a look later, you'll like it. That's little old me. A. E. Marshall. Mum changed our name back to her maiden name when we moved back to the farm. It was easier that way, after Silas was named in the paper. If only we'd been called Jones or Davies, right? The Cracknells were all dead to her anyway.

'Then Mum died not long after Silas did. She had a heart attack. I was sad but it worked out for the best. Turns out an eco-energy company wanted a strip of the farmland for an access road to a new wind farm – it's good to be green, right? Grampy had been turning them down for years but, once I inherited, I took the cheque right away. It was never a home to me and I got a nice bit of money to start over and applied for an adult arts exchange visa, to come to Portland, thanks to the book.

'So here I am,' she leans back with satisfaction, her face softening a little from the vodka, becoming chummy. 'When I get a job with Bright Brothers, they'll let me stay on a work visa,' she says. 'You can arrange that for me, can't you, a soon-to-be-partner's wife? I'll be good at it. I'm a great graphic artist. We can be together again, Lolly. And you need a real friend. Someone who knows you, who you really are. No one knows you like I do. No one knows where we came from. We can be real sisters now.'

She's not joking. She thinks we can be a family. 'But Abi . . .' I start, the words stalling on my tongue, my hand clenching around the glass.

'You can't call me Abi now though, *Grace*,' she smirks. 'It's not my name any more, and I guess I should stop calling you Lolly Pop.'

'What should I call you then?' I take the bait.

'Don't you know?' she grins. 'Come on, you do know if you think about it . . .' She points to the E in A. E. Marshall, waiting for me to catch on. My middle name's Eleanor, remember?'

And I do know, what's been sticking in my airway all night finally loosening into truth. How have I not seen it until now?

'Nell,' I say. 'You're Anoushka's friend Nell.'

'Hole in one,' she laughs. 'Pleased to meet you, Grace,' she reaches her hand across the table for a formal introduction, then drops it, settling for, 'Too soon? You're impressed though, right? Well, what better way to find out all about you than to be friends with your daughter's nanny? One who studies art and hangs around in the Portland student coffee shop, like me? Whoops, don't say "nanny" though. I mean *assistant*.

'Bit lazy though, not to vet your daughter's nanny's acquaintances,' she mock frowns. 'What would Mrs Baby Babcock say?' making a face very like the teacher's post food-fight frown. 'I kept waiting for you to ask to meet me, ask me to dinner, but you never did. I think your mum would consider that rude. I can do that now, though, officially, come and meet Elias? He's so great, Lolly. He loves you so much. Anyone can see that, just watching you together. And she's a lovely girl, your Tilly. Just like you were. Bold and brave and full of guts. She's a great swimmer too and kayaker. A year or two and she'll put you to shame in the water.'

Could we teach Noushki and Nell to kayak? echoes Tilly's excited voice in my head, through her mouthful of meatballs, when I was too distracted to think it odd that she'd include Anoushka's friend in her request. Suddenly I'm floating out to sea on the wind-winged back of the Cyhireath with no way to 'process' this, not even the vodka helping me pull my fucking self together. Everything inside is stretching apart into the blackness around me. I'm on the underside of the Eskimo roll and time is running out to right everything.

'The great thing is, you don't have to tell them anything about the old days now, if you don't want to,' continues Abi, oblivious to my drowning. 'We're already friends. This is a great place to start over. I'll need somewhere to housesit for a bit, of course. Until I can sort the paper-work, then find a little place of my own.'

She clearly means here, as she gazes around at the almost finished interior. She wants to move into the Project, into my house. My blank slate. My story-less space.

'Think about it,' she explains. 'Anoushka's in the city so much. She finishes her college course next summer, hardly that useful to you, for school runs and pickups, if she goes back to Salem. But I can be here all day, every day. I've got a job at the bookstore, starting next week. It's the perfect solution. Especially when you start your big commission in January, the Garibaldi fish cannery project – you'll need a regular sitter then, when you're down the coast redesign-ing the best hotel in the Pacific Northwest.'

She smiles proudly. 'See, you're the star architect, but I can make myself useful in so many ways. That man was a pig anyway. It was yours by right.'

'What man?' I manage to mutter.

'You know, Poliakoff, the mincy little twat who almost

got the job. Not after he fell down those steps, though. He was such a dick with his headphones in. He wasn't looking anywhere else, and it was so easy.'

'What was?' reduced to two-syllable questions.

'Well, let's just say, if you run in the city at night, alone, you're asking for trouble these days, even if you're a man, if you don't watch your step,' she winks, pouring herself another tot of Stoli, downing it. 'You see, I've been looking out for you and Tilly for a long time. I bet that little girl-scout bitch doesn't bother and bully Tilly any more either,' she winks again. 'Or is it like this?' pulling down the side of her left eye as I realise she means Ashley Weathers.

'Yeah, that was luck, really,' muses Abi. 'It wasn't a good place for her to hide. Right by the edge up there on Hug Point. I came up behind her and just kicked her feet out. Gave her just one little shove. She didn't even see me.'

My face freezes, as I recall the steep bluffs of the bay outside town, the sharp-edged tidepools, the wheeling eagles of my walk with Belle, imagining a little girl falling, falling . . .

Eventually, I say, 'Well, you're full of surprises. You had me fooled all this time.'

'I did, didn't I? You didn't guess I was Anoushka's friend, even when I gave the book to Tilly, well, when I put it in the bin at the bookstore? *Fairy and Folk Tales of the South Wales Coast*? I thought for sure you'd get the hint then, see the joke, carrying on the tradition.'

Giving myself time to think, I get up and walk to the window, because I can't look at her right now. A great white moon, missing only its last sliver, rises above the headland, what Tilly and I call the Captain's Moon. Just around the bay sits the original Terrible Tilly, the infamous lighthouse in her well of rocks and surf, and sometimes I'll tell my girl stories of that moon lighting the ships to harbour. If you stand on the promontory on the headland, it rises behind the lighthouse and looks like it's glowing to guide the seafarers home. I need a guiding light now, for sure.

Something flickers in my chest then, a memory of a feeling, but its colour is the opposite of moonlight, whatever that might be, vibrating with the blackness behind the glass. It feels cold in my stomach, tastes of metal and salt on my tongue.

'Well, all that seems great, *Nell*, we should make that toast,' I say after a moment, gathering steel into myself as I turn and raise my glass. 'To old friends.'

'And new beginnings,' adds Abi, as we toss the vodka back before I add, 'We have to take things slowly, though. I don't want to bother Eli until the Slabtown project is completely settled and the awards ceremony is over. Let's keep things between us for now. We've got plenty of time to catch up, haven't we? And there are so many places here I need to show you. So many magical things.'

I'm telling her what she wants to hear, buying time with pleas for patience, but tell-tale tears are in Abi's vodka-swimmy eyes, even as Grace swallows the lump in her throat the stinging Stoli can't dislodge.

'Well, I should get back home. Are you OK to drive? You've put a few of those away,' gesturing to her glass. 'Your car is parked somewhere nearby, right?'

'Oh yes, I'm fine. It's not far. Drunk driving is almost socially acceptable out here as long as you don't hit anyone.

I left it at the turnout just in case those bloody rangers are nosing around.'

'You're staying in town now, then?' I confirm, knocking off the lamp, steering us to the stairs.

'Yes, I'm staying in the arts centre next to the bookstore this weekend – they have a residential floor for visiting painters and daubers. I arranged it with the owner, you know the one who looks like Father Christmas, after they started selling some of my gift baskets. It's tat but they pay good money for it. It's a short-term measure, obviously.'

'Well, I must go, Tilly and Eli will be wondering where I am.'

'Story before bed? I understand.'

We hover by the door until I say, 'Say, why don't we get together on Thursday evening?' the flicker of an idea forming behind the words. 'Elias will be up in town before the awards ceremony. Why don't we meet in the rest area up on Ecola Point, where the path dips into the woods? It's easy to find.'

'Why?' she asks. 'Why can't we just come here and chat or go out for dinner?'

'Because I want to show you something special, and we have to do it when the moon is full. It's a Lookout Beach ritual, one of its oldest stories from the founding fathers' days.' Thinking on my feet I add, 'It's got everything, pirates, shipwrecks. MK and Belle have never been that interested in local history but there's a secret spot I want to show you, I know you'll love. It'll be like old times, our secret. Then next week we can take Tilly to Otters together and you can come for meatballs.'

'OK, great, what time?'

'Make it about four-thirty,' I say, as I guide her out and set the alarm. 'It has to be getting dark for the full effect.'

'What is it?' She's excited now as we crunch up the gravel drive. Part of her is thirteen years old again and, at last, she's been invited to the party.

'Wait and see,' I smile. 'Wrap up warm, though, and don't tell Noushki. She'll want to come and she'll only ruin it. It should be just us. I'll bring some booze. We'll have to sneak into the nature reserve, bypass the rangers, so park in the public layby and walk up, OK?'

When we part at the Project gate, she throws her arms around me and says, 'It's going to be great, Lolly, like old times,' and I nod.

Right after Abi turns south towards Lookout Beach, her headlights fading away down the coast road, I get in my car and drive north in the inky darkness, ratcheting up Nine Inch Nails on the speakers. Then I scream myself hoarse, hitting the steering wheel over and over as I run over what I should do next. Probably go straight to the police. I should call up Lieutenant Andy right now and reveal I'm an imposter, let rip with my fantastical tale of old murder and betrayal (at least the official parts), watch his friendly racoon face react with horror as I lay Laura's past bare. Then I'll explain that the sister of a cult teen killer is here, in our little town, stalking me.

'It must run in the family,' Danny and Dolores, partners in crime, will whisper loudly, as no-longer-Grace hugs the scratchy angora cardigan closer around her shoulders, playing the victim. But if I do, I know it will all come out; if there's an investigation, if there's a restraining order like Americans always seem to be getting courts to issue in movies, tongues will wag, people will know. Everything I left back there on the wind-lashed Welsh coast will have followed Grace here, after everything she's done to outwit it, staining and degrading the house she's built on these shifting sands, worming its way into Eli's heart, hollowing him out trunk and branch.

And what if they don't believe me? There's no evidence of anything Abi has done, not what she did to Priss or Silas back then, not even what she did to Ashley Weathers on the bluffs or Andreas Poliakoff in the city. What if the police do nothing, *can* do nothing, and she stays here, setting up home as she's promised, sketching pictures, writing stories, only angry now that I've betrayed her too?

I can't have her anywhere in this state, or even on this continent. I've made the plan with her to distract her, because I don't want her calling me, texting me or popping up at the house before then, leaving a trail, being careless. She wants me to herself for a while and I'll give her just that, at the same time keeping her away from everyone I love.

There's so little time to fix this. Abi thinks she's the one who's going to write the end of this story with me, but she isn't. This isn't *The Laura Llewellyn Show* as she once knew it. *The Grace Jensen Story* has to get the next chapter it deserves, though I have a feeling I'm going to need good old Lolly's help to make sure of that. Because, even though Grace might be able to live with the aftermath of honesty in all its forms, start over, with a new house, new blouse, new lipstick, I'm pretty sure what's left of Laura can't – not now I know, we know, that Abi has spoken to my girl, touched my terrible, wonderful daughter with her father's eyes and none of my shadows. She shouldn't have done that.

Then I think of Belle, just yesterday evening, when the world still hung straight and true. I remember her with the gun raised, then afterwards, saying, 'Sometimes you have to take matters into your own hands. You run or you stand, you know.'

Maybe she's right. I've run once before, it obviously didn't work. Perhaps it's time to decide if I can stand.

Twenty-two

Incantations and Offerings

It's not difficult to persuade Eli to go up to the city a day early without me. He understands perfectly when I say I need to prep some unexpected drafts for the Garibaldi project before I can leave and Anoushka's more than happy to step in for a few hours, taking Tilly for pizza in the Pearl District. After waving them off with kisses, I'm alone and I'm ready.

As soon as I arrive at the Project, I turn on all the lights and take a good look around, checking my earlier cleaning efforts before changing into my yoga pants and sweater. Then I apply some lipstick, suck in my breath and call the Lookout Beach police house. I already popped in there this morning, seemingly to shoot the breeze with Andy about my unsolved case, but really to find out who's on duty tonight. Luckily, it's Officer Danny, and he answers immediately when I call the office number.

'Hi Danny, this is Mrs Jensen,' I say. 'Listen, I'm sorry to be a nervous Nelly, and it's probably just me panicking, but I'm up at the Project working and I thought I saw someone in the grounds, inside the fence. I don't suppose you could just drive by and check, could you?'

Twenty minutes later, I'm fortifying him with coffee in the gallery and thanking him for poking around the undergrowth before giving me the all clear.

'Thanks, Danny,' I smile. 'I know this isn't your job now, but, well, I need to work on here for maybe another hour or two. If it's quiet, do you think you could just keep watch outside for a bit? I mean, if duty doesn't call, of course. I'd just feel safer with you out there. This home invasion thing has left me a little nervous.' I wring a tissue in my hands. 'Eli is in the city tonight. Would it be too much trouble?'

'Of course not, Mrs Jensen,' he nods. 'It's dead quiet, as always. I'm off shift in two hours but I could escort you home after that?'

'That'd be wonderful,' I nod.

'I'll park outside the security gate. If I need to attend a call, I'll text your cell so you know. You can keep the gate locked until I get back.'

'You're so kind,' I smile again, glad that he's suggested exactly what I was going to.

Once his reusable quart coffee cup is topped up with Guatemalan roast, I lock the door behind him and change into my winter wetsuit and booties. Then I pop my backpack on and head out of the ground-level rear door into the ferny slough. It's four o'clock on a winter's evening, darkness settling as I pick my way along by the gallery glow that falls into the ravine.

The tide is inching in already, the white heads of the

waves cupping the rocking hollows as I change into my wetsuit, waiting on the sand. As I strike out in the kayak, hugging the granite cliffs towards the bay beyond, I'm not wasting any time. Abi is waiting for me.

Halfway around the point, I take Abi's folk-story book, the one she left on the coffee table the other night, out of my backpack and soak it in the surf. I've already cleaned all the surfaces she touched while she was inside the Project and washed the glass she used. As I push the waxed cover down into the rocking blackness beneath me, all traces she was ever there sink with it. I follow it with the copy of my father's book, retrieved from beneath my car's passenger seat, holding my breath as the Maid of Sker, the Cap Goch and all their illustrated companions are consigned to a watery grave.

My arms are stinging with effort by the time I reach the beach on the other side, my back slicked with sweat, but my head is singing with oxygen and purpose. On the gravelly sand, I drag the kayak up behind me, away from the highest reach of the waterline and pull it into a cleft. Then I change into the dry clothes and sneakers I've packed in my backpack, leaving the suit with the kayak.

I use my pen torch to master the steep path, coiled through the trees to the layby, eighty feet above, behind the bluff. The trail's almost invisible unless you know it's there and I know it well. But I can't miss my footing in the gloom and take a fall. How would I explain being here, like this?

Abi is waiting for me, just as I emerge from the trees from the access road, approaching the entrance to the State Park as if I'm coming from the tourist pullout. It's a bright enough night up here, thanks to the moon rising, but no one will see us in this winter dusk, no one is out here in this darkest and most secret of seasons.

'It's bloody freezing,' says Abi, dressed for the Northwest chill, as I'd told her to. 'It must be five degrees. This surprise had better be worth it, Lolly.'

But she's not annoyed, she's expectant. As am I.

The ten-minute walk through the gate and across the headland warms us both up.

'Where the hell are we going?' she pants, out of shape, winded from the incline. 'You know it's two-for-one fried oysters and tequila shooters at the Schooner tonight?'

'Wait and see,' I grin, following the path marked with the official signs until we reach the parkland boundary, indicated by a ring of wire and a sign asking people not to cross into the endangered bald eagle nesting site. I ignore both.

'Who'd have thought,' says Abi admiringly, 'Grace Jensen, breaking the law?' as she follows my lead and swings her legs over the boundary, one at a time. The rough track, once worn by the feet of birdwatchers and hikers, is easy to see in the white light, then we emerge onto the ragged promontory. Out across the heaving surge of water is Terrible Tilly, backlit by the rising moon, just as I'd hoped.

'Wow,' says Abi, stopping short at my rear, 'that's quite a sight.'

So it is, one of wind and water and the glowing Captain's Moon, guiding the weary and lost home from far shores. The stage is set, the incantations and offerings ready, but there'll be no photographs tonight.

'Take care,' I say to Abi, pointing my pen torch in front of her, 'it's a bit shaley here,' as we head over the false lip of turf that looks like the cliff edge but actually dips down towards the water on a thread of worn stone. A few moments later, a great punchbowl of rock and black water emerges below us and Abi gasps.

'Told you it was worth it,' I say. 'I've kayaked around the coast here but I've never been able to persuade MK or Belle to get their Ugg boots dirty on this walk. They're such *girls*,' I add, and Abi grins, as intended.

The night is empty of human noise now, the roosting seabirds silent too, only the wash of the rising tide, sliding backwards and forwards against the unyielding cliffs, accompanies the deafening ticking in my head. I dump my backpack and sit down on a smooth plate of exposed rock, gesturing for Abi to do the same. The wind is like a knife through my fleece, which couldn't be better for my purposes.

'This'll warm us up,' I grin, as Abi sits beside me and I pull open the front of my backpack, waving two small bottles of bourbon, Lookout Beach Distillery's favourite tipple, from MK's last bag of freebies. Unscrewing one, passing it to her, I say, 'Here's to old friends and new ones,' opening mine and appearing to take a long draw, making sure Abi complies. 'Welcome to the Oregon party,' I toast.

'This is amazing, Lolly,' she smiles. 'Thank you for bringing me here. For showing me this.'

'Well, this is just the first part. Now comes the story,' and then it's time to lean in, to lower my voice and weave the tale I've concocted just for her, of sailors far from home returning with precious cargo, of pirates beset by curses and betrayals, at every key point of the tale, swigging from my bottle and nodding that she must do the same.

What she doesn't know is that I'm inventing this piece of supposedly long-told Lookout Beach history more or less on the spot. I was always good at that and though Grace hasn't written a story in years, Lolly hasn't lost the knack. What she also doesn't know is that I'm pouring a little of my own already watered-down booze out behind me every time I grab her arm for emphasis or point to the lighthouse, the rocks, the road back to town, with the classic magician's trick of misdirection.

After the story reaches its climax, after the sailors have sighted Terrible Tilly, realised themselves within reach of home only to founder in a storm, she applauds.

'That's a great story, Lolly. Almost as good as one of your old ones,' but since it's the first time she's spoken in twenty minutes, she's surprised to hear herself slurring. 'This is strong stuff,' she observes, blinking sleepily at the Lookout Beach Distillery label on her half-empty bottle, 'it's got, like, a herby taste to it.'

'That's the seagrass they put in the vats here. Their secret ingredient,' I laugh, miming another swig. 'To the return of Captain Carruthers!' and she complies.

'This is just so great, the two of us,' Abi says, intense concentration on her face. 'It's magical. I can almost see the pirate ship out there. The poor drowning sailors.'

'There's one last thing we must do, to complete the ritual,' I say. 'We have to give a doubloon back to the sea, to honour the sailors who drowned here. They say their souls are trapped in the punchbowl down there but can be assuaged with gold, well, a quarter in this case, not to take revenge on the living of the town.'

I draw the shiny silver coins from my pocket and hand her one, saying, 'Come on.'

'Where?' she slurs, thicker now.

'Just down there,' I wave at the edge. 'Kids from town used to come out here all the time before they created the conservation area last year. It was a rite of passage, you know, to show you belonged here. Come on. It's fine,' I add, seeing her strained expression as she tries to focus.

'I dunno, Lol. I feel a bit wobbly. I think this stuff has gone to my head.'

'Don't worry,' I add, offering my hand. 'The ledge is solid. Besides, if you fall in, who better to pull you out, right?' I flash my best affectionate smile, the one I usually reserve for Tilly. 'Come on. You can tell Tilly you've passed the initiation like she did last year,' and that's enough to make Abi lever herself to her feet and let me lead her the twenty yards to the edge.

The punchbowl is full now, glassy as the tide evens off, at the height of its reach. Tomorrow the level will fall again and the water surge out to the Pacific beyond, as the whole pot boils like a cauldron. But it looks inviting in this light, like you could jump in and enjoy a swim.

'We bathe here in the summer, when we kayak round the bay,' I lie. 'I'll bring you to see the baby sea otters in April. They're so sweet.'

I sidle up to the edge, making a show of taking care, coin in hand. 'Spare us, souls of the drowned. We offer you this coin for your sacrifice,' I say theatrically, then flip my coin into the eye of the punchbowl.

242

Now it's Abi's turn to edge towards the lip of rock.

So we are really here, in the space between the seconds, after my night spent staring at the bedroom ceiling listening to Eli's metronymic breathing. Sleep was an ocean away for most of it, but I'd dozed, dreamed, at some point, in the deepest darkness, fitfully, fearfully, of water gushing into my nose and mouth, of Abi bobbing in the water ahead, sopping red curls and snot, clinging to me begging, 'Don't let me go.'

Then Abi had become Tilly, only she was floating away from me on a riptide I couldn't best, no more than a fingertip touch out of reach but enough, as she yelled, 'Mommy, help me!' That was when the tsunami rose up and carried us on its humped back up the slough, washing away the house, the whole of Shore Street and Lookout Beach before it. I woke with sweat and snot coating my own face and my mind grasping a black, metallic idea I'd been afraid to acknowledge until that moment.

As I lead Abi to the edge, hear her make the offering as I just did, see the sliver of silver coin slice the surface before sinking out of sight, I know this is now my story alone. I have to finish it. I *can* finish it. It means accepting the truth about what I am, what I've always been deep down inside, my role in this tale made clear at last, but that can't be helped, *like it or lump it*, as Mum would say.

As Abi smiles back at me, I step into her and give her just a small push with my hip and right hand. It's not even a push really, it could have been accidental bump even, which is what Abi seems to think as her balance shifts and she drops, without a sound, into the punchbowl below. She's not afraid when she surfaces, seconds later, coughing at the cold rush of water, wiping her hair from her face.

'Jesus,' she yells, 'what the fuck?' old habit kicking in as she starts to tread water. She looks up expectantly, for me to yell, to help her out, only realising, as she sees me looking down, that it's too far for me to reach. There are seven feet of sheer granite between us, all around the punchbowl sides.

'Jesus, Lolly,' she cries, 'help me out, pull me up with something.'

She must be wondering why I'm just standing here, as she looks for ledges or niches to pull herself up, watching as she finds none, watching as the cold starts to bite into her legs and arms, gnawing the breath from her chest.

'It's all right, Abi,' I say, though not in the way she thinks it is. Lolly remembers. Lolly is not panicking this time. Lolly thought she understood then, about heroes and villains and which she was. She knows better now.

'What the fuck are you doing?' demands Abi. 'Do something, it's fucking freezing in here.'

Of course it is. It's the Pacific Northwest in November. It must be no more than two or three degrees tonight, Eli could warn you of that, and with the windchill it's lethally cold.

'Lolly,' she yells, 'help me. What's wrong with you?'

What's wrong with *you*? I want to ask in return. I pulled you out of the waves once before and look what happened. If I'd left you there maybe Priss Hartford would still be alive, maybe Silas would be too, your parents even. It's my fault as much as yours, all this trauma, and it's time to rectify that. But not with words. There's nothing left to say.

To save Grace and what she has built here I can't run or plead or lie, or hope. I just have to stand. Here. And wait.

Abi's still treading water below me but it's getting harder now, as her dense jacket fills with salt weight. Alcohol makes you lose body heat much faster, dilates the blood vessels, not a good match with swimming as Coach Turner always warned us. 'No teenage drunken dips, OK? Even if you think the water's warm and you're good swimmers.'

But Abi's not a good swimmer any more, no sea in Abergavenny to keep up her practice. This shouldn't take long. As her legs and arms start to solidify, she's struggling to keep her chin up above the foam, the first rush of reviving shock dissipating as she winds down like a doll, running out of battery. Abi is scared now. Abi is pleading, 'Lolly, please. Please help me!'

But Lolly is calm. Grace is calm. Neither responds. No one else is around to answer.

After what seems like an age, Abi stops struggling and her head dips down into the water. The thrashing ceases, the pool is becoming glassy again. But still I wait. Rule of three. Three minutes without oxygen . . .

I give it a few more minutes just in case. I make it ten, to be sure. In that time, I watch the strobe of the lighthouse beam striking off the segments of time, dividing the water then vanishing, like a second hand sweeping across the rock face. It's so quiet now, apart from the suck of the water below, almost as if something is missing. That's when I realise the ticking in my head has stopped. The night is finally silent.

When I'm certain it's over, I gather my thoughts for the next step, pulling on the pair of thin neoprene kayaking gloves from my rucksack pocket before gathering up Abi's things, her bag, her bourbon bottle. Like a good little camper, I leave no litter, no trace. Then I slip back up the path towards the boundary of the nature reserve, no torch this time. I am the shadows. I am the night.

After I cross the fence, I find a good spot on the legal side of the State Park sign to drop Abi's bag over the cliff edge. It lands on a ledge below, as intended, with Abi's phone and car keys still inside. I've added a flyer for the State Park and its various beauty spots, along with a free hiking map, both of which you can pick up from the magazine-strewn tables of any coffee shop in town, already smudged with fingerprints. Then I trot back to the remaining strip of sand, to the kayak on the shingle bank, get into my wetsuit and push off.

The churn is harder to ride now that the tide is full, competing in its age-old battle with the cliffs, but I have the strength of two women to carry me back. Grace watches, sitting as still as a rat on a life raft, as Lolly beats time with her paddle. Halfway around the granite corner I drop the little blue bottle into the sea, after I've emptied it out first, the one MK gave me ages ago that I'd kept tucked into a box of her CBD oil freebies.

'This is a non-standard product for an exclusive customer,' she'd grinned, back last summer. 'A few drops in water takes the edge right off. Don't mix it with Pinot or anything else, though. It gave me the best night's sleep I've ever had without vodka and it's got a nice herby taste, seagrass or some trendy shit.'

When the bottle is sunk, I empty the bourbon bottles we drank from, also weighted with water, so they will not bob about, will carry no message beyond this moment, and sink them to the sea floor.

Now comes the tricky part. I pull myself up and balance myself with my back against the rock, on a little stone lip, feet in the kayak. It's battered and old anyway, so it's not so hard to push down with my feet to scuttle it with water. As it goes down, it lists at the front end and I lean on the other until it sinks, then slip into the bitter wake and kick out into the night sea. The winter suit comes into its own here, though I still gasp as the water hits my face, my hands burning. Luckily the rucksack is much lighter now, with only my change of clothes inside its waterproof pouch.

Still, less than half a dozen people in Lookout Beach could make this swim in summer, let alone in November, and Grace Jensen is not one of them. She doesn't wild swim at all and always restricts her kayaking to the lazy bends of the Tillamook river. Besides, she's tucked up tight in her elegant, almost complete, new house right now, working on some schematics – the policeman outside will confirm it if anyone asks. The drive is the only way to leave the Project, unless you go by the open sea, but there is no gate at the back and no boat, let alone a kayak moored on the slip of jagged rock teeth of the slough. So, if she ever needs one, Grace will have the perfect alibi.

As I heave myself up onto the shingle of the slough, there's no time to catch my breath, powering up the rocky slit on shaky legs, checking my phone in its rubber envelope. I've been gone 112 minutes. Once inside, I peel off my suit, put my clothes in the newly installed washing machine on a quick cycle, ensuring the mechanism has engaged, then set the wetsuit to dry. Then I redress in the outfit I was wearing earlier, squirt some perfume, re-apply some lipstick and run the tongs to smooth my hair. Re-costumed, I lock up, go down to the front gate to tell Officer Danny, with my most charming and grateful smile, that I'm done for the night. Then he escorts me home.

Twenty-three

What's in a Name?

The awards evening turned out to be unexpectedly lovely. I thought I'd hate every minute of it but the venue was very impressive and the 'morning mist' sheath dress and 'hint of seafoam' stole were exactly the right choice for a dedicated wife. Right before the reception, Eli surprised me with my birthday gift, a perfectly elegant pearl on a silver chain that glowed softly at my throat as I beamed through the standing ovation as he accepted his award. Everyone was all champagne smiles afterwards and, to our relief, no one asked any awkward questions about the provenance of the Project and its building materials, or mentioned redwood felling or permit frauds, because Neil Morrow did not attend and hasn't called us since the night Belle almost shot him.

Other reporters have been in touch over the weekend, though, via messages from Bridgette at the office, asking for follow-ups on the Slabtown project and the Garibaldi fish cannery conversion, other clients too, requesting consultations and quotes. Suddenly we are in demand, of the moment and hot property, pardon the pun.

Tilly has gone back to class today, after my belated birthday pizza party for just the three of us, sulking because Bosun Seb is not at school again. He's gone with Belle to visit his sick auntie in San Francisco, according to a message she left on my phone while I was in Portland. Eli is back in the city today and the house here on Shore Street is wonderfully quiet. My head too, for a change. Since that night on the beach, the countdown has stopped.

I'm just wondering what to prepare for Thanksgiving dessert in a few weeks' time when my mobile buzzes and I recognise Noushki's number. I answer cheerfully, then am careful to seem surprised when she tells me she can't get in touch with her friend Nell.

'It's so weird,' says Noushki, worry radiating through the phone connection. 'She didn't show up at our last class on Friday and hasn't been in touch since. We were supposed to meet up at the bookstore today, after she started her new job, but they say she didn't show and she wasn't in the artists' residence over the weekend. Scary Agatha's kinda pissed with her.'

Unable to help her, I promise to let her know if I hear anything in town, reasoning, 'I'm sure she's OK. I'm sure she'll call you soon.'

'I don't get it,' she ponders. 'Where was she this weekend if she wasn't at the arts centre? Her last bag of stuff is still here. She's been crashing at mine since September, more or less living out of her bag after she left that college flat with the creepy landlord. I was going to bring it up for her. It has her clothes and shoes and all that stuff in it.'

When she eventually rings off, I stare around my perfect kitchen where everything is neat and in order, giving Elias's new award, an understated sweep of curved glass, a quick polish on the dresser. Then I wait for the next call, the one that will decide how this all ends. I wait for a Lookout Beach cop or Portland police officer to knock on my door and say they just need to ask me a few questions.

But somehow seven days pass, through a stream of orderly school runs and Otter sessions, cookie baking and conference calls, the hours practically portioned out and predictable, still safe and secure. It's a week later, just as I'm settling down to read the schematics for the fish cannery at the kitchen table, that the doorbell rings, and I steel myself when I see Detective Olsen outside, her face frozen into a now familiar frown.

I guess it's time. *She's going to enjoy this*, I think, as I call her in and politely seat her in the kitchen, smelling today of expensive coffee and finality.

'What can I do for you, Detective?' I ask, accomplished now in this role play.

Instead of answering, she heaves one of the impressive sighs I've come to know so well, drums her fingers on the tabletop then hands me an envelope.

'What's this?' I ask, confused, trying to read those crow-black eyes. She looks very uncomfortable for some reason, far less no muss no fuss than usual; she actually looks like the dog ate her homework.

'I'm afraid you won't understand right away, but I need you to read this letter, here, in my presence, then I have to destroy it,' she says.

'What?' I almost laugh. 'Is this a joke?'

'Decidedly not, no.'

'Is this something about my intruder? Has there been a development in the case?'

'Yes and no. It's really much easier if you read the letter first, Mrs Jensen. It's from your friend Belinda.'

'Belinda?' It takes me a second to realise she means Belle. 'Belle has written me a letter?' How quaint. But how strange. I can't imagine Olsen willingly playing postman. 'Is she back from her sister's in San Francisco, then?' I ask. 'Why doesn't she just pop over and tell me herself? Or text, like a normal person?'

'Because she's not living in the cottage any more, Mrs Jensen, and she can't contact you in any other way.'

'What? Don't be ridiculous.'

'Just read the letter. Then we'll talk.'

I open the letter:

Dear Grace,

This is all going to come as a big surprise to you but, believe me, it's long overdue. I don't expect you to understand, but you've been a good friend to me and Seb and I owe you this much as least. I'm afraid I'm not who you think I am. I haven't been honest with you. I can't tell you my real name but it's not Diana Belinda Cooper – yeah, it was sort of a joke, but that doesn't matter now.

A long time ago, when I was young and stupid, I got in with some bad people, fell for a bad guy and saw something even worse happen. I saw a man get killed and, instead of doing the right thing, I ran away because I was scared. The man who committed the murder swore he would track me down and kill me because of what I'd seen and, believe me, I believed him.

When I left home, I took some CCTV footage on some CDs, as evidence, and a lot of his money as a safeguard. I changed my name and my life and moved to San Francisco, where I eventually met a nice guy who, in the end, didn't stick around to raise the son we had together. So I came here with Seb and learned to be happy.

I thought everything was behind me, that I was safe and forgotten. But when the incident happened at your place I started to panic that he'd tracked me down, that he was sending me a message, that he was going to hurt me. I realised I'd never stopped looking over my shoulder, living in fear. I've been jumping at shadows for over ten years.

Then that numb-nut reporter made me realise how I almost did something stupid that night, in the garden, so it's time to stop hiding. I have the evidence to put my old boyfriend behind bars. Detective Olsen is helping me. She promises she'll make sure Seb and I are safe until I can testify. Then we'll have another new name, less stupid, and a safe place to live.

I know you will understand this better than most, Grace — you've started a new life too, far away from your first home, for reasons of your own and we all know it can be done. We can start over.

Don't think too badly of me. I was just trying to
stay alive and protect my son. I never told you a lie
that mattered. I will miss you and Tilly and maybe,
one day, we can all be friends again. Seb says Tilly
is to keep his pirate hat and badge just in case there
is another party.

Much love, your friend, B.

As I reach the last line I stare at Olsen, her eyebrows
disappearing into her bangs as she says, 'Mind fuck, huh?
Pardon my language. I know you must have a million
questions but I can't tell you much more, beyond the fact
your neighbour was not quite who she seemed to be.'

'No fucking kidding,' I laugh, though I'm not really
amused, but the profanity seems to make Olsen relax, her
gaze raking me up and down, toe to crown, more gently
than before.

'As she explained, she's helping us with an important
case now,' she waves for me to hand the letter back. 'She's
going to live somewhere else and start over.'

'So? What? She's going into witness protection or
something?'

'I can't say.'

'But she . . . she was really involved with criminals?'

'Let's just say she grew up in a rough neighbourhood
like lots of kids do, was running with the wolves for a
while, fell for the wrong guy. She got up to some question-
able pursuits herself, until things went badly wrong. She
witnessed an armed robbery. A man was killed. That was
her wake-up call.'

'Seriously? Belle?' I snort. Belle with her boho blouses and bangle stacks, the hippie girl who gets offed by the serial killer in the first half of the slasher movie. Then I think of her ease with my Glock. The mettle in her stature, the steel in her voice as she stared Morrow down.

'So, she's been on the run all this time,' I think aloud, the words absurd in my mouth, 'took something incriminating as protection. Smart, I guess. But, why this now? I know Belle was on edge but do you really think the incident here in September was linked to her past? To this bad guy?' pretending that I don't know better.

'We don't know for sure if that's true,' says Olsen thoughtfully, getting to her feet, setting fire to the letter with a lighter from her pocket, watching it flare, before dropping it into the kitchen sink and rinsing away the ashes. 'So far it's the only half plausible explanation we have for what happened here. This man she's been hiding from, well, his local cops have had him in for questioning and he denies everything about Mr Lennon's assault, but he would, wouldn't he? He has an alibi for Mr Lennon's attack but he's the kind of guy who'd get others to do his dirty work for him. The sort of guy, shall we say, who makes Tony Soprano look like a legitimate businessman.'

'Yes, but it's a reach, surely, that he'd come here and just, what, leave a surprise?'

'Apparently, your friend says he used to buy her cupcakes all the time, ones with little red ribbons on top, from the bakery in the city they lived in. It was their romantic thing, so that could be a link.'

'But how did Belle know about the ribbons here? That never came out in the press and I never told her.'

'Detective White did,' she says sheepishly, 'my partner. He's not very experienced, I'm afraid. We were asking her about the day of the incident, if she'd seen anyone, if she knew anyone who might want to hurt you. She told us about those eco-protestors who papered your car, then White, trying to be a smart ass, asked if a red ribbon meant anything to her or if it had any significance for you.

'We were trying to keep the finer details to ourselves but I didn't think it mattered hugely at the time, though it obviously triggered something in Ms Cooper. I don't know if it's relevant. I mean, red ribbons could mean something to almost anyone. There's a red ribbon for HIV aware- ness, a Drug Enforcement red ribbon against narcotics trafficking, even a Mothers Against Drunk Driving ribbon in Texas, not to mention four Red Ribbon bakeshops on Google.'

'Yes, I suppose you're right. Why my house, though, not hers?' I play along.

'Well, I'm told people are always mixing up your addresses, right? For deliveries, the zip codes are twitchy? The GPS is not reliable?'

'Ha!' I let out a laugh that she misunderstands.

'I know. This town, right? Sleepy old town. I tell you, Mrs Jensen, I thought the city would be challenging, but you guys . . .'

'Poor Walter, wrong place wrong time, then?'

'Seems that way. We probably won't make anything much out of that side of the investigation, your intruder I mean. No fingerprints, no witnesses, remember? But that won't matter. We have what we need. It'll be quite the legal case.'

'This guy is that big a deal, then?'

'Oh yes, the evidence Ms Cooper has on CD will put him away for a good few years. Kind of like getting Al Capone on tax evasion but if it worked for Eliot Ness . . . Obviously she needs to go dark now, with a much better alias than Diana Belinda Cooper.'

I shake my head. 'Sure, but what did she mean about her name being a joke?'

'Think about it,' she smiles, the first time I've seen one on her face. 'D. B. Cooper? Even an ex-Brit will have heard that story, if you've lived here for more than five minutes. Seems the first guy who got her fake documents had a dangerous sense of humour when he gave her a new last name.'

Then it clicks, D. B. Cooper, Oregon's biggest fugitive, still supposedly missing in the wilds of this state with an empty parachute and bundles of cash.

'Well, I guess the show's over for today,' says Olsen, heading for the door. 'Obviously, you can't mention this to anyone. *Anyone.* Well, your husband I guess, but no one else. I only said I'd give you the letter because I think you have a right to know. Your own case will officially remain open but as it's *unofficially* linked to the new investigation, we'll carry on behind the scenes only.

'Oh, by the way, there was a reporter called Morrow sniffing around. Ms Cooper says he was hassling you both? He had some idea that Walter Lennon was involved in dodgy business dealings, that your husband was involved in forging some permits.' She looks sheepish again. 'We spoke to him a while back and, at one point that was an avenue of investigation, for the assault. But, well, it turns out it was probably some malicious gossip Morrow got from a guy called Andreas Poliakoff, who seems to think Bright Brothers stole a commission from him, stirring the pot. Not a very nice guy. I can't vouch for the credibility of all Lennon's business dealings but everything in relation to your project is above board.'

She was hoping to find something, I realise. She wanted to be the one to shatter the Jensen empire as she sees it. She catches my eye, sees I know and pretends to study Eli's award for a few seconds, before adding. 'In the light of this new development with Ms Cooper, Morrow's been warned off pursuing anything with the Lennons or you, in case it compromises the investigation. If he gets in touch, don't speak to him, call me. The good news is, you're safe. You can rest your mind. And I should let you get back to work.'

I show her to the door, flooded with relief, when she turns, scratches her nose, pushes an imaginary piece of stray hair behind her ear and says, 'I was sorry to hear about your nanny's friend by the way.'

'Nell? Yes. Anoushka rang this morning. It's so sad,' I nod.

'Indeed.'

'Those poor kayakers who spotted her body. Anoushka says it looks like she fell from one of the viewpoints up in the park. Do you know what happened?'

'It's not exactly my case,' begins Olsen, 'but, well, the Lieutenant has shared his initial findings with me. He thinks she was sightseeing and went too far out onto the cliff. A ranger found her purse on a rocky ledge, her wallet, her keys inside; no theft, no assault, which seems to support the theory. Maybe she dropped it over, leaned too far out trying to get it. People don't appreciate the terrain here. My grandmother was Nisqually, you know, her tribe used to say the ocean here has teeth and it's always hungry. Between you and me, the coroner told me she had quite a lot of alcohol in her system and some cannabis too. Not a great mix. God knows this hippie, trippy state of ours has made its bed – legalising that shit will be the end of us all one day.'

She wrinkles her nose as if she can smell patchouli and hates it, and I nod in agreement asking, 'Have you tracked down any of her family yet?'

'It seems she was here on an expired arts visa from the UK. No next of kin they can find. She only had one bag and a little suitcase with her and was living out of that. Her mom was her only relative on record and she died last year, no siblings. No family photos or anything with her, except a couple of childhood snaps. Her phone was too water damaged to retrieve anything. The college had only the bare details on file. Guess there wasn't much for her back in the UK. Shame, seems like she was trying to make a fresh start.'

And this is the moment she doesn't ask me anything else, if I knew Abigail Eleanor Marshall well or that she was once Abigail Cracknell whose brother killed a girl, because Abi Cracknell stopped existing years ago. Abi Marshall lived in Abergavenny and neither of us were ever from a town called Gwyn Mawr. Thanks, Detective Inspector Maureen. Who'd have thought I'd ever need your insight into the disposal and arrangement of evidence and circumstances – the simplest explanation usually being the right one.

'The Foreign Office might ship her home to the UK,' adds Olsen, and I get the sense she's reluctant to leave, 'but, considering the expense, the local authority is more likely to pay for a burial here.'

'Perhaps we could help pay for it, if it comes to that,' I say. 'My daughter had taken quite a shine to her. It might be the decent thing to do.'

'Well, I'll bear that in mind. Thank you, Mrs Jensen. Listen, I'm sorry about the whole home-invasion thing. I made assumptions. I got an idea in my head and tried to make the facts and everything fit it. That was lazy. Not good procedure. I won't let it happen again. Good luck with everything. Stay safe.'

We shake hands and I close the door.

Epilogue

Blank Slate

So that, as Mum is inclined to say, is that, at least for now, as the season rolls on and winter shivers thick and grey over Shore Street and Belle's empty cottage. Thanksgiving is in a few weeks and I'm already ordering an organic turkey and locally sourced cranberries, supporting the farm-to-table ethic.

I miss Belle, her steady hand, her recipes, her lifesaving offers of pie, even her carob balls and *I brake to bake* bumper sticker. I still can't quite believe she took us all in so completely. I knew this was a place where people came to hide, the tail-end of the continent where North America folds down to the shore and falls into the sea, but I still thought I was the only one who'd reinvented myself so completely here. Yet all the while she'd done it so much better, her disguise all the more perfect and complete because she lived it instead of just wearing it. I think I can learn a lot from her, even if it's only with hindsight.

On the plus side, Walter is on the mend, the jigsaw of his memory slowly reassembling itself, his waking hours exceeding his sleeping ones. We've invited him and MK over for Thanksgiving dinner and he's determined be up for it, and to being ready for some beach soccer with Tilly by the spring, so he can get his ass handed to him again.

MK is deeply attentive to him but has also started making me awesome 'practising gratitude' margaritas on Thursday nights, to repay me for my silence. She's accepted my explanation that Belle has had to remain in San Francisco to nurse her sister through the winter. Though how long she'll buy that as the weeks pass and she doesn't call, is anyone's guess. Cross that bridge when we come to it, as Mum used to say.

'I didn't even know she had a sister,' says MK, toasting me with a perfected salted rim in front of the crackling log burner, now the nights are sharp and unforgiving. 'I miss the old hippie.'

So, the mist billows in and out and the rain falls, and sometimes the ocean reveals itself in all its heaving, seething majesty before the clouds roll down from the trees, hiding us in silence again, covering the spot where Abi is buried in the municipal cemetery with a few old photographs inside the coffin – one of a group of cheering children on a beach, one of a girl in a pirate costume in front of a giant octopus.

You might think it would be hard to stay here now, in Lookout Beach, but I've a daughter to raise, one who misses her best friend Bosun Seb but still loves her school, her village, the charge of the ocean at our backs. It's certainly a great place to raise a family and Elias has just been made junior partner at Bright Brothers, so this is not a good time for a relocation.

Anyway, in March, we'll move into the Project and I'm looking forward to it already. There's a big split-level wine fridge in the new kitchen I intend to half fill with teeth-achingly sweet Pinot Gris but also some smoky reds I much prefer. And I'm going to get a pontoon installed at the mouth of the slough, so I can take Eli and Tilly kayaking along the coast when the weather is right, tethered at my bow like ducklings. I haven't told him yet but I'll win him over when my parents come out in April. I'll say, 'If Granny Lew can do it, it must be perfectly safe.'

I want it now. All of this. My life. This new start, this blank slate. No more running.

The Cyhireath may sing its fretful song around the triple glazing in the long, dark months before spring but it can't trouble me. I've already weathered the storm. Another woman's face may stare back at me in the glass from time to time, when I gaze into the heaving, seascaped night, but she can't hurt me any more. Because I know who I am and I know where I belong.

My name is Grace Jensen, good wife, good mother, good friend, and I am home.

Acknowledgements

I would like to thank my indomitable agent Peter Buckman, of The Ampersand Agency, for the faith he put in the work of a Welsh journalist who, ten years ago, decided she really wanted to write fiction instead of news stories. His continued encouragement and dedication over the last decade, as well as the application of red wine and, occasionally, hankies, has kept me returning to the keyboard when times have been tough. Thanks also to the lovely Rosie Buckman who has helped my novels cross into translation in Germany.

Then there's the team at Little, Brown, particularly Krystyna Green who signed me for my first three-book deal and whipped my previous novels into shape. The credit for getting *The Beach House* into its final glory goes to Hannah Wann, for her excellent feedback and eagle eyes, not forgetting Amanda Keats and Howard Watson for spotting all my sloppy mistakes.

A shout-out to Jess Gulliver too, for sticking with me through four novels and handling the PR.

I couldn't have hoped to have worked with a lovelier team of people. Many thanks to you all! And one final mention to the group of writers that is Crime Cymru, especially the enthusiasm and support of Alis Hawkins, who invited me to join this brilliant fiction tribe.